P9-CEN-032

Now You See Her,
Now You Don't

William Murray's Shifty Lou Anderson Novels

Tip on a Dead Crab

The Hard Knocker's Luck

When the Fat Man Sings

The King of the Nightcap

The Getaway Blues

I'm Getting Killed Right Here

We're Off to See the Killer

Now You See Her, Now You Don't

Other Books by William Murray

The Americano

Best Seller

The Dream Girls

The Fugitive Romans

Horse Fever

Italy: The Fatal Gift

The Killing Touch

The Last Italian

Malibu

The Mouth of the Wolf

Previews of Coming Attractions

The Self-starting Wheel

The Sweet Ride

The Wrong Horse

Now You See Her, Now You Don't

A Shifty Lou Anderson Novel

♥ ♦ ♣ ♠

WILLIAM MURRAY

Henry Holt and Company
New York

Henry Holt and Company, Inc.
Publishers since 1866
115 West 18th Street
New York, New York 10011

Henry Holt® is a registered
trademark of Henry Holt and Company, Inc.

Published in Canada by Fitzhenry & Whiteside Ltd.,
195 Allstate Parkway, Markham, Ontario L3R 4T8.

Library of Congress Cataloging-in-Publication Data
Murray, William.
Now you see her, now you don't / by William Murray. — 1st ed.
p. cm.
"A Shifty Lou Anderson novel."
1. Anderson, Shifty Lou (Fictitious character)—Fiction.
2. Horse racing—United States—Fiction. I. Title.
PS3563.U8N69 1994 94-13433
813'.54—dc20 CIP

ISBN 0-8050-2971-0

Henry Holt books are available for special promotions
and premiums. For details contact:
Director, Special Markets.

First Edition—1994

Designed by Betty Lew

Printed in the United States of America
All first editions are printed on acid-free paper.∞

1 3 5 7 9 10 8 6 4 2

For Alice,
who used to dream winners.

"Never bet on anything that talks," Jocko once advised me. "Stick to the ponies. They're as close to a cure for futility as you'll find."

—Brendan Boyd, *Blue Ruin*

1
Wiseguy

♥

I'd been seeing her around from time to time since the start of the Hollywood Park summer race meet, but I had no idea who she was. I only knew that I wanted to know her. Not so much because I found her physically attractive, but mainly because I liked the overall look of her—the way she carried herself, the way she moved, with the quiet confidence of someone in touch with herself. She was tall, at least five foot nine, with fine legs and square shoulders. She also had beautiful arms, firm but not overly muscled, with the strong hands of a pianist or a surgeon. She had a fair complexion, lightly freckled, and red curly hair that she wore cut short, like a boy's. She had a long, slightly hooked nose that kept her from being conventionally beautiful, but a wide, brilliant smile and hazel eyes. When she laughed, she threw her head back and let it all out, taking an animal pleasure in the emotion.

I hadn't seen her laugh very much; most of the time she seemed preoccupied, serious, concentrated on some problem or cause she hadn't yet come to grips with. She dressed simply, sometimes in jeans, but most often in dresses or pants suits in basic greens and dark browns.

I still don't know why, from the very first time I saw her, I felt so compelled to introduce myself to her. Nor why it took me so long to get around to it. After all, I'm a public performer and not shy about approaching strangers. There was just something about her that made me hesitant, cautious. I wanted to know a little more before I made a move, and that's usually not my style at all with people.

"Hey, Shifty, did you hear this one about my doctor?" Angles Beltrami asked, interrupting my reverie.

"What?"

"My doctor. He goes up to this friend of mine yesterday, after the ninth, a guy who's got to have heart surgery in a couple of weeks, and he says to him it's a very delicate operation."

"Come on, Angles," Jay said, "give us the punch line."

"I'm getting to it," Angles continued. "But the good news, he tells my friend, is that he had the superfecta in the ninth."

"An apocryphal tale if ever I've heard one," Arnie Wolfenden observed. "Where do you pick up this stuff?"

"Marty Joyce, he told me."

"Marty Joyce isn't even a good tout," Arnie said. "Come on, this is a tough card. Jay?"

"Nothing till the fifth, Arnie," Jay said. "Except for Angles. He'd bet on cockroaches if we let him."

"You guys are a pain," Angles said and disappeared toward the grandstand betting windows.

I didn't pay much attention to this exchange. I had spotted her again, this time not far from our box. She was standing in the aisle, talking to a couple of trainers I knew, and seemed relaxed, ready to enjoy herself. She even had a pair of small binoculars slung around her neck and had apparently come to play. I decided this would be my day with her. "I really like the look of her," I said, to no one in particular.

"Who?" Jay asked.

"That lady in the aisle down there," I said, "talking to Mel Ducato and Willie Vernon."

"You've been mumbling about her all week," Jay said. "Why don't you introduce yourself?"

"Why don't you?"

"Not my type, Shifty. I like them a little smaller. You know, cute and fluffy and all. This one looks too serious."

"Yeah."

Arnie looked up from his *Racing Form*. "Women, deadly at the track," he said. "Why bother betting at all? Just go and give them the money."

The bugler came out in front of the stands and blew the call to the post for the first race. The horses, cheap fillies and mares running in a sprint for a small opening pot, appeared from under the stands. Although, like Jay, I had no intention of risking any money on this race, almost as a reflex action I raised my glasses to have a look at the animals. After they had passed us and begun to trot or gallop toward the starting gate across the infield, I lowered my binocs and looked for the woman again. She had gone, but I didn't let it bother me. I knew I'd find her later.

After the race, which was won by the favorite in about as unexciting a contest as I've ever seen, I left our box and went to the men's room. On my way back, I spotted Vernon at the clubhouse bar, buying himself a beer, and joined him. "Drinking on the job, Willie?" I asked, smiling.

"Well, well, Shifty, what's going on?" he said. "I haven't seen you around much the past couple of weeks."

"I had a gig in Vegas," I said. "A week at the Xanadu."

"How'd it go?"

"The room was too big. I bombed."

"What do you mean, too big?"

"You know me, Willie—cards and coins and little stuff. It doesn't really work all that well in a big room."

"Want a beer? A real one? This stuff I'm drinking has no booze in it."

"No, thanks. I never drink when I'm betting. You on the wagon?"

"Just till after the fourth, when I run that maiden filly."

"You going to bet on her?"

He grinned. "Sure, I bet on all my horses, don't I?"

"That could be dangerous, Willie, the way you're going this meet."

"Yeah, I got a barn full of nothing, Shifty. But it's better than Vegas. First time I ever went there, I won a bundle. I thought I was a king. But Vegas has a paddle for everybody's rear end."

I liked Willie Vernon. I didn't think he'd live long, because he smoked and drank heavily and wagered too much money on his own horses. But he was a pretty good trainer and a decent guy who had been around for years on the California circuit. He'd only ever had one big horse, a gelding he won the Preakness with some years back, but he didn't seem to mind. He didn't like to travel, so he was content mainly to run his cheap stock at the local Southern California tracks—Santa Anita, Hollywood Park, Del Mar—with occasional forays to the fair circuit during the summer months. He was in his mid-fifties, I guessed, with a round, good-humored, wrinkled face and a gap-toothed smile. He liked to party and he was fun to be around when he was winning.

"I wanted to ask you about that lady you were talking to," I said.

"What lady is that? I don't know any ladies. Just women and girls."

"Before the last race, you and Mel, down in the box section."

"Oh, Megan Starbuck, that the one?"

"I guess so. A tall redhead."

"Yeah, that's Meg. Aw, she's a nice girl, Shifty. You don't want to go working your magic on a nice girl like that."

"How nice is she?"

He laughed. "Hell, I don't know," he said. "I've just known her ever since she was about twelve. Her folks are horse people, up around Hemet, have a nice little ranch. But Meg moved East to go to college ten or twelve years ago and I haven't seen her since. I guess she's back for a while." He looked me up and down and grinned. "Ain't you a little old for her?"

"Never too old, Willie," I said. "I'm over forty, but I'm not crumbling yet. Anyway, she has to be thirty or so, right? It's not like I'm robbing the cradle."

"Aw hell, I gave up chasing women a long time ago."

"You're married."

"Yeah, that's right," he said. "Kind of puts a crimp in a guy, don't it? You want to meet her?"

"That's the idea."

"Come on by the paddock for the fourth. She said she'd be there."

"What does she do?"

"For a living? How the hell would I know? Something for the government, I guess. She told me she's been living in Virginia and commuting a lot."

"Thanks, Willie, I'll see you later."

The horses were on the track for the second race and I wanted to see it, even though, like Jay, I had no intention of risking any money on it. Jay and I often differed on how to bet on a race, but rarely on when.

I'd been back from Las Vegas for nearly a week now and was enjoying my time at Hollywood Park. During weekdays, the place seemed nearly empty, with no more than ten or twelve thousand people in the stands, which made it easy to bet, to get something to eat, or just wander around basking in the aura of another racing day.

I used to hate Hollywood Park, the ugliest of the region's hippodromes, but control of the premises had recently changed hands and a lot of improvements had been made. The infield had been restored to its former glory, with lakes and banks of flowers and a pretty blonde, chosen to serve as that season's Goose Girl. She was all dressed up in a sort of Dutch dairymaid's costume and tended her flock of honkers from the safety of her swan boat. Only Hollywood could have dreamed up such a scenario, and it fitted in perfectly with the track's history as a playground for the show-biz crowd. Funkiness and fun had always been the theme here, and R. D. Hubbard, the track's CEO, knew how to conjure up the atmosphere. He also knew something about aesthetics. Out in back of the grandstand, he had built a new paddock, with real grass and a big walking ring under the trees where the horses were saddled before every race. Best of all, he knew how to please the wiseguys and the hard knockers, the gamblers on whose backs the entire industry rested. He provided every betting option they wanted and was in the process of throwing in an on-premises card club, so the boys and girls could go and play poker and beat one another's brains out before, during, and after the racing. Not glamorous, not the sport of kings anymore, but so what? For those of us who cared about quality, the best horses still raced here; the rest of it we could ignore.

The entries for the second race were being loaded into the starting gate when I returned to my seat, next to Jay in the front row of our box. He had his glasses focused on the gate crew beginning to lead the contestants into their stalls, narrow little enclosures from which they would spring out at the press of the starter's button and begin to run, a drama within a drama, since no part of a race is more crucial than those few seconds during which the animals burst into the clear. More races are lost in the starting gate than at any other part of the track. "Look at those jerks," Jay said. "You can forget about him."

"Who?"

"The two horse," he answered. "He won't go in and they're whipping and slashing at him and getting him all worked up, so he'll be a mess by the time they do get him in there."

"Foreman, the Gantry horse?" Angles asked.

"Yeah, that's him."

"That's because he's never seen a starting gate before," Arnie said. "D. L. Gantry doesn't think it's important to take his horses to the starting gate in the morning."

It took the crew several minutes to load Foreman into his stall, by which time he'd become a sweaty, wild, unmanageable beast. When the race went off, he reared into the air, unseating his rider, and galloped off by himself.

"Shit," Angles said.

Jay lowered his binoculars and glanced at him. "You didn't bet on him, Angles?"

"Nah, only in one exacta."

"D. L. Gantry," Arnie observed. "That man couldn't train ivy up a wall."

It was the maid who found the bodies of the Goldman family in Rancho Santa Fe. Her name was Juanita Madero. She was a small, dark woman, originally from San Salvador, who had worked for the Goldmans for only a few weeks. She had come by at about noon, an hour and a half later than her usual time, and had found the front door locked. No one had answered her ring, but that had happened before. Mr. Goldman was rarely at home and his wife, Penny, was often out in the garden, tending to her roses. She had more than forty rose bushes, all kinds of roses, and they required a lot of attention. So Juanita had done what Mrs. Goldman had told her to do if no one answered her ring. She had let herself into the grounds through the side gate and walked toward the back of the house, expecting to find Mrs. Goldman either in the garden, on the patio, or in the kitchen.

No one was about and the French doors in the rear were shut, the slats of the vertical blinds drawn tight against the light. Juanita told the police later that she had not known what to do. She had returned to the front door and again rung the bell and waited. Nothing. Then back to the rear again, where she had rapped on the door with her knuckles. Silence. She had thought about leaving and coming back later. Perhaps the Goldmans had gone away on a trip somewhere and neglected to inform her. Mr. Goldman traveled quite a lot. But usually alone. Mrs. Goldman had joked with Juanita about not wanting ever to leave her roses. "They are like my children to me," she had told the maid. "I can't leave them." Juanita knew that the girls, Richie and Carla, went to a day camp every morning and didn't come home until five o'clock, an hour or so before dinner. Perhaps Mrs. Goldman had become tired of waiting for her to show up and had driven into town to do some shopping. Juanita had been unable to call her, because she'd had a flat tire on Via de la Valle, about five miles from the house and not near a public phone, so she had had to walk two miles back to the Texaco station near the freeway to call Hector, her husband. He had driven her to work, then left her to go back and rescue his wife's car.

Juanita knocked again, then tried the French doors. To her surprise, one of them was open. The Goldmans must have forgotten to lock them the night before, though they were usually very careful and security conscious. Mr. Goldman himself had warned Juanita on her very first day of working for the family never to leave windows wide open or doors unlocked. "You never know," he had told her. "It just takes one maniac to come in. So please be careful, Juanita." And she had promised to be very careful and had always made sure the windows could not be opened more than six inches or so and the doors were always kept locked.

Once inside the kitchen, Juanita had not known what to do. She had hesitated and called out for Mrs. Goldman. No answer. She had snapped on the kitchen light and looked around. No breakfast dishes, no coffee machine on. But it was afternoon now. Mrs. Goldman must have given up on her, cleaned up herself, and gone out. Juanita headed back through the hallway toward the front of the house and the garage, where she kept most of her cleaning tools—the vacuum cleaner, brooms, dusters, furniture polish. To her surprise, Mrs. Goldman's car, a Volvo station wagon, was still there, parked in its usual place on the left side of the garage.

Juanita hesitated again, then she picked up a broom, a feather duster, some rags, and the furniture polish. She intended to begin, as she usually did, by cleaning the upstairs bedrooms and bathrooms. The stuff to clean the latter was kept in the cabinets under the sinks, so she didn't have to worry about remembering to bring anything up there from the garage. Yes, she would begin cleaning upstairs, as usual. If Mrs. Goldman's bedroom door was closed, Juanita would not disturb her. Perhaps she was sick or had not slept well. Mrs. Goldman was a pale, blond lady, very nice-looking for a gringo, but she became tired easily; she slept a lot.

The maid hurried up the stairs to the landing and, to her surprise, saw that all the bedroom doors were closed. She did not know what to do. She put down the vacuum cleaner and the broom, went to the girls' door, and knocked. Nothing. She opened the door a crack and peeked in. It was dark in the room, the only light filtering in through the closed Venetian blinds, but as her eyes adjusted to it, Juanita could see both the girls lying in their beds. One was facedown, an arm dangling over the side. The other lay on her back, her eyes open. Juanita called out to the one on her back, Carla, the older girl. "Miss Carla? Is Juanita," she said. "You sick?"

And then she saw the blood and screamed. She ran down the stairs and out the front door, shouting and waving her arms. Mr. Greenwood, a neighbor on his way back from town, saw her and stopped his car. Juanita was crying and sobbing and pointing back toward the house. Mr. Greenwood did not go inside. He left Juanita by the road, drove quickly to his own house, only a quarter of a mile away, went inside, calling out to his wife as he came through the front door, then telephoned the police.

When I arrived at the paddock, about twenty minutes before the fourth race, Meg Starbuck wasn't there. Under a tree toward the rear, Willie Vernon and one of his grooms were putting a saddle on their horse, but the only other people present were the owners of the animal, a middle-aged couple named Bob and Betty, who were standing close together, looking more worried than excited. Willie introduced me to them, then finished tightening the cinch and making sure the tiny racing saddle sat properly on his charge's back. "Where's Miss Starbuck?" I asked.

Willie looked up. "Right behind you," he said.

I looked around. Meg Starbuck was walking quickly toward us. I decided that I loved the way she moved, with those long legs in a purposeful, athletic stride. Willie instructed his groom to walk the horse around until it was time to mount up, then turned to introduce me to Meg. For once I couldn't think of anything amusing or interesting to say. The woman dazzled me. She must have seen this in my face, but she chose to ignore it. "Now, Willie, fess up," she said. "This horse of yours has a chance in here?"

Willie looked mildly pained, as if fighting off a sudden attack of gas. "Aw, Meg, you never know with these maidens," he said. "She can run some, but she don't have much speed." He turned to his owners. "Like I told you, Bob and Betty, she may need to go long. But I expect her to break better today and she's doing real good."

"You mean she's eating a lot," I said. "Is that going to help her run fast?"

"Darn you, Shifty," Willie answered. "You trying to give away my racing secrets? It just means she's feeling good. She'll run okay." He turned to his owners to reassure them about their horse's chances, feeding them the sort of placating patter that I knew was intended to prepare them for another losing effort. Meg and I stood quietly by as Kevin Worland, the innocent-looking young apprentice engaged to ride the filly, now joined us. The paddock judge called for the riders to mount and Willie gave his boy a leg up into the saddle. "She'll break good," he instructed him, "but she ain't got a whole lot of speed. Try to come with her on the outside, as she don't like the dirt in her face. She'll give you everything she's got."

"Everything she's got isn't much," I said as I fell in beside Meg on our way back to the grandstand.

"Willie said she could run a little bit," Meg said. "And she's fourteen to one."

"You aren't going to bet on her?"

"I always bet on Willie's horses," she said. "I cash quite a few tickets, too."

"You aren't going to cash any today," I said. "Save your money." I glanced behind me. Willie was walking back toward the stands with the owners, still trying to reassure them. "When Willie works this hard with trainer talk, it means he thinks his horse has no chance."

"What do you mean, trainer talk?"

"You know the patter," I said. "Willie told me you grew up around horses. You must know about it."

"Who are you, anyway?"

"I'm a magician."

"You're kidding. You saw people in half and make them disappear and all that?"

"No, that's pots and pans, Meg," I said. "It's all show biz and construction. I'm in close-up. Cards, coins, small objects. I'd like to show you sometime."

"Well, maybe."

"Willie says he's known you since you were a kid."

"That's right, a long time."

We emerged from under the stands into the winner's circle, then headed for the stairs leading up to the box section. The horses out on the track came back past us toward the starting gate. Willie's filly looked nice out there, a dark bay with a white blaze between her eyes, but then most Thoroughbreds look glorious to me. "She looks good," I said. "Too bad she can't run."

"Oh, Willie'll find a way to win with her."

"Not today and probably not here. Maybe up north or on the fair circuit."

She lingered at the top of the stairs just long enough to take a good look at me. "Are you always so negative about everything?"

"No. Right now just this particular horse. May I call you?"

"I don't think so."

"Was it something I said?"

She smiled, but not very warmly. "You're sort of a wiseguy, aren't you?"

"No, I've been trying to impress you. I guess I'm not doing a very good job of it." I reached into my pocket, pulled out a tiny bouquet of violets and a playing card, and handed them to her. "My number's on the card. Please call me."

She looked surprised. "There's nothing on this card," she said. "It's the king of hearts."

I pretended astonishment. "Really? Let me see." I took the card back from her, pressed it between my hands for a second or two, then handed it to her again. "There, see?" My telephone number appeared now along the edge of the card.

"That's pretty good," she said. "How did you do that?"

"I told you, I'm a magician."

"You're also a wiseguy."

"Not really, Meg. Honest. I wish you would call me."

"I don't know." She did, however, slip the card into her shoulder bag. "I'll think about it."

"Thinking is what gets people into trouble. Feeling is better. Even at the track."

She walked away from me toward the pari-mutuel windows and I watched her go, moving up the steps between the grandstand boxes with that long, athletic stride of hers. I decided that she looked almost as good from the rear as the front.

Willie's maiden filly broke next to last in the twelve-horse field, moved up some on the turn for home, but came lumbering in eighth. I don't think the event did my cause much good, because Megan Starbuck paid no more attention to me the rest of the afternoon.

2
Names

♦

She didn't call me, either. I went out to the stable area early every morning, hoping to find her, but I kept missing her. Either that or Willie Vernon was putting me on. I'd stop by his shed row or hunt him down at the cafeteria during the break, around seven o'clock, but he'd tell me that she had just left or hadn't arrived yet. Finally, after five days of this, I decided he was lying. "Come on, Willie, tell me the truth," I said as we stood together at the rail of the guinea stand, sipping tepid coffee out of Styrofoam cups. "You haven't seen her at all, have you?"

"Who?" he asked, giving me his famous gap-toothed, innocent grin.

"You know damn well who."

"Oh, Meg. That who you mean?"

"Look, Willie, I just want a date with her, that's all."

"Well, Shifty, you're in luck. There she is."

And sure enough, Meg Starbuck had just emerged from the cafeteria directly behind us. She was dressed very casually, in jeans, boots, and a red cowboy shirt; she looked terrific. She smiled, mostly at Willie, I guessed, and joined us. "We was just talking about you," Willie said.

"We?"

"Well, mostly old Shifty here. I guess he's got the hots for you, Meg. I wouldn't waste my time on him, if I was you. Magicians and horseplayers ain't up there in the Fortune Five Hundred."

"Neither are trainers," I said. "Hi, Meg. I was hoping you'd call me. I'm not usually as obnoxious as I was the first time we met."

"You weren't obnoxious," she said. "A little too cocky, maybe."

"Watch your language, Meg," Willie said. "There's gentlemen present."

"Where?" I asked.

"I would have called you, but I was out of town for a few days."

"Willie kept telling me all week I'd just missed you. How are you?"

"I'm fine."

"You look wonderful."

"Thank you." She turned to Willie. "You have anything out here?"

"No, just an old plater out for a gallop," he answered. "Let's go get some fresh coffee. Shifty?"

"You bet."

"Business?" I asked as we headed for the cafeteria.

"Yes," she said. "In San Diego."

"Oh. Do you get down there a lot?"

"It depends. Sometimes, sure."

"That's good."

"Why?"

"Because the Del Mar meet opens next week and I'll be down there for the whole seven weeks."

"Don't you ever work?"

"You think picking winners is easy? It's the hardest job in the world. Ask Willie. He trains these animals and even he doesn't know if they're going to win or not."

"Is that what you are, a horseplayer who does magic tricks?"

"No, I'm a magician who plays the horses," I explained. "But during the Del Mar meet I try not to take any engagements. A pal of mine and I rent a condo down there for the season."

We lined up at the counter inside the cafeteria, picked up fresh coffee, this time in real cups, and joined a small group of trainers sitting at a big round table near the window looking out on the guinea stand. They all seemed to know Meg or who she was, but the only person to stand up when she joined them was Duke Vernon, Willie's older brother. His real name was Walter, but I'd never heard him called anything but Duke, and it suited him. He was a lean, wiry man, always impeccably groomed even during working hours, and he had old-fashioned good manners. He also had a pair of sharp blue eyes that could turn to stone when he became angry or impassioned about something, usually politics. I knew he distrusted me, because he suspected that as a show-biz personality I had to be a liberal, which to Duke was just this side of being an out-and-out Marxist. Nevertheless, I liked him. He was at least in his late sixties, but he still galloped most of his own horses in the morning and was as fit as a cowboy just off the range. I tried never to discuss controversial topics with him, though Willie always baited me, hoping I'd get into it with Duke. Willie enjoyed brouhahas of any kind, the louder the better.

"Meg, honey, how have you been?" Duke asked, pulling out a chair for her. "Willie said you were out of town."

"Yes, just for a few days. I may have to go back down there."

"It's sure nice to have you here," Duke said. "Like the old days, when you were a kid and your folks was training for Westwood." Duke introduced her to the other three men at the table, all trainers, who nodded and smiled at her. "You're not hanging around with this magician, are you?"

Meg laughed. "No. I just met him."

"Well, watch out for him. He's one of these damn liberals, like all those Hollywood people."

"Yeah, if it were up to me, Duke, I'd make myself commissar of the whole country and put all you nineteenth-century throwbacks into a gulag."

"A what?"

"A concentration camp, Duke. Just the place for an old right-wing horseshit artist like you."

There was more of this sort of banter, but none of it harmful or taken seriously. A couple of the boys told some mildly funny but definitely racist jokes, then the talk turned to the rising costs of keeping horses in training these days, now about two thousand dollars a month, exclusive of vet bills. Duke was especially incensed about workers' compensation, which he considered a complete fraud perpetrated on the public by left-wing politicians, a corrupt legal system, and crooked insurance companies. "Hell, I had a hotwalker who claimed stress, for God's sake," he said. "Stress! He'd only worked for me about ten days. When I found out about it, I punched him right in the mouth. Now he says he's going to sue me."

"He don't have any teeth, Duke," one of the trainers said. "He ain't got a case."

"Damn insurance companies," Duke said. "It just makes you sick. It's pitiful."

I'd heard all this before, but I still found it entertaining. I loved being able to hang around the backside, I loved hearing the stories, the jokes, the horse talk. Like magic, it took me out of myself, away from the hostile outside world. Sarajevo, Somalia, Rwanda, riots in the cities, AIDS, unemployment, the deficit—sure, the world is a hostile, terrible place, but hey, who do you like in the double? If the world can't be a rose garden, at least there are racetracks you can escape to.

I tried to explain how I felt about it to Megan Starbuck as we walked back toward Willie's shed row. She had kept quiet at the table, except to answer a couple of questions about what her parents were doing now. And she heard me out, then said, "You're a gambler, aren't you?"

"Only on the horses," I said. "I don't bet on anything that talks, I don't try to go up against the casinos, I don't buy lottery tickets, and I don't play cards. I used to like poker a lot, but nobody would play with me now anyway."

"Why is that?"

"There isn't much I can't do with cards, Meg," I explained. "Want to see?" I reached into my pocket and produced a deck.

"Now?"

"Sure. Why not?"

"No, I'm just going to have a look at Willie's string and go on my way. I have an appointment at ten o'clock."

"Will I see you at the races?"

"Not today."

"How about Friday night? Hollywood races at night on Fridays. We could have dinner, I'll show you a few safe moves, and we could catch the last few races."

"Well, maybe," she said as we reached the corner of Willie's barn, a big, gray, graceless stone structure that looked more like a prison than a stable. "I hate these new barns, don't you?"

"They're nice and airy, good for the horses," I said, "but I agree with you. Aesthetics has never been a backside strong suit, not in California, anyway."

"I'll call you," she said.

"Please do, one way or the other, okay?"

"Okay." She turned and shook my hand. "I guess you're okay, Shifty. May I call you Lou?"

"Sure, if you'd like to. Lots of people do."

"I'd prefer it. Shifty sounds, I don't know, a little shifty, if you know what I mean."

"I got the nickname after a kind of deal I'm pretty good at," I said. "The Erdnase Shift. Maybe I'll show it to you Friday night, if you'd like."

"We'll see. If I'm in town." She looked at me thoughtfully, as if trying to decide once and for all about me. "You may not be a gambler, but you're certainly a player," she said.

"Yeah, you're right," I told her. "I'm going to waste my life having a good time."

"So, Shifty, what are you up to now?" Max Silverman asked as I passed him that morning on the way to my apartment. He was sitting in a straight-backed chair by the swimming pool, sipping a cup of coffee and reading the *L.A. Times.* The sun was out, just peeping over the top of the building, which encircled the pool. Max had placed his chair in the shade of one of the old palm trees that had been there ever since the complex had been erected, back in the early 1950s. Sunlight didn't agree with Max, who was at least in his mid-eighties, but who had changed hardly at all in the decade I'd known him. An ex–classical violinist who had played with several of the world's best symphony orchestras, he was a tall, thin old man with a wrinkled, kindly face almost always topped by a black beret from under which protruded wisps of gray hair. I suspected he was bald, but I hadn't seen him for years without his hat on, so I couldn't be sure. He managed the building and lived in a cluttered two-room flat near the street entrance, which enabled him to keep an eye on his tenants, not all of whom had proved to be of impeccable character. I hadn't seen him for a couple of months.

"I've just come from the track, Max," I said. "I'm going to clean up and go see my agent."

"They're running in the mornings now?" he asked in alarm. "Shifty, this will destroy you."

I laughed. "No, Max, it's all right. They only have workouts in the morning. The racing's still in the afternoon."

"Ay," Max exclaimed. "Shifty, why do you do this to yourself? You have a great talent. Why do you waste it? Gambling, it ruined Dostoyevsky."

"He still wrote some great novels."

"The greatest," Max agreed, "but think what he could have written if he had not been a gambler."

"My guess is he wrote such long books because he needed the money to pay his debts," I said. "Max, if he hadn't been a gambler, he might never have written anything."

"That is ridiculous," Max said. "Sit down, Shifty. You want a cup of coffee?"

"No, thanks, Max, I've had my quota today." I sat down anyway, on the edge of the diving board facing his chair. "What's up?"

"Up? Nothing is up. I wished to talk to you, that is all."

"You okay?"

"I'm fine," he said. "I have not seen you for a time. So?"

So I told him a little about my recent doings, keeping it light and amusing. I enjoyed talking to Max. Unlike me, he took the world very seriously. The continued misadventures and follies of the human race distressed him and I think he was fascinated by my ability to dance away from this scene of misery. We had one thing in common, Max and I: we both loved life. But he was one of those people who had always striven to make the world a better, more civilized place to live, whereas I had always taken Voltaire's great closing statement in *Candide* to heart: " 'Tis well said, but we must cultivate our garden." I had once quoted this line to Max, but he had dismissed it as irresponsible. I think he enjoyed my conversation, however, because I offered him some relief from the dreary accounts of wrongdoing and mayhem that he culled daily from his newspaper.

"So what about that girl you were seeing?"

"May Potter? That's all over with, Max."

"You were so crazy about her."

"She had another agenda," I explained. "Anyway, she moved on. I think she went back to Florida."

"And are you owning any horses now?"

"No, Max. The only one I ever had was Mad Margaret, and that was because that rich old man gave her to me."

"The one who killed himself, I remember," Max said, sighing. "Ah, such a waste. All that money and so much to do with it."

"He was bored, Max."

"Bored? It is a sin to be bored in this life."

"I thought you were Jewish, Max."

"I am. So?"

"So what's this talk about sin? Guilt, yes, but sin?"

"Don't be a smart aleck," Max said. "You play with words like you do with cards. How is your magic?"

"I still work at it, Max. Two or three hours every day, sometimes more. I'm going to have some new moves to show you pretty soon."

"Ah, that will be wonderful. That is what you should be, an artist, not a gambler."

"I'm not a gambler, Max. I'm a horseplayer."

"An uneasy distinction, Shifty. So this horse you had, where is she now?"

"She's a broodmare, on a ranch a couple of hours away from here. She just had her first foal, a filly that looks exactly like her. I go up and see her from time to time. She gave me a little financial security, Max, with all the money she won and the price I got for her. I owe her a lot. I'll never lose track of her, and I'm not going to let anything bad happen to her."

"Don't throw the money away gambling."

"Hey, Max, give me a break. Racing's been very good to me."

"Yeah, I believe you. Here." He held out the paper for me.

"It's okay, Max, I subscribe, too. I just don't read the front page, unless it's a really sleazy crime story. I enjoy those."

"I know that. Why do you think I hand it to you? There's a really good one in here. About this man who murdered his wife and children and then shot himself." He stood up and stretched. "What people don't do to each other. It's a scandal." He shuffled away toward his flat. "Thanks for talking to a boring old man. You're a good boy."

"I'll see you, Max. The pleasure was mine."

That was how I heard about the Goldman case. When I got back to my apartment, I washed up and showered, then lay down on my bed to read about it. The story repeated the maid's account of how she had found the bodies of the two girls, shot at point-blank range through the head by a small-caliber pistol, probably a .25. The wife, Penny, had apparently tried to come to their aid, but had been gunned down before she reached the door. She had fallen forward on her face, almost certainly still alive, then had been dispatched like her daughters, by a bullet through the head.

Bob Goldman, the husband and father, had been found dead twelve hours later in his Mercedes sedan, parked fifty miles or so to the east, off the road to the mountain community of Julien. It appeared that he had killed himself. He had placed the twin barrels of a shotgun inside his mouth and pulled the trigger. The police had found a sealed envelope, presumably a suicide note, on the seat beside him, but they had so far refused to divulge its contents.

At first reading, it struck me as merely the simple but sordid tale of a businessman reacting savagely to failure and consequent stress. Goldman had been a small-scale wheeler-dealer in the Reagan eighties, another ruthless corporate raider who had financed his operations with junk bonds and loans from several now-insolvent savings institutions. None of his attempts at major takeovers of half a dozen large firms had succeeded, but every failure had enriched him through stock manipulations and buy-offs. In 1990 he had been indicted for fraud in one of these schemes, but after two years the government had dropped charges against him. Goldman had expressed bitterness at the cost of having to defend himself in the case, saying that the claims against him were false but nonetheless had lost him his credibility in the financial markets. He had been unable since then to put any kind of a business deal together and had been living, his friends and acquaintances said, on the remains of the fortune his maneuverings had earned for him, an estimated fifteen or twenty million dollars.

Goldman could not have been in need and so it was hard to understand why he would have wanted to kill himself, much less his wife and children. He had, however, been depressed recently and during the past year had disappeared for weeks at a time on mysterious trips. Not even his wife had known of his whereabouts, one neighbor recalled. Mrs. Goldman had told the neighbor her husband needed to be alone for a while and she had not questioned his absences. After all, he had always come back to her and the children, hadn't he? Penny Goldman was a devoted Jewish housewife and mother, primarily concerned with the family's welfare and her rose garden. Everyone felt certain that poor Bob must have been under terrific pressure to do what he had done; he must have had a reason, perhaps a financial one. Who knew for sure how much money the Goldmans really had? Bob had been angry and full of hate, especially at the politicians; he had contributed money to many conservative causes and groups, most notably the Heritage Foundation, the National Rifle Association, and America One.

Something about the story bothered me and I began to understand, as I dressed to go and see my agent, why Max had thought I might be interested in it. Max was a connoisseur of the sordid and the sensational, and he knew I had a weakness for scalawags and dirty doings. Here was a man who until then had led a humdrum, upper-middle-class life, who believed devoutly in the capitalist system and had exploited it to earn himself some money and put his family on easy street. He had experienced some reverses, but still seemed to have plenty of loot left to live well. He had every reason to think that he might eventually be able to get back in the money game, once the economy began to loosen up a bit and the speculative fever started to simmer again.

Of course, there might have been hidden reasons for the murder-suicide act. And, as his neighbor Tom Greenwood put it, he could have just gone crazy. "Bob definitely had a paranoid streak in him," Greenwood said. "He hated a lot of people and he hated hard. He thought the whole country was being taken over by the wrong people. You couldn't reason with him about it, but he was a pretty nice Joe and a real good neighbor. I don't think he could have done this unless he'd really flipped out. Why drive fifty miles away to kill himself? Why didn't he do it right on the spot?"

I thought Greenwood had a point there. Goldman, however, may have just fled, not knowing what to do, and then taken his own life a few hours later, when the enormity of his deed had overwhelmed him. Still, it was odd. Odder still was the fact that he had apparently been hit several times. The police had reported bruises and a couple of small cuts on his face. And why hadn't he used the handgun, which was found in the front hallway? Why the shotgun, which had necessitated a trip to his gun rack in the den and the unlocking of cabinet doors? Well, I was probably making too much out of illogical but basically small discrepancies. A man in great mental distress would not act coldly and calculatingly. Interesting, though. I thought I'd talk it over later with Max, who loved that sort of discussion.

I was halfway out the door when my phone rang; I picked up the receiver in time to cut off my answering machine. "Lou?" her voice said. "This is Megan."

"Hi. You've called to say yes."

"No, I can't see you Friday night. I have to go back to San Diego."

"That's too bad. When *can* we see each other?"

"I don't know," she said, "but I'll call you Sunday morning, I promise."

"I believe you. Is Megan what you like to be called?"

"Oh, Meg's okay. And now that you told me where Shifty comes from, that's okay, too."

"I don't care what you call me. Just call."

She laughed and hung up.

3
Thespians

♣

The whole meet has been a disaster," Angles Beltrami said after the fifth on Sunday, when his key exacta horse finished out of the money again. "I can't understand it. I started so good. The first half I had nothing but winners, but now I can't even pick my nose."

"You're pressing," Jay said. "You're on a losing streak and you're pressing. Back off. Cut your action down till you get your touch back. It always turns around eventually, Angles. Your problem is you won't wait for it. You try to force it too much."

"I'm picking good horses," Angles said. "I got a real opinion in every race, but something always happens. My horses stumble out of the gate, they get fanned on the turns, they get shut off on the inside, the jockey drops his whip at the eighth pole. Twice I get disqualified. I mean, what's going on here?"

"You need freshening, Angles," Jay said. "Go home, take the rest of the day off. Give yourself a break. Wait for Del Mar. That good sea air down there will clear your head and turn things around for you."

"Yeah, but the hell of it is I got a great angle and I can't cash in. I got this guy who's paying me to pick winners for him and I can't pick any."

"Why would he persist?" Arnie asked. "The man must be a masochist."

"No, he ain't religious," Angles said. "The thing is, I pick a thirty-to-one shot for him two weeks ago and he cashes a huge ticket, so he tosses me a couple of bills. And then he says he wants me to pick horses for him and he'll pay me twenty percent of his winnings. He's a potential gold mine, but ever since then I can't come up with a live bet. I mean, what the hell's going on?"

"Why don't you turn him over to Jay?" Arnie suggested. "Let him do it and you take a finder's fee."

"What, are you crazy? I got this walking gold mine and I should pass it on to Jay?"

"I don't need any more clients, Arnie," Jay said. "Who is this guy, Angles?"

"Some old actor," he said. "You seen him in a hundred movies. You should hear the guy talk. It's like he's from overseas or something. Half the time I don't know what he's saying. But he's a big bettor and I could make a bundle. Only I can't pick a winner."

"As I understand it," Arnie said, "your losing streak began about the time you met this actor, right?"

"Yeah. Just before I come up with the long shot," Angles said. "I haven't had a winner since."

"Lose him," Arnie said. "The guy's a jinx."

"Yeah, I considered that," Angles said, "but he bets with both hands. What an angle! I could win a fortune without risking a dime of my own."

"OPM," Jay commented, "the ideal betting situation."

"Which is?" I asked.

"Other people's money," Jay said. "Angles, who is this guy? An old actor, you said. What's his name?"

"Everybody calls him Reggie, that's all I know."

"Reginald Montrose," I guessed. "He used to own horses."

"I know him," Jay said. "He plays all these character parts. You've seen him, Shifty."

"Oh, sure, he's great. He's an expert on Shakespeare."

"Who?" Angles asked.

"An English playwright, Angles," Arnie explained. "You've heard of *Hamlet?*"

"Hamburger Hamlet," Angles said. "Yeah, yeah, I know. I had to read them terrible plays in school. All that funny language. That's how this guy talks. I got to get him a winner."

"Give him the six horse in here," Jay said. "First time on the turf, but she's bred for it. She'll run well and she'll be a decent price."

"Yeah, thanks, Jay," Angles said. "I like that horse, too." He stood up and started out of the box. "What have we got, twenty minutes? I got to go find Reggie."

"Where does he hang out?" Jay asked.

"The clubhouse bar. He watches the races on the monitors. And how he roots, you should hear him. He sounds like one of them terrible plays." And Angles left in pursuit of his benefactor.

"Terrible plays, he calls them," Arnie said, shaking his head and snapping his *Racing Form* open to look at the entries again. "Angles must have been educated in a zoo."

"An orphanage, actually," Jay said. "One of the nuns taught him to handicap. But he knows more than you think he does, Arnie. He hides it from people."

"Nobody's going to mistake him for a genius," Arnie said. "Where are you going, Shifty?"

"To walk around a bit," I said. "I don't like this race and I'm not going to play it."

It was a cool, clammy day, with an overcast and a lot of hazy smog in the air, more like mid-June than late July. I was bored with the racing that day, nothing but mediocre horses and small fields, and I wanted to take my mind off it by moving around. Also, of course, I was looking for Megan Starbuck. She had called me that morning, as she had promised, and said that she'd probably be at the races for the second half of the card. She'd be in the Turf Club with some people and I could look for her there, or I could pick her up after the races at the Westwood Marquis, where she was staying. She was going to let me take her out to dinner, but only if she could pay her half of the check. "Equality for women, I love it," I had said to her. "I'll even let you split the drinks."

"Why not? You either believe in equality or you don't."

"I'm adaptable, Meg," I said. "I play it as it lays."

"What does that mean, Lou?"

"Old gambling term. Go with the flow, how's that?"

"Exactly. I'll see you later. I'll be busy with these people in the Turf Club," she said. "Can you get up there?"

"Sure. I'll dress more reputably than usual, that's all."

"Okay, but I may not be able to spend much time with you, Lou."

"That's all right," I said. "We'll have the evening."

I walked over to the stairs leading from the grandstand area to the Turf Club and was glad to see that, as usual, the usher on duty was Jack Biggs, an affable good old boy I had known for years. "Jack, I need to get upstairs," I said, coming up to him.

He glanced quickly around, then let me through. "Jay likes the six horse in this race," I said as I passed him.

"Thanks, Shifty. I'll get down on him."

Upstairs it didn't take me long to spot Megan. She was sitting at a large table above the finish line with a group of well-dressed middle-aged men, among whom I immediately recognized Wayne Copeland. The star was sitting at the head of the table, but seemed to be totally uninterested in his party. He was gazing through a large pair of binoculars at the horses for the seventh race, now on their way past the stands and around the clubhouse turn toward the starting gate. I hesitated, wondering whether I should approach their table, then decided not to. While Copeland was concentrating on the horses, the men around him were talking animatedly to one another. Meg was listening to them, but not contributing very much. I stood at the end of the aisle, looking back and forth from my program to the animals and waiting for her to notice me. As the odds on Jay's selection in the race began to drop, however, I found myself wondering whether to risk some money on it, so I didn't notice Meg coming up beside me.

"Hello," she said. "You look very nice all dressed up. I didn't know you were a member."

"I'm not, but I know racetracks. Or, as my friend Angles would put it, there's always an angle."

"Want to meet Wayne?"

"Not especially. Are you with him?"

"Sort of. I mean, I'm not dating him or anything like that."

"That's good. I don't think I could compete with a movie star, even if he is twice your age."

"You think so?"

"Sure. He's got to be in his early sixties."

"He's sixty-three. I'm thirty-one."

"I was right. He's married, isn't he? Or did his wife die? You never hear about her."

"No, she's alive. She just stays in the background. I don't think Wayne's all that interested in women. I don't mean to imply he's gay. He isn't."

"So what are you doing for him?"

"A little PR, that's all."

"Really? You're in the movie business?"

She laughed. "No. I'll tell you about it later. You can drive me home from here, if you want to."

"Fine, I'd like that. How about stopping at my place first, so I can clean up?"

"You're not that far away from me," she said. "Can't you drop me off and then go home? I have to change, too, and I also have to make some calls. Pick a time and a restaurant and we can meet there."

"All right," I said, "but we could have gone together in one car."

"Not this time, Lou."

"How'd you get here?"

"Bill McDame drove me," she answered. "I work for him. He's the big blond guy with the mustache." She touched my arm briefly. "I'll see you later, Lou. Meet me downstairs at the Turf Club entrance after the feature, okay?"

"Sure."

I watched her go back to her table. Nobody stood up, pulled her chair out for her, or acknowledged her reappearance in any way. They were all still very busy talking to one another. Wayne Copeland had his binoculars focused on the starting gate, where the horses for the seventh were now being loaded into their stalls. I hurried back downstairs to watch the race.

"Do you believe that, Reggie?" Angles was saying. "Nosed at the wire! One more jump and we'd have had him! At five to one, too! I can't believe this!"

"To weep at losing is to make less the depth of grief," Reginald Montrose said, gazing intently up at the TV monitor then providing a replay of the seventh race, in which the horse Jay had selected had gone five wide on the turn for home and had just missed catching the winner, the six-to-five favorite. "If that dumb jock just waits, we get through on the inside and win by two. I knew they shouldn't have put Otay up on him. He can't ride the Turf Course, the bum!"

"There's small choice in rotten riders," Montrose said.

"I'd like to kill the little bastard."

"We may pity an incompetent ride, though not pardon it." Montrose sighed and stuffed his program back into his jacket pocket.

Angles turned around in disgust and noticed me. "Shifty, did you see that ride?"

"Yes. I was standing right behind you."

"If the jockey don't do that, we win by two. We make a bundle and the whole day turns around."

"*Et tu,* brute," Montrose said. "I doubt some foul play."

"Reggie, this is my friend Shifty."

"Enchanted, lad," the old actor said, extending his hand as if to bless me. "Art thou of the inner confraternity?"

"If you mean do I bet on the horses, the answer is yes," I said, smiling. "I'm happy to meet you, Mr. Montrose. I've admired your work for years."

"In the cinema?"

"Yes, mostly."

"A dismal medium that reduces the sublime to the merely vulgar."

"I've also seen you onstage," I said. "Years ago, when you played Banquo in *Macbeth.* In Pasadena, wasn't it?"

"Ah, yes," the actor said. "A glorious production, that one, except for the infamous Macbeth himself, Mr. Wayne Copeland, a movie thespian of limited resources and barely a smidgin of talent. Yes, I remember it well, the mangling and the mumbling of the Bard's most eloquent flights."

"You were fine."

"Yes, I was, but then I am an actor, not a lout ennobled by a lens. Out, out, brief candle!"

"I told you," Angles said to me. "Sometimes I can't hardly understand him. Reggie, we're in a bad streak here, but we'll come out of it, I promise you."

"I 'gin to be aweary of the game," the actor intoned, "and wish the estate of the world were now undone."

"Hey, Reggie, don't take it so hard."

I decided on the spot that Reginald Montrose was someone I wanted to see more of, with or without Angles. He was tall, very thin, with a long, aquiline nose, dark eyebrows, obviously dyed, and the ruin of what must have been a classic profile, something on the order of a John Barrymore or a Richard Burton. A black toupee sat on his head like a small prayer rug, tilted slightly to one side, and he was dressed in dark gray slacks, loafers, and a bright red cashmere sports jacket. He had to be at least in his early seventies, but he had the energy of a much younger man, set off by a booming baritone voice that he could evidently project to the rear rows of the grandstand if he had to. He had obviously been as dismayed as Angles by the loss of the last race, but his cheerful, optimistic nature had apparently survived the ordeal, not only of the one race but the long losing streak he and Angles were undergoing. Angles was trying hard to reassure him, but the actor cut him off in midpitch. "Tomorrow and tomorrow and tomorrow creeps on apace," he boomed. "Today is a tale told by an idiot, full of sound and fury, paying nothing." He raised an arm in salute, then turned to go.

"See you tomorrow, Reggie?" Angles asked.

"When night's candles are burnt out and jocund day stands tiptoe on the misty tote board," he said. "Good night, sweet princes, and may flights of winners sing you to your rest."

"I told you," Angles said after the old man had gone, walking briskly out through the crowd as if parting the Red Sea, "he's a real character. I hope he ain't gone for good."

"He'll be back, Angles. Don't worry about it. How much did he lose?"

"At least a grand. He's got bucks, believe me. If I could just get him some winners . . ."

"Don't give up, Angles," I said. "And above all, to thine own choice be true."

Angles looked at me in horror. "Not you, too," he said. "What is this? A contagious disease?"

"It's called culture, Angles. Revel in it."

"So what do you do for Wayne Copeland?" I asked her as we headed up the freeway toward Westwood.

"Not much yet," she said. "I work for Bill McDame. Copeland may want us to represent him."

"For what? I thought you lived in Virginia."

"I do, in Alexandria. But I work in Washington."

"For this guy McDame?"

"Yes. It's a consulting and public relations firm, Flaherty and McDame."

"I've heard of it," I said. "Politics. Didn't they work for Bush?"

"During the first campaign, not the second one."

"He fired you?"

"Well, not exactly. I wasn't with the firm then, but Bill told me they couldn't get along with the people around Bush during the reelection campaign," she explained. "They were pretty arrogant. They thought, after Desert Storm, that they had it in the bag. By the time they woke up, it was too late, of course."

"So that's what you do, manage political campaigns?"

"Not exactly manage," she said. "We advise, we concern ourselves with the candidate's image, we try to deal with the press. You know, anticipate what they want, make sure they get it, and try to keep things under control. We also do a lot of cleaning up of the messes candidates make while they're out there shooting their mouths off. That's the hard part of the job."

"I'll bet." I glanced at her. She was sitting beside me, looking out the window at the smog-shrouded landscape of L.A. It was so bad we couldn't even see the Santa Monica Mountains on either side of the Sepulveda Pass, but I'd become so used to living in bad air that I hardly paid any attention to it anymore. "Well, well, I'm having a date with a spin doctor," I said.

She smiled. "Yes, a really corrupt individual."

"I guess I'd rather think of you as a hired gun, one of those Western roles Copeland's so good at playing."

"That's better. Yes, I guess that's what I am."

"For conservatives only?"

"I'm afraid so," she said.

"But *you're* not right-wing, are you?"

"No, I'm an independent. I don't belong to any party." She smiled. "I've always voted mostly Democrat, though."

"Shocking, Meg. Do they know this about you?"

"They've never asked. It's none of their business. For all I know, my boss also votes left. It's not an issue. We just do our job as well as we can."

"Which is to make saints out of sinners."

"I like that," she said. "It makes what we do sound, I don't know, magical."

"Metamorphosis. What kind of animal are you going to change Copeland into? An elephant?"

"Something like that. He's thinking about it."

"No, really? Running for what office?"

"I really can't talk about it yet, Lou," she said. "It's much too early."

"I hear he's really way over on the right. I mean, really extreme."

"Lou, I just can't discuss it with you. If he doesn't hire us, or if he decides not to run, I'll tell you."

"Run for what? Mayor of Palm Desert? Isn't that where he lives?"

She didn't answer.

"Uh-oh," I said, "it's big, right? My God, is the country in that bad a mess? Another movie star to the rescue. What will they think of next?"

"Talk to me about horses or magic," she said. "It's safer. And also more interesting."

By the time I dropped her off at her hotel, she knew pretty much all about me—my fairly dismal childhood growing up in a small town on the South Shore of Long Island, the obsession from my teenage years with magic, the jobs in magic shops in New York while trying to become a magician, my move to L.A. in the late seventies and the years I put in there at the Magic Castle, mastering and perfecting my craft. "And that's how magicians are made, not born," I concluded as I pulled into the hotel driveway. "Of course, like a jockey or a concert pianist, you have to have good hands."

"And the horses?" she asked. "Where do they fit in?"

"Ah, that's another story, Megan," I said. "You sure you want to hear it?"

"I'm fascinated."

"Really? I didn't know I was such a charmer."

"Don't bullshit me, Shifty Lou Anderson," she said as she got out of the car. "Where are we having dinner? I'll meet you there in an hour."

I gave her the address of Dudley's, one of my favorite hangouts in West L.A., and drove home. It wasn't until I pulled into the carport under my building that I realized I hadn't learned much of anything about her. She'd encouraged me to do all the talking, which was admirable of her, but she made me a little uneasy, as if I were being auditioned for a part.

4
Moves

♠

This is a neat place," she said as she joined me in one of the rear booths next to the bar. "Been waiting long? I'm sorry I'm late. Too many phone calls."

"You're only ten minutes late and I came early," I said. "Don't worry about it. What do you want to drink?"

"I want to eat. I'm starved. Do you mind?"

"Drinks and dinner coming right up," I said, signaling to the waitress at the far end of the bar.

Meg was gazing about her with evident delight. "It's great," she said. "Who's Dudley? Not the ex-jockey?"

"The very one," I told her. "He opened this place about five years ago, after he recovered from that bad spill at Hollywood Park, remember?"

"I wasn't here then, but I heard about it. He broke his leg."

"Shattered it," I said. "He still walks with a limp. But he's doing better with this restaurant than he ever did as a rider, so he's not complaining."

"Is he here?"

"I don't see him, but he'll be in later, I'm sure."

"He rode a couple of horses for my dad. I remember him as a real sweet guy. English, right?"

"Yes."

The atmosphere in Dudley's was always convivial, in a very informal way. The bar stretched along the whole length of the dining room, which consisted of large booths that could seat up to eight people. Beyond this room was a second one containing a single pool table, with more dining tables around it on a raised platform. The walls were festooned with track memorabilia—posters and blowups of great races and horses, jockey silks, whips, caps, boots, even horseshoes. The prices were reasonable and the place was nearly always full, the pool table always in action. Whenever Arnie Wolfenden needed money, I could always find him in Dudley's, hustling. Arnie had been a pool shark in his youth, had played with the best and could still beat the casual players out of a few hundred bucks on any given night. I was relieved to find him absent, since I wanted to be alone with Megan Starbuck on this first date. I wasn't sure how she would respond to my colorful but raffish friends. She had a background in horses, but she dressed and acted like a person solidly entrenched in the corporate world. Ordinarily, I'm not attracted to the type, but something about her, some quality disguised by the middle-class exterior, sang to me. One of the talents of a good close-up man is an ability to make quick judgments about people, react instantly to their personalities and adapt to them. I also liked to use magic to test people, bring out the best in them if I could.

It wasn't going to be too difficult with Megan. No sooner had we ordered a couple of glasses of the house red than she said, "Show me something, Lou. I'd like to see what you do."

"Well, here's one of my favorites," I said, reaching into my pocket and producing five golden thimbles on the fingertips of my right hand. "I haven't done it for a while, but it's a lot of fun. When I first started practicing, I could never decide how to start. I thought maybe that instead of five on one hand"—a little crossing pass at chest level—"four and one might be better, first one on the left, then one on the right." I moved the thimbles from finger to finger, hand to hand to match the patter, keeping it low-key and gentle, as good patter should be. What Megan saw was a ballet of fluttering hands, with the little thimbles moving in perfect time from finger to finger. Then, without having touched each other or moved below the level of our table, the thimbles simply vanished. I held out my empty hands for her to look at.

"Wow," she said. "What do you call that?"

"Golden Thimbles," I said. "You like it?"

"It's beautiful, sort of like a ballet."

"May I borrow your ring?" I asked her, indicating the silver one she wore on her right hand. "Nothing significant about it, is there?"

"My dad gave it to me for my high-school graduation," she answered. "Why? Are you going to make it disappear?"

"Not exactly. And a pen or a pencil. Do you have one?"

She tugged the ring off her finger and handed it to me, then opened her purse and produced a golden Cross pen. "This all right?"

"Sure. I want you to use yours, just so you'll know it's not rigged to make this work."

"What work?"

"You'll see. Now, Meg," I told her, "pick up the pen and hold it very tightly at both ends." She did so. "Just as hard as you can, out toward me, okay?"

She smiled warily, not knowing what to expect. "You're going to take it from me."

"Why would I want to do that, Meg?" I asked. "No, I'm going to give you your ring back, that's all." I held up the ring for her to look at. "This is it, isn't it?"

She didn't answer, but concentrated on the pen, clutching it fiercely in front of her. I made a quick pass and put the ring on the pen. She saw it dangling there, between her hands, and looked up at me in amazement. "How did you do that?" she asked. "I just felt like a little tap on the back of one hand."

"Magic," I said, "that's all. Magic."

"That's incredible. Do it again."

I did it again. She said nothing this time, then slipped the ring back on her finger and returned the pen to her purse. "Wonderful, Lou, just wonderful," she murmured at last. "What do you call that?"

"Ring on a Stick. Not very romantic or awe-inspiring, but apt, don't you think?"

"Do some more."

The waitress appeared and we ordered, after which, during the ten minutes or so that passed before our food arrived, I showed her three moves with coins. When our orders came, I raised my glass and toasted her. "Here's looking at you, kid."

"That one I know," she said. "*Casablanca.*"

"My all-time favorite movie. Pure magic."

"Yes, I can see how it would be. How many tricks do you know, Lou?" she asked.

"They're not tricks, Meg," I explained. "They're moves. Oh, maybe a thousand or so."

"Incredible."

"Not really. My friend Vince Michaels in Vegas has at least two thousand, but then he doesn't play the horses."

"Who's Vince Michaels?"

"The finest close-up artist I know," I said. "The fastest hands in magic."

"Faster than yours?"

"Maybe not at cards, but he's the best."

"You haven't shown me any card moves."

"There's plenty of time," I assured her. "I'm hard to stop, once I get started."

The food at Dudley's is basically meat-and-potatoes, but the quality is first-rate and the cooking superb. Megan ate a pepper steak, very rare, and wiped her plate clean with a big slice of sourdough bread. She also had a Caesar salad, a fruit tart, and drank more than half of our bottle of Napa Valley cabernet. "I have this terrible appetite," she said. "Always have had."

"You're a big girl," I said, "but where do you put it all?"

"Please don't say big, I hate that. When I was a kid, everybody called me a big girl, including my parents." She sighed. "I guess I was and am."

"You don't look overweight, though."

"I work out a lot. How about you?"

"Not much. Once a week I take a women's defense class."

"Women's?"

"Sure. It's taught by a friend of mine, Mary Conroy. As you can see, I'm *not* big." She grimaced. "Sorry about that," I continued. "I work at it the way I do at my magic, for misdirection and speed. I've learned to use my feet pretty well."

"You get into fights?"

"Hardly ever." I held up my hands. "This is the only capital I have, Meg. I try not to get in harm's way."

I showed her some shuffles, including the Erdnase Shift. "Now I understand," she said. "You know, Lou, watching you work, I get this feeling about you."

"What kind of feeling?"

"That you could alter my perception of reality."

"That's what the best magic is supposed to do, Meg. The world is a pretty heavy load most of the time. I try to lighten it a little."

I was waiting for Meg to finish her fruit tart, so I could show her a few more moves, this time with cards, when Bobby Dudley stopped by to say hello. "Shifty, how are you?" he said. "All set for Del Mar?"

"I'm leaving right after getaway day," I said. "Bobby, I want you to meet Megan Starbuck. She says you used to ride a few horses for her dad."

"You're Jim Starbuck's daughter? Good Lord, I haven't seen you since you were a toddler," Dudley said. "Slide over, Shifty. Let me have a good look at her." He sat down beside me and leaned toward Meg. "Of course I rode for your dad, more than a few times, too. Westwood Farm, wasn't it? How is Jim? And your mum? I haven't seen them for years. Where are they?"

Megan filled him in on the family news. Her parents were doing all right, she told him. They lived on a small spread near Hemet and bred a few horses, which they sold privately. They rarely came into town anymore. "Dad's in his mid-sixties now and Mom has a bad ticker. She can't do too much and she may have to have surgery," she concluded. "I see them as often as I can, but I live in the East now and don't get out here all that much."

"Well, you've grown up to be quite a beauty," Dudley said. "How did you happen to fall into the clutches of such a reprobate as Shifty here?"

"He picked me up at the track."

"That figures. Excuse me a moment," he said, getting up and limping out of our booth. "They're calling me from the kitchen."

"He's a nice guy," I said after he'd gone. "Too bad."

"What do you mean, too bad?" she asked. "His leg?"

"No, I was hoping he'd ask you about you."

"Why?"

"It would save me the trouble," I said. "I don't know anything about you, really. I mean, how you go from being a California horse person to becoming a PR flack for politicians. That's quite a transition, Meg. What happened?"

"Nothing dramatic," she said. "All very mundane and uninteresting, basically. I married a guy from the East, someone I met in college, and moved there to be with him. He was a doctor, an allergist. Actually, he was still in medical school and I went to work to help him get through it."

"And?"

"And nothing. We were together nearly two years and he began to have an affair with a nurse. Fairly sordid stuff, really. When I found out about it, I left him."

"But you stayed in the East?"

She shrugged. "Yes, I got to like it. I was working in advertising, first as a copywriter, then I began to have my own accounts. I was doing fine till the recession and our business shrank in half. Then Bill asked me to come to work for him. And that's my whole story. Not very glamorous or interesting, is it?"

"You and Bill?"

She laughed. "That is none of your business, Mr. Anderson," she said. "But I'll tell you anyway. Sure, he asked me out a couple of times, but I said no and he's never bothered me since. He's my boss and we have strictly a working relationship."

"He's married."

"Of course." She laughed again. "Most men make at least one pass in every relationship. It's the nature of the beast. What happens afterward is another matter."

"Okay, I'll make mine now," I said. "Would you like to come back to my place and see my posters?"

"Your posters?"

"And other decorative touches. I only live a few blocks away. We can have coffee and a nightcap and then I'll bring you back here and you can drive home to your hotel."

"Wow, a dazzling offer."

"We don't have much time, Megan. Tomorrow's getaway day. I leave the morning after for Del Mar. Who knows when I'll see you again? Anyway, I'd like you to see my place. I promise not to touch you."

"Make no promises you can't keep," she said. "Your hands are a little too fast. Fine. I'd love to see your place. Let's go."

I lived on the ground floor of the two-story complex, in a corner at the rear of the building. "Kind of a funky place," Meg said as we threaded our way through the rickety aluminum beach chairs strewn carelessly around the pool area. "Who lives here?"

"A lot of fringe people," I said. "Actors, models, retired folks on fixed incomes, a few losers trying to hang on. It's fairly cheap."

"It looks it," she said.

Once inside my front door, however, her attitude changed. "Oh, Lou, this is nice," she said. "It's definitely you."

The apartment reflected my basic enthusiasms. It was one large room, furnished very simply, with a queen-size bed, a big stereo, a TV set, a single armchair, an old chest of drawers, and several big floor lamps. In one corner I kept my more recent *Racing Forms*, a stack about four feet high. The tools of my trade—packs of cards, cups, rubber balls, little plastic animals, coins, bits of string, a row of basic books on prestidigitation—rested on a long table next to my bed. Blowups of great horses in action took up the far wall, while on the other were portraits of famous conjurors. Framed posters of my two favorite magicians, Houdini and Giuseppe Verdi, occupied the space above the stereo and dominated the room. "Verdi, the composer?" Megan asked. "What's he got to do with horses and magic?"

"You might as well say life and magic," I answered. "That great Italian understood more about both than anyone else."

"You're an opera fan?"

"Giuseppe turned me into one," I said. "Basically, I'm a Verdi fan."

"Where do you practice?"

I pointed to the kitchen table. "Out there," I said. "There's great light in the morning, even on overcast days. Want a drink?"

"Maybe a beer."

"Coming up." I went into the kitchen and came back with two open bottles of Dos Equis. "This okay? You want a glass?"

"It's fine." She took a couple of swallows from the bottle, then strolled around the room, taking in the sights. "Tell me about the horses," she said. "This is Sunday Silence, isn't it?"

"Winning the Breeders' Cup Classic," I said. "I made a bundle on him that day."

"I loved that horse," she said. "I cried when he lost the Belmont."

"He looked like a giraffe, some Eastern trainer said about him before the race. He looked like a god to me."

"I saw the Triple Crown races, every one of them." She turned around to look at me. "This is a wonderful room, Lou. I think I really know a lot about you now."

"Want to see a few more moves?" I asked, reaching for the pack of cards in my pocket.

"No, not now," she said. She walked up to me and kissed me, very sweetly and gently, then put her hands on my shoulders and looked into my eyes. "Would you like to go to bed?"

"With you?"

"Who else? Are you expecting anyone?"

"Oh, no. I guess I'm surprised."

"It's what you want, isn't it?"

"Well, yes, but you—"

"I'd like to, if you would."

I kissed her this time and her arms went around me. It was a passionate kiss and her body pressed into me. "I guess I ought to kill some lights."

"Why? Don't you want to see what we're doing?"

"Well, yes, but—okay. How about precautions? Are you okay? I mean, I have condoms. . . ."

She stared into my eyes. "Lou, do you sleep around a lot?"

"No."

"Neither do I. Now will you please take my clothes off, or do I have to do it for you?"

5
Getaway

♥

Getaway days at racetracks are usually melancholy affairs, because they bring to a close another long-running drama of horses and people, successes and failures, opportunities taken and missed. They leave behind them an aura of regret, if for no other reason than that of time passing. Every race meet begins in an atmosphere of anticipation, a bustle of arrivals, with the giant horse vans unloading their precious cargos, and the feeling in the air, amidst the noise of shouted instructions and music blaring from the radios of the stable hands, that tomorrow's miracle is at hand. The big traveling circus that is the world of the Thoroughbred is back in town, its wonders to perform, and you had better be there so as not to miss any of it. But by getaway day the glories have passed into history, the dreams have faded, and the caravan is packing up and moving on. There is no music to be heard where only echoes linger and every passing breeze stirs up small clouds of dust along the empty stalls.

But for me, at Hollywood Park, getaway day is a fiesta, because it means that I'll be leaving for Del Mar, where for the seven weeks of the summer meet I'll be once more totally involved in the day-to-day affairs of the racing world. The town is small, about twenty miles north of San Diego, and is flanked by an endless line of fine beaches. From the grandstand and the open terraces of the track you can watch the long Pacific rollers breaking on the white sand. The worst losing day can be soothed and quickly obliterated by a half hour spent in the surf or by what Jay calls the wine ceremony, a quiet hour or two of sitting on a blanket, sipping white wine, and watching the sun set beyond the horizon. Losing in such a setting becomes another way of winning, because, as Jay once put it, "a shitty day in paradise is better than a good day anywhere else." And best of all, as far as I'm concerned, is the fact that in Del Mar the horse people don't disperse, as they do in larger cities. For twenty-four hours a day, every day, the racing world reigns supreme. We think, talk, and act on little else but horses, and as always in racing, there are no endings, only beginnings. "There's always fresh," the gamblers say.

So I showed up at Hollywood Park on getaway day brimming with hope and high expectations. In our box, Jay sat, methodically poring over the stats in his notebooks, while in the row behind him Arnie placidly perused his *Racing Form*. "Gentlemen," I said as I joined them, "and I use the term advisedly, this will be a great day. I can sense it in the air. We will depart for the south in a great cloud of green bills."

"A reckless prediction," Arnie said, not looking up from his paper. "The Dummy God is on his throne."

"What dummy god?" Whodoyoulike asked, thrusting his face over the railing in front of us. "What do you mean?"

"Ah, the ubiquitous suppliant," Arnie observed, gazing with distaste at our visitor. "He comes in ignorance to gather crumbs of wisdom."

Whodoyoulike, whose real name nobody knew, was dressed as usual in his baggy brown suit and food-stained necktie. One of life's minor parasites, he survived at the track on information and opinion, no matter from what source or how ill-founded. Now, having overheard Arnie's dour prediction, he lingered before us, his face a blur of indecision and anxiety. "What do you mean? Who do you like?"

"The Dummy God protects the innocent and the foolish alike," Arnie continued. "Go thou and wager on the obvious, for the day reeks of potential chalk."

"What's he saying? Who do you like, Jay?"

"He means it looks like a day for obvious favorites," Jay said. "I wouldn't bet against them."

"Oh," Whodoyoulike said, his eyebrows arching upward in consternation. "You mean that?" But before Jay could confirm his estimate of the card, Whodoyoulike had vanished, scurrying off in pursuit of Marty Joyce, a professional tout from whom he'd wheedle more information on the day's doings.

"Sad," Arnie observed, watching him go. "Incorrigible."

"He'll probably cash some tickets today," Jay said. "It does look like a very obvious card, with few potential surprises."

"So," Angles said, suddenly exploding into our box from his own round of information gathering, "so listen to this! I heard from two sources that the shipper in from Golden Gate has got a big shot in the feature. How about that, huh? He'll be twenty to one, at least. The sucker can really run. Twenty to one, what an angle!"

"Who are your sources?" Jay asked.

"I can't tell you, but believe me, they're good ones. They know this horse from up north."

"He broke his maiden against claimers and in slow time," Arnie objected. "Then he wilted after a fast half in the stakes race. Where's the angle? He ought to be fifty to one."

"No, no, you don't get it," Angles said. "The first race he was in hand. The jock never touched him with the whip, and he won in a breeze. In the stakes race, he drew the rail and he bled. See? They're adding Lasix today and he's drawn outside. I'm telling you, this horse can run."

"You mean Walpole?" I asked. "Angles, he's trained by Dunne. The guy never wins."

"He couldn't spell *horse* if you gave him the first four letters," Arnie said.

"It ain't Dunne," Angles said. "It's Robertson, who trains up north. He's good. They just sold him to these owners, who use Dunne. But he ain't had time to screw him up yet. I'm telling you, this horse can run."

"And what are you planning to do about the favorite?" Arnie asked. "You going to shoot him?"

"You mean the actor's horse?"

"Superpatriot will be even money or less and should win, Angles," Jay said.

"So you box him with Walpole," Angles insisted. "Exactas, you remember exactas, guys? Where you pick these pigs to run one-two? What's the matter with you? I come up with a great angle to beat this race and you act like I'm trying to trash your day or something. I don't get it. Anyway, I had my say. I'm boxing them, and that's the way it's going to be."

"Someday, Angles, they'll box you permanently underground, you get buried so often," Arnie said.

Like Jay, I saw no reason to buck what looked on paper like a very obvious card full of probable winners going off at low odds, so I spent most of the afternoon wandering around and schmoozing with my friends. After the fourth, I bumped into Angles again. He was ecstatic because he had managed to put Reggie Montrose onto a couple of winners and ensure the continuation of his potentially profitable relationship with the old ham. "We ain't making real money yet," Angles informed me, his black eyes alight with greed, "but at least we're cashing a couple of tickets. Look at the old boy." Behind him, I could see Montrose declaiming to a small knot of admirers at the corner of the clubhouse bar. "I had to get away from him for a few minutes, Shifty. This guy can talk your ears off, and most of it I don't understand. It's like poetry, you know? Crazy stuff."

"Full of sound and fury, signifying nothing."

"Cut it out, Shifty. I can't take too much of that shit. Lay off, will you?"

I left him to go upstairs in search of Megan. She was sitting at a large table in the Turf Club, overlooking the finish line. There must have been thirty people in the party, mostly a Hollywood crowd, with the exception of Bill McDame, another tall, middle-aged blond man named Ed Drumheller, whom I'd seen around Copeland before, and Megan herself. The star presided at the head of the table. He was dressed in tight black pants, a wide belt with a huge silver buckle, a black-and-white-striped cowboy shirt and black string tie, and a light blue jacket that fitted snugly on his big, square shoulders. On his head he wore an immaculate black Stetson of the kind he'd sported in the early Western flicks that had launched him on the public consciousness a generation and a half ago. He was smiling and nodding to two overdressed, ripening beauties on either side of him, but his sharp blue eyes were focused elsewhere, on some distant panorama visible only to him. He hardly spoke at all, but then he didn't have much to say in his movies, either. He had become a star by playing those strong, silent men who had once, we imagined, stalked our frontier lands, slow of speech, fast to draw in the pursuit of justice and right. Even I liked those early movies, perhaps because we all had such a longing in this country for a return to simple values and an easier time, when every problem could be solved, every villain eliminated by a single upright, courageous man devoted to the common good. Dreamers, that's what we are, a nation of dreamers.

I lingered at the top of the aisle above Copeland's table until Megan spotted me, then went inside to the bar, where I thought she might come looking for me. I ordered a ginger ale and waited.

"That was lovely, Megan," I had said to her after we'd made love at my place the night before. "Did you enjoy it?"

"Why do men always ask that question?" she said, propping herself up on one elbow to look at me. "It must be insecurity, a congenital male failing."

"Probably," I agreed. "Or maybe we want to feel we've made our partners happy, that's all."

"Not all men," she said. "Not even most men."

"How many men have you known?" I asked. "Are you speaking from experience?"

"Observation," she said. "And I read a lot." She sat up and swung her legs to the floor.

"Where are you going?"

"A glass of water."

"How about a glass of wine instead?"

"No, I've had enough. Water will be fine."

"Stay put. I'll get it." I went quickly into the kitchen, opened the fridge, and poured a glass from my Sparklett's jug. When I came back, I found she had propped herself up against my pillows, with her arms behind her head, leaving herself only partly covered by the top sheet. She had small, nicely shaped breasts with large, light brown nipples.

"Stop staring," she said as I handed her the glass. "You've had enough for one night."

"How do you know? How do you know I'm not insatiable?"

"Are you?"

"When inspired, yes."

"And you're inspired, I can tell."

"How?"

"I can *see* it. And because you're very nice in bed," she said. "You're very considerate."

"Want to try again?"

She laughed. "My God, Lou, three times? You'll wear us out. Can't we just talk and be friendly for a while?"

"Absolutely," I said, climbing back into bed with her. "Okay, so tell me something."

"Like what?"

"About you. About your family. I don't know anything, really."

"There isn't much to tell," she said. "I had a secure, loving relationship with my folks, who are sort of conservative, old-fashioned, you know. My dad kind of shielded me from the track and I spent most of my time away from school on the ranch."

"In Hemet?"

"No, that came later. We had a little three-and-a-half-acre spread in the Sierra foothills, near Santa Anita, but we called it the ranch."

"Anything in California bigger than a lot is a ranch."

"Right. But we had horses there, never less than three or four, so I grew up in that world. Not much to tell, Lou. I was an only child, so I had it all my way from the start. I guess just about the only time my folks didn't approve of me was when I decided to get married."

"They didn't like him?"

"They thought I was too young. And Dick was very arrogant. He came from Boston, from a very good family—prep schools, Ivy League, all that. And I was just a simple country girl from an L.A. suburb."

"How did you meet?"

"Through a friend of mine, who was also a premed. Dick was on vacation, driving around. I guess I knew even then he was kind of a snob, and my folks sensed it right away. Also, he was a liberal, which to my dad was like being a Communist. I didn't care. He represented a new world for me and he was very charming. I thought he'd get over the snob part."

"And everything was okay until he had this affair with a nurse."

"Not really. I was already pretty sick of him by then," she admitted. "Dick was a taker."

"And you're a giver."

"You want to know the worst thing about him?"

"He beat you."

"No way, I'd have killed him. No, he wouldn't eat vegetables."

"He what?"

"Can you imagine living with someone who won't eat vegetables?"

"Nothing from the garden?"

She held up a hand and made a big circle with her thumb and forefinger. "Zero. I think I started to lose interest in him when he made a scene one night over having to eat his green beans."

"How about zucchini? I love zucchini."

"He'd eat lima beans and that's the one vegetable I don't like much."

"And you had to cook for him."

"It was hell, Lou, pure hell." She smiled and held out her arms; I descended into the curve of her embrace and rested my head on her breast.

"I like this," I said. "I think I could get used to it." I started to make love to her again, but she pushed me away.

"Hey, I've got to get out of here."

"What's the rush?"

"Rush? Lou, it's nearly midnight. I have to get up early."

I lay in bed and watched her dress, which was nearly as much fun as watching her undress.

"Stop staring," she said. "It's rude."

"I've never had any manners, Meg, but you'll get used to me."

"Maybe. Hey, get up."

"Me? I live here."

"You have to drive me back to Dudley's, remember?"

"Oh, yeah, I forgot. Why don't you stay here? I'll drive you back for breakfast."

"Can't do it, Lou. I have an early-morning appointment."

"So? I'll get you there on time."

"Don't argue with me, please. And hurry up, will you?"

I got out of bed and went into the bathroom to wash up. When I came out, she was sitting on my bed, fully dressed and looking at the *L.A. Times*. I began to climb into my clothes, but she ignored me. "What's so interesting?" I asked.

She looked up, a little startled. "Oh, nothing. I just happened to pick up the paper. Hurry up, will you, Lou?"

"That's an old issue. You like crime stories?"

"Not especially."

"You were reading about the Goldmans, weren't you? A really snazzy family murder-suicide, don't you think?"

"I don't know. I was just looking at it while waiting for you. Are you ready?"

"Almost."

"What's *your* interest in the story?"

"None, really. Max, my friend the manager of this building, gets off on sleazy crime stories. He brought it to my attention. It's a good one, I have to admit."

She shrugged and stood up just as I zipped up my pants and

stepped barefoot into my moccasins. "One last kiss, for the road," I suggested.

"Not a chance," she said. "I don't trust you, Lou."

"I wouldn't either, if I were you," I agreed, following her out the door. "I'm a thoroughly unreliable type."

I waited at the Turf Club bar for nearly ten minutes before Megan found me. "Lou, get out of here," she said as she walked up to me. "I can't see you today."

"You're working?"

"Can't you tell? We have twenty-seven people at Wayne's tables and we're trying to keep all of them happy. It isn't easy. So I can't linger."

"When am I going to see you?"

"I don't know. I'll call you."

"I still don't have a phone number for you."

"I said I'd call you. When are you leaving?"

"Tomorrow morning, early." I handed her a slip of paper. "My summer number. We have a condo overlooking the racetrack."

"We?"

"My friend Jay Fox and I."

"How convenient." She thrust the slip of paper into her purse and started to leave.

"Not even a parting peck on the cheek?"

"Are you kidding? Grow up, Lou. This is work."

I went back downstairs, made a couple of small losing bets on mediocre horses in uninteresting races, more to break the monotony of a Dummy God day than anything else, then went down to the paddock before the running of the Juvenile, a six-and-a-half-furlong sprint for the best two-year-old colts and geldings on the grounds.

Copeland's Superpatriot had drawn the eight hole, a great post position for the distance, and was being saddled under a tree toward the rear of the walking ring. I strolled in with a group of owners and went over to have a look at him. He was a big, strong dark bay with a small white blaze between his eyes, and he looked like a champion. Undefeated in four races, all of which he had won easily, he was already the favorite to win the Breeders' Cup in the fall and was being considered a potential leading contender for the Triple Crown races the following spring. His trainer, William Short, better known in the racing world as Billy Bob, was reportedly very high on him. "He's done everything I've asked him to do and then some," he had told reporters earlier. "Of course, you never know in this game, but I'd say the colt will go long. He's bred for it. I'm sure glad Mr. Copeland gave him to me to train." Standard trainer talk, but Billy Bob Short was good at it. I'd met him a couple of times through my friend Charlie Pickard, who had once trained my filly for me, and been told by Charlie that he was a good horseman. "He ain't got the brains of a newt," Charlie had said, "but he can get a horse to run. Don't talk politics to him, though."

"I wasn't planning to, but why not?"

" 'Cause you're a damn liberal," Charlie had said, "and Billy Bob's a redneck from the Kentucky hills. He once told me the 'Battle Hymn of the Republic' was a nigger song."

I had never had occasion to talk to Billy Bob, since he was a loner who tended to keep to himself, but I saw no reason to, anyway. Short was about sixty, with a tight-lipped, mean-looking face and the arms of a blacksmith; he also had a reputation as a barroom brawler. He struck me as the perfect guy for Wayne Copeland and his aptly named horse. I glanced at the tote board. Superpatriot was already three to five to win the race.

As I stood there, looking at the colt, Copeland and a portion of his entourage appeared. The actor went up and patted his animal affectionately on the neck, while his friends milled about on the grass off to one side. McDame was there, but not Meg. Copeland turned away from the horse and grinned. "Doesn't he look just great?" he said to his group. "We're going to win one for America again."

I was still trying to figure out what he meant by that, since I couldn't imagine what winning a horse race could possibly have to do with patriotism, when the paddock judge called out, "Riders up!" Billy Bob gave his jock, Kelly McRae, a leg up into the saddle and the horses began to move out under the stands toward the track. I trailed along behind Copeland's army of admirers, watching him wave to the crowd as he headed for the Turf Club. He certainly looked like an authentic Western hero, even if he only acted the part.

It wasn't much of a race. Superpatriot broke alertly out of the starting gate, then dropped back a couple of lengths behind the two leaders, speed horses going the first half-mile in fast time. At the three-eighths pole, McRae asked Superpatriot for his run and the colt put his head down and responded. One light tap of the jockey's whip and he blew past the leaders, opened up two lengths by the head of the stretch, and won by eight, well in hand, as the chart caller for the *Racing Form* put it the next day. "Very nice," was Jay's comment as the horses came back toward the finish line. "We may be looking at an eight-hundred-pound gorilla here."

"Too bad we couldn't bet on him," Arnie said. "Twenty cents on the dollar is not my price."

"I keep reminding you guys," Angles said. "Exactas, exactas. I put him on top of the two speed horses. You see who ran second, don't you? Walpole. So it only pays eight bucks, that's three to one, right? Nothing wrong with that, is there?"

"Angles, Angles," Arnie said, "I wonder what will become of you?"

"Yeah, well, the story here is I'm cashing and you're not." Angles laughed and left us to rake in his loot.

I went down to the winner's circle to have another look at the now-ecstatic crowd around Wayne Copeland and his horse. Again I couldn't find Meg in the group. After the photographs and the ceremony, a reporter stuck a microphone in the actor's face as the TV cameras focused on him. "Well, Wayne, you must be very pleased with your colt's race," the reporter said. "Billy Bob really had him ready to run."

"Yes, he did," the actor said, smiling into the cameras. "This was a great win. Not only for me and Billy Bob and the folks here, but for Americans everywhere."

"Why is that, Wayne?"

"Because this is America's horse," Copeland explained. "Like I said before, all of Superpatriot's earnings go into a fund I've started for underprivileged children, to make sure they get a good education and a good start in life. It's called the Superpatriot Scholarship Fund, and it's administered by America One. It's to give America's kids a head start in life, and there's not one cent of government money in it." The actor took off his hat and waved it to the crowd. "Those folks out there know what I'm talking about. We've had too much government meddling and too much wasting of the taxpayers' hard-earned dollars in this country. It's about time we took our nation back from the politicians, boys. And setting up this fund in Superpatriot's name is just a small beginning, a little taste of things on down the road a ways."

"Sounds like a terrific idea, Wayne," the reporter said, a little uneasily; he obviously hadn't prepared himself for a speech. "Where do you figure your colt may run next, Wayne? The Futurity at Del Mar?"

"That's all up to Billy Bob." The actor put an arm around his trainer's shoulders. "But wherever he runs, it's for America's kids, just remember that."

"Well, thank you, Wayne, and good luck to you and to Superpatriot."

The reporter lowered his mike and the actor began to move back toward his table, waving and shaking hands with members of the public as he went. I returned to our box, where Jay was concentrating on one of his notebooks. "Jay thinks we have a bet in this race," Arnie said. "The horse on the rail. It's a good stretch-out fig."

"Did you hear Wayne's little speech?" I asked.

Jay looked up. "Speech? What did he say?"

"He's running for office."

"Really? Where? For what?"

"I don't know."

"Does it surprise you?" Arnie asked. "We elected Ronnie, didn't we? Why not some celluloid gunslinger?"

"Not for president, Arnie," Jay said. "Come on, that's three years away still."

"It's never too early," Arnie said.

"What about congressman or something like that?"

"Are you kidding?" Arnie answered. "Wayne Copeland waste his time in Congress? That would be like asking Wyatt Earp to skip the shootout at the O.K. Corral to play marbles in the school playground."

"I'm not sure I understand you, Arnie," I said. "You don't really think Copeland wants to be president, do you?"

"What else?" Arnie asked. "He didn't start up America One just for the fun of spending his money."

"Perot tried it and lost," Jay said. "You'd think they'd learn."

"They never learn, Jay," Arnie said. "And I'll tell you something else. The country's a lot sicker and angrier than it was two years ago. We're looking for a man on horseback."

"Arnie, I sure hope you're wrong," Jay said.

"What difference would it make?" Arnie replied. "Forget it, it's what they call real life. America in action, two hundred million boobs leading lives of shrill desperation. So tell me, why do you like this rail horse in the ninth?"

6
Sucker

◆

Meg didn't call me, but I was so busy enjoying myself that I didn't miss her all that much. My whole year is built around the Del Mar racing season, which runs from late July through the middle of the second week after Labor Day. I try not to take any engagements during that time, which angers my agent, the irrepressible Happy Hal Mancuso, and I dedicate myself to a schedule of beach and horses and a little partying at night. Not too dismal a way to pass time, and isn't passing time the reality we all face? We must cultivate our gardens, Voltaire told us. Well, my garden is the racetrack and, most specifically, the one nestled on the floodplain next to Del Mar. Who cares what the rest of the world is up to in its madness and cruelty. The golden girls are on the sands, the sky is blue, the ocean clean, and the horses are running at Del Mar. "Life is what you make of it," that great philosopher Arnie Wolfenden once said. "Life for me is a fast horse, five lengths in front at the eighth pole, with my money on his nose."

After the first five or six days, however, I began to wonder if I would ever hear from Megan Starbuck again. I also couldn't understand why she persisted in refusing to give me a number where I could reach her. It didn't make any sense to me, especially after our one wonderful evening together. At least it had been wonderful for me. Had I offended her in some way? What was there about me that made her so cautious, so reluctant to commit herself even slightly? "Don't try to understand women," Arnie said to me on the beach one morning after I'd mentioned that Meg seemed to have vanished from my life. "They are not of our species. They have their own mysterious agendas that have little or nothing to do with us, except as providers and mates. They are in the grip of the Life Force, Shifty, and we are merely servants to their ultimate goals."

"Oh, knock it off, Arnie," Jay said. "Shifty just wants her to call him, that's all." He looked up from his stats in time to see two nubile young women jog past our position in tiny bathing suits apparently held together by dental floss. "And as you can see, the area teems with possibilities."

"Yeah, she wasn't that good-looking anyway," Angles said. "She's got a big nose. I seen her."

"I happen to love big noses," I said. "A big nose is a sign of a warm heart. Besides, it's not big, just a little bumpy in one place."

"You're weird," Angles said. "All this free-floating pussy available here and you're waiting for some chick with a huge schnoz to ring your bell. Weird."

I decided to drop the subject of Megan Starbuck with my racing pals, who were clearly not attuned to women, but only to bodies. I stood up and ran into the surf, swam for twenty minutes or so, riding some nice waves into shore, and when I emerged it was to find Megan Starbuck sitting on my beach chair, waiting for me. "I thought you might be here," she said, smiling. "I was running along the beach and I saw your friends, so I decided to wait for you."

"The water's great," I said. "Want to come in?"

"No. When I finish my run, I have to go into town."

"San Diego?" I picked up my towel and began to dry myself.

"Yes, business, as usual."

"I gather you've met everyone."

"Yes, I introduced myself."

She looked beautiful, sitting there on my beach chair in the bright sunlight. She was dressed in white shorts, a blue jersey, and running shoes, and her red curls were tucked under a visored cap. Her skin gleamed and her legs, stretched out in the sand before her, seemed endless. I glanced at Angles. He was sitting on his own chair, about eight feet from her and off to the side, gazing at her in admiration. "So where are you staying?" I asked.

"At the Hilton," she answered, "but only tonight. I'll be at the Embassy on La Jolla Village Drive tomorrow night and for about a week. Want to take a walk with me?"

"Sure. But I thought you were running."

"I am. I've got about two miles to go, but I'll walk with you as far as the lifeguard tower. You want to run with me?"

"No, thanks, Meg. Surf and sand for me this morning."

"And then the track."

"Well, sure, they're running today, aren't they?"

Megan stood up and flexed her long legs to make sure nothing would cramp up on her. "So long, guys," she said. "It was nice meeting you."

"I wish you were entered in the seventh today," Arnie said. "It's for classy fillies and mares on the turf at a mile. I'd bet on you."

"I take it that's a compliment," Meg said.

"It's Arnie's way of saying you look good," Jay explained. "He relates everything to horses."

Meg laughed. "You guys are sick."

"No, just obsessed," Jay said.

We walked toward the lifeguard station along the edge of the water; the tide was out and it was easy going on the flat, hard sand. The beach was crowded, a typical summer day full of families with children of all ages and clusters of teenagers basking in the sun. "I remember this beach when it used to be nearly empty, even in summer," Meg said. "I'd come down here with my folks during the racing season and it was great."

"It's still pretty good, just too many people in the world."

"I guess."

"Meg, when are you going to give me your phone number?"

"When I have one," she said. "I've been living out of hotels now for weeks and I'm never sure where I'm going to be from one day to the next."

"You don't have an answering machine somewhere I can leave a message?"

"Back home, sure. But I only check it every two or three days."

"Then why don't you call me?"

"Lou, I get busy," she said. "You have no idea how demanding this job can be. But I'll be in and out of here all summer."

"I gather your client is getting ready to run for office."

"Something like that. He's thinking about it."

"What office?"

"No comment. Don't ask me, Lou. I can't talk about it now."

"Well, it can't be worse than the last movie actor we had for president. That's it, isn't it?"

"I said no comment."

"I can't believe you're working for him."

"Why not?"

"Because, from what I hear about him, he's to the right of Pat Buchanan."

"Well, how do you know I'm not a right-winger?"

"You told me you weren't. Anyway, I don't know. I just assumed."

"That's a dangerous thing to do these days, Lou."

"Well, are you?"

"What?"

"A right-wing freak."

"No."

"So why are you working for him?"

"I get paid, Lou. I'm a working stiff, remember? We can't all be artists and horseplayers. Some of us have to earn a living. And I like what I do. I have fun doing it. Really."

"You have fun telling lies about people?"

"Hey, that's pretty extreme, Lou. They're not all lies."

"You doctor the truth a bit, is that it?"

"Lou," she said, taking my hand and tugging me to a stop so that she could turn to face me, "you're going to have to stop questioning me and criticizing what I do for a living. That is, if we're going to see each other again."

"I'm sorry, Meg. I'm a naturally inquisitive type. I didn't mean to offend you. Actually, I don't know anything about what you do."

"Right. So why don't we keep it that way for now?"

"I agree. So . . ."

"So how about tonight?"

"Great. What time do you want me to pick you up?"

"I'll meet you somewhere. Anywhere you say."

"How about the Enoteca, the wine bar outside on top of the shopping center in downtown Del Mar? You know where it is?"

"I'll find out. What time?"

"Seven o'clock?"

"Okay, I'll see you there."

"We'll have a glass of wine and then go eat. There are several good restaurants in the complex."

"Good. Now I'll finish my run." I looked around and saw that we were standing in front of the crowded dining terrace of the Poseidon, next to the lifeguard tower. "Bye, Lou." She smiled, turned, and began to run away from me toward the south. She moved with the grace and power of a trained athlete, and I found myself wondering how she found the time to stay in such wonderful shape. It made me want to begin running, too, but I resisted the impulse and walked back to my friends.

"Hey, Shifty," Angles said, "I take it all back. She's got some figure. I've never seen a better pair of pins."

"What about her schnoz?" Jay asked. "I thought you said she had a big nose?"

"Who's looking?" Angles answered. "You ever see pins like that?"

"A few times," Jay said.

"Dans la nuit tous les chats sont gris," Arnie observed placidly.

"What the hell is that?" Angles asked.

"It's French, Angles," Arnie explained. "It means that at night all cats are gray. The French understand these things."

"What things?"

"Women come and go, Angles," Jay said. "Only the horses are forever."

"No shit. Even I know that."

I was late for our date that night. A car broke down and caught fire halfway up the exit ramp from the track and it took me nearly an hour to get back to our condo, a trip that ordinarily consumed no more than a few minutes. I showered and shaved in ten minutes flat, threw on a pair of clean slacks, a shirt, and a sports jacket in another five, but it was still nearly seven-thirty by the time I came panting up the stairs from the garage onto the terrace outside the Enoteca. It was crowded, festive, and noisy, but I spotted Megan right away. She was standing in the doorway of the little bar, holding a glass of white wine in her hand and talking to a couple I had never seen before. I waved and began to maneuver my way through the swarm of people partying on the terrace, which had become a popular meeting place for the younger crowd during the summer. The sun had begun to set and the ocean lay flat and still under its golden glow. "Hi, I'm sorry I'm late," I said as I came up to her. "A car broke down on the exit ramp and I got stuck in traffic for nearly an hour."

"It's all right, Lou," she replied. "I'd like you to meet Janet and Tom Greenwood. We just ran into each other. They're about to have dinner at Il Fornaio, next door here."

I shook hands with the Greenwoods. She was a big blonde of about fifty who I could tell had once been very beautiful, but she had the ruined face of an alcoholic, with watery blue eyes and a slack mouth. He was tall, lean, in his mid-fifties, with neatly combed white hair parted on one side and a small, tight face; he reminded me of a ferret. "Lou's an old family friend," Meg said. "We're going to have a drink and catch up on old times."

"Yes, that's right," I said. "I've known Megan since she was this high." I lowered my hand to my knee. "Well, maybe this high." I raised it to my hip.

"How cute," Janet Greenwood said. "And how tall were you?"

"Oh, I've always been this tall," I said. "I was born tall, like Athena sprung from the brow of Zeus, as a friend of mine would put it."

"That's silly," Janet Greenwood said.

"You're right. I guess since we were—well, what, Megan?"

"I guess you were in your teens," Meg said. "We met you at Santa Anita, when my dad was training there."

"That's right, how could I forget? What do you do, Mr. Greenwood?"

"I'm a banker."

"Good for you. One of the safe ones, I hope."

Greenwood's face flushed slightly, as if I had insulted him. "Of course it's safe," he snapped. "What are you implying?"

"Nothing, nothing," I answered hastily. "I was being facetious, that's all. All these bank failures lately, the savings and loans scandals. Nothing personal, Mr. Greenwood."

"You're a funny man," Janet Greenwood said. "How you talk!"

"I guess I'll get myself a drink," I said. "Excuse me a moment, while I remove my foot from my mouth."

I went inside the bar to get away from them and bought myself a glass of merlot. By the time I rejoined Meg, the Greenwoods had gone. "What was that all about?" I asked.

"They're backers of Wayne's," she explained. "I met them at a couple of fund-raisers. They're not my favorite people."

"Is he always that uptight or was it me?"

"I don't think he has much of a sense of humor."

"Maybe that's why she drinks a lot."

"How do you know she drinks a lot?"

"She's loaded right now."

"I guess you're right. Anyway, his bank is under investigation. That's why he was so defensive with you."

"Why did you tell them we're old friends?" I asked. "Aren't you supposed to go out on dates if you work for Copeland?"

"I don't know, Lou. I don't know why I said that. Maybe I don't want my private life to get mixed up with what I do for a living." She raised her wineglass to me and smiled. "The hell with the Greenwoods. Aren't you hungry?"

"Yes. Let's eat."

I took her down to the Poseidon, the only restaurant in town with an open dining terrace on the beach. It was a warm night and we sat under the stars, watching the surf break on the pale sand. The food wasn't very good, but it didn't matter. We drank a bottle of excellent California zinfandel and talked about our lives. She talked openly about her early days and school and marriage, but managed always not to talk about her more recent activities. It was a little strange and I had to remind myself that I had already made love to this woman, because she seemed so distant, abstracted, as if she would have preferred to be somewhere else. Finally, I decided to confront her. "Are we just going to be friends?" I asked.

"Why? What a strange question."

"I mean, what we had the other night, what was that?"

"Sex. And it was very nice, Lou."

"Ah, friendly fucking, I see."

"What are you getting at? Are we supposed to be engaged or something, just because we spent a couple of hours in bed?"

"You're so distant, Meg," I said. "I sense a sort of wall between us tonight. Are you ashamed of me?"

"Of course not. What a funny question!"

"That whole business tonight with the Greenwoods . . . By the way, where have I heard that name before? Has the bank stuff been in the papers?"

"I'm not sure, maybe. Aren't you being a little paranoid or something?"

"Maybe, maybe I am. But why did you tell them I'm an old family acquaintance?"

"I already told you, I don't know."

"You've been wound up like a coiled spring all evening. What did I do?"

"Nothing, Lou, really. I guess you'd better take me home. I'm not much fun this evening."

"It's your work, isn't it?"

She nodded. "Yes, but I can't talk about it. It has nothing to do with you, believe me."

"I believe you." I reached over and took her hand. "And I'm sorry if I seem pushy or overeager. I'd like to keep on seeing you. I don't suppose you'd like to go dancing or for a nightcap somewhere?"

"Not tonight, Lou. Next time."

"There will be a next time, then?"

"Sure. I like you, Lou."

"And *you'll* call *me*."

She smiled. "Yes."

"I guess I'll begin to believe we could be more than friends on the day you give me your phone number. Can I call you at your hotel?"

"I'd rather you didn't. I'm working and my hours are fairly irregular. I'll call you in a day or two and we can make a date."

"Okay, and again, I'm sorry to be pushy. I'm usually not."

We walked down to the garage together and I escorted her to her car, a rented white Pontiac. She gave me a quick peck on the lips, climbed in, and began to back her vehicle slowly out of her parking space. I hurried up the stairs to the level above, where my own car was parked, and arrived at the exit two cars behind her.

We both turned right out of the structure and headed north up the coast, then bore to the right where the road split. To my left, the empty grandstand of the racetrack loomed out of the darkness, and the musky smell of horses, hay, straw, dust, and manure blew in through my window. The Hilton lay between the freeway and the track, directly across from the stable entrance, but as I cruised along toward my condo, which was located on the hillside straight ahead of me, I saw the white

Pontiac speed on past the hotel entrance. On impulse, I swung my Toyota quickly over to the right lanes and followed.

Megan drove inland along the Via de la Valle toward Rancho Santa Fe. I kept a discreet distance behind her, hoping she wouldn't notice me; it was dark, I had the top up on my convertible, and she had no reason to believe I would follow her. She drove past the turnoff to the town center and proceeded for another half-mile or so, then turned left onto a country road that wound along between a series of large, walled estates and ranches, interspersed by groves of fruit trees. I lost sight of her around a sharp curve, then caught up to her again as she was turning into the driveway of a large white house with a small, classical portico.

I kept on going for a couple of hundred yards past another curve, then made a quick U-turn and came cruising slowly back. I eventually parked what I thought was a safe distance beyond the house and under the branches of a large overhanging pine. I turned my lights off. The two-story building directly across the way was dark. I took my racetrack binoculars, a small pair of Zeiss ten-by-twenty-fives, out of their leather case, got out of my car, and walked back down the road. I stopped some distance away and focused on the portico, where Megan Starbuck now stood, waiting for someone to open the front door. No sooner had I brought her into a clear picture than the door opened and Tom Greenwood appeared. He didn't seem surprised to see her, but he didn't invite her inside. He said something, turned, and left. A half minute or so later, Bill McDame and another man, whom I recognized as Ed Drumheller, stepped into the picture. A hurried conversation ensued, after which Drumheller went back into the house. Megan and Bill McDame talked some more, then he leaned over and whispered in her ear, after which he took her by the arm and led her inside, shutting the door behind them.

I took note of the number of the house, 3727, went back to my car, and drove to the end of the road, where I stopped long enough to write down the name of the street, Valencia Drive, before going home. I don't know why I do these things, but I'm a naturally inquisitive type and misdirection is one of the basic skills of my profession. I had felt all evening long, from the moment I'd joined Megan Starbuck outside the Enoteca, that she had not been dealing with me that night from the top of the deck. Something had happened, but I wasn't sure what. All I knew for certain was that I'd been the victim, even if only mildly so, of a sucker move, making me believe something that wasn't so. And I already cared too much about the lady.

Jay looked up as I came through the door. He was sitting at our dining-room table, hunched over his *Racing Form* and with his notebooks spread out around him. A row of red, green, and black markers lay next to his right hand and his reading glasses rested on the tip of his nose. "Well, you're home early," he said. "It's not even eleven o'clock. What happened? Has the lady proved to be a sprinter and not up to a classic distance of ground?"

"I don't know, Jay, but I do know I'm not going to talk about it," I said, heading for the fridge. "How's the handicapping?"

"Slow tonight, Shifty. It's a tough card tomorrow, a lot of cheap maiden and claiming races," he answered. "Not much to go on, but I'm digging out a small nugget of information here and there. Fish me out a beer, will you? I need a break."

"Maybe we should pass the card tomorrow," I suggested, tossing him a can of Budweiser from our stash on the second shelf. "Maybe we should all go to the beach instead."

"It's too early to write it off," he said. "I still have four races to handicap."

"Too much work, Jay. The track is supposed to be fun."

"It's no fun when you lose, Shifty. I'm not going to lose because I show up there unprepared. The racetrack is a very unforgiving place." He popped on the TV set and sank back in his chair. "Let's see the news and then back to work."

I went into my bedroom, undressed, and had a shower. When I came back out, in my bathrobe and holding the last of my beer, Jay had moved to the couch. On the screen, a reporter was doing a stand-up on a memorial service for Robert Goldman, which had taken place that afternoon. "Isn't that your girlfriend?" Jay asked.

"Where?"

"Oh, you missed her. She was standing in a row of people at the back. I guess that must be the house."

On the screen, behind the reporter, was the Goldman house, which I realized was the one I'd parked across from that night. The mourners sat on chairs on the front lawn facing the house and Wayne Copeland, who was apparently delivering a eulogy. The phrases "great American" and "true patriot" could be heard through the drone of the reporter's story. "Robert Goldman, one of the founders of America One, was obviously a deeply troubled man," the reporter said, "whose faith in this country was strong but not strong enough to protect him from the personal demons that haunted him."

"It probably was Megan you saw," I said as a commercial came on and Jay punched the muting button on the remote control. "Goldman was a pal of Copeland's and she works for Copeland."

"Really? Doing what? What an asshole he is."

"He's an asshole with money," I said. "And he wants to run for president."

"It's scary," Jay said. "It's the scariest thing I've heard since somebody told me that little Ronnie Reagan wanted to be in the White House. I still can't believe it. Wayne Copeland, the poor man's Clint Eastwood."

"America is the land of opportunity," I said. "Anyone can become president, even Wayne Copeland."

Jay stood up and headed back to his figures. "That's why I love horse racing," he said. "It's crazy, but it's not as crazy as real life."

7
Vanishes

♣

"So you haven't heard from her," Willie Vernon said, watching his horse begin to run at the head of the stretch. "I guess she's got things to do."

"I guess so, Willie. She seems to have a life all bound up in her work and it doesn't have much to do with me. Only I'm not sure just what her work is." I raised my binoculars in time to pick up Willie's horse as it reappeared from behind the infield tote board. The animal was running strongly along the inside, the exercise boy low in the saddle but not asking too much from his mount. "Who is that?" I asked.

"Little two-year-old colt I picked up at the Keeneland sale last fall, might be a nice one," Willie said, glancing at the stopwatch he held in his left hand. "Still about a month away."

"I like the way he moves," I said.

"Yeah, he's a runner," the trainer said. "At least, in the mornings. It don't count in the mornings, though. You got to wait till the afternoons. That's when it counts."

"I guess a lot of these two-year-olds don't like all that dirt kicked up in their faces for the first time," I volunteered.

"Hell, who would?" Willie's little colt made the turn, still running strongly, then began to ease up as the boy in the saddle relaxed and allowed him to gallop out. The trainer looked at his watch. "Not bad, maybe a tick slower than I wanted him to go."

"What did you get him in?"

"Forty-eight. That's about right. And he's galloping out good. I wanted a strong half out of him."

We were standing at the top of the old rickety wooden guinea stand looking down over the racing surface. It was about 7:00 A.M. and cold, with a drizzly fog sweeping in off the Pacific and blurring the outline of the grandstand across the way. Willie had a cigarette dangling from his lips, as usual, and was wearing a windbreaker and a cap against the chill. "A lot of people like this Del Mar climate," he said, "but I damn near catch pneumonia every year I come down here."

"It'll burn off by noon and it'll be a glorious day," I predicted. "Typical Del Mar summer weather."

"Yeah, well, the hell with it," Willie said. "You lazy bastards don't have to be out here every morning before dawn, when it's a damn freezer. Half my horses are coughing from this stuff. What do you call it?"

"Fog."

"Well, the hell with it. Come on, let's go back to the barn and get some coffee. We're on the break now." He tucked his hands inside the pockets of his jacket and headed for the stairs, along with most of the other watchers in the stands. The horses were coming off the track and the harrows were beginning their work of digging up and smoothing out the racing surface. We had about half an hour before the horses would be able to resume their training chores.

As I followed Willie down the steps, his colt came trotting back toward us along the outside rail. "He's a pretty little thing," I said. "Is he going to grow any?"

"Who knows?" the trainer answered. "He's sure a doer. He eats so much I'm thinking of sending him to Jenny Craig."

I love the smell and the feel of a racetrack in the early mornings, when the public is absent and only the animals and their entourages are on hand. It's like being backstage at the theater or in a circus, a world concentrated totally on itself, full of clubby banter and reeking of boundless hope. The animals move silently like indifferent aristocrats through this landscape, their keepers bustling about them on their endless chores, a sound of voices and music and occasional laughter in the air, the rub rags hanging out to dry looking like small pennants in the breeze. The wars will be fought in the afternoons; the mornings are dedicated to routine and gossip and anticipation and remembrances of things past, the sort of tales related around campfires. It's a world I've always found nourishing, even at its worst, when unforeseen large and small disasters strike and the stable champions sicken or die and disappear, never to be seen again. It's a cruel world, too, but no more so than any other. The animals, in their innocence and beauty, ennoble it.

Willie's barn was about halfway between the guinea stand and the cafeteria, not far from the gap where the horses go back and forth from the track. A large electric coffee machine rested on a corner of the desk in his tack room. Willie poured us both a cup, then indicated the open cardboard box of pastries next to it. "Help yourself," he said, grabbing one, "unless you're into some kind of health-food crap."

I picked up a doughnut and walked out to see what was going on, while Willie settled himself behind his desk to make some phone calls. "Time to call the owners," he said. "Treat 'em like mushrooms, you know. Keep 'em in the dark, feed 'em a little shit."

"Why don't you try telling them the truth?"

"What, and lose all my clients?"

I stood at the corner of the barn and watched several of Willie's horses being hot-walked in a long oval around a central group of outside pens containing three or four other animals. Down the shed row from me, several grooms were working around the stalls to the accompaniment of a Latin beat from somebody's boom box. Just another routine working day for everyone. I hunched into my sweater against the chill air, sipped my coffee, munched my doughnut, and tried to figure out what had happened. Was I becoming paranoid about this woman or was she really involved in something dangerous? Either that or she was a real flake and I'd better forget all about her.

I hadn't seen or heard from Megan Starbuck for eight days. On the fourth day, I had called the Embassy Suites, but she had moved out and nobody knew where she had gone. Then, from my condo, I had called the Washington, D.C., offices of Flaherty and McDame. The receptionist didn't know who she was, but eventually I was told by somebody's assistant that she'd be checking in. I left my name and phone number, but she never called me back. I decided to abandon the search and had just about given up on her when I suddenly ran into her in downtown Del Mar.

I had stopped at the local branch of the Wells Fargo Bank to withdraw a couple of hundred dollars from the ATM machine, and I was on my way back to my Toyota. It was about ten o'clock and I was planning to hit the beach as soon as the early-morning fog burned off. Megan Starbuck was sitting at the wheel of her car in the corner of the lot nearest the exit. I strolled over to speak to her. "Hi," I said. "Long time no see, long time no hear. How are you?"

"Beat it," she said. "Get out of here."

"Was it something I said?"

"Please. Go away. Now." Her face was tense and she gripped the steering wheel with both hands.

I backed away. "Okay, okay. I just thought we might have a cup of coffee together. They make a very good *caffè latte* up the street here. Sorry."

"I can't talk to you now. I'll call you."

"Sure you will."

"Lou, damn it, please leave me alone."

I backed away, holding both hands out in front of me. "I'm going, I'm going. I'm in full humiliating retreat."

I went back to my car, then changed my mind about leaving. It would be another half hour at least before the sun broke through the cloud cover, so I decided to have a *caffè latte* by myself, but at the small sidewalk café next to the bank. From my table, as I sipped my coffee, I had a clear view of the Wells Fargo parking lot and Megan Starbuck, still sitting quietly behind the wheel of her car. And it was then I realized she must have been waiting for someone.

A couple of minutes later, two men came out of the bank and walked across the parking lot toward a black Mercedes sedan parked up at the far end. One was Ed Drumheller, the other a thin, small, blond man of about fifty whom I'd never seen before. I glanced toward Megan, but she had disappeared. The two men climbed into the Mercedes, Ed Drumheller behind the wheel, and the car backed slowly out of its slot, turned, and moved silently toward the exit. No sooner had it headed out into traffic toward the stoplight on the corner than Megan bobbed into view behind the wheel again. She must have been lying on the front seat in order not to be seen, but now she started up her own car and headed quickly out of the lot. She barely made the light in time and sped away in the wake of the black Mercedes, two or three vehicles behind it.

All I knew for certain was that Megan had not wanted me to be there when the two men appeared from inside the bank, which accounted for her otherwise inexplicable hostility. I felt reasonably sure that now I'd hear from her sometime soon.

But I didn't. I began to think I might never see or hear from her again. And it struck me, from Megan's recent curious behavior, that being in PR seemed to be not unlike carrying on undercover police work. Unfortunately for me, it's this kind of behavior that never fails to pique my curiosity. It gets me into trouble, especially if I happen to care about the person or persons involved.

Willie came out of the tack room and began calling instructions in a mixture of Spanish and English to his foreman, Pablo, a tall, paunchy

Mexican with a mustache. "You want to see my big horse work?" he asked me. "It's about time they reopen the track."

"Who is your big horse these days?"

"You're looking at him," Willie said, pointing to the rangy chestnut Pablo was saddling. "That's Cremona."

I knew all about Cremona. He was a six-year-old gelding who ran mainly at long distances on the turf, in allowance races and unimportant stakes and handicaps. He was what is known in the game as a useful animal, a money-earner who never failed to bring home a piece of the pot, but who rarely won. I had never cashed a ticket on him and Jay never used him except in exactas; he often ran second. "Not my favorite horse," I said. "That's the star of your barn, Willie? You *are* going through hard times."

"I wish I had five more like him," the trainer said. "He's a goddamn money machine. Not like most of these common sonsabitches I got. You remember that colt I claimed last month off of Mel?"

"No, what about him?"

"He works like a demon, but I can't get him to run a step when it counts. I never should have claimed him. After I did, Mel comes up to me and he says, 'Squeeze him.' "

"Squeeze him? What does that mean?"

"Squeeze him like a lemon, he meant, because that's what he is."

"What did you pay for him?"

"Thirty-two thousand. I took him out of his first race and there was eight other bids in for him. Damn bum worked like Secretariat, for Christ's sake. Just my luck to win the shake for him. He's run twice since and spits it out top of the lane every time, just when the race gets going. Now I got an owner who's pissed off at me."

"Have you tried putting blinkers on him?"

"I tried everything but a damn jet engine up his ass. Hell, I should have known better than to try and take a horse off of Mel. He never would have run him for thirty-two if he was any good."

As we stood by the corner of the barn, waiting for Pablo to finish saddling Cremona and for Francisco Perez, his jockey, to show up, a big, dark bay colt, with Kelly McRae up in the saddle, walked past me on his way to the gap. Billy Bob Short came trotting up beside him on a honey-colored pony and said something to McRae, who nodded. "Hey, Willie, isn't that Superpatriot?" I asked.

"Yep, sure is. They're stabled over there, two barns down."

"I'll see you up in the guinea stand," I said. "I want to watch this colt work."

"They never work him fast, you know."

"I don't pay much attention to workouts, Willie. I just want to see what he looks like."

"You better pay some attention."

"Why's that?"

"Horse works fast, it might mean something. That is, if the clockers are honest." He grinned at me.

"Hell, Willie, I've been around the track too long to trust clockers."

"You're not as dumb as Duke says you are."

"We're not talking politics here, Willie," I said. "We're talking racing."

"I'll see you, Shifty. And if I run into Megan, I'll tell her to call you."

"Don't bother, it won't do any good."

"I hate to see a man go to pieces over some woman."

"Aren't you married?"

"That's what I'm talking about. Only place I can get away from her is here."

I left Willie and hurried off after Superpatriot. By the time I reached the guinea stand, the horse was out on the track, one of the first after the end of the break. Accompanied by Billy Bob Short on his honey-colored pony and under a tight hold from McRae, he was jogging purposefully toward the head of the stretch. I went up to the top row of the stand and focused my glasses on him. He was about halfway around the far turn when I felt someone come up beside me. "Hi," Megan Starbuck said. "I'm sorry about the other morning."

I turned to look at her. She was wearing sneakers, a pair of khaki pants, a windbreaker, and a baseball cap. "Well, well," I said. "You're being friendly this morning."

She smiled. "I'm really sorry, Lou. I didn't mean to be rude. I was waiting for someone."

"It must have been someone very important."

"It was, but I can't tell you about it."

"There seems to be a lot you can't tell me about."

"I guess there is."

I raised my glasses to pick up Superpatriot again. "Anyway, you do a great vanish."

"Is that a noun? Don't you mean vanishing?"

"It's a magic term. It's usually done with construction and mirrors, but you're terrific at it."

"I was going to call you—"

"I was hoping you would."

"But I had to go back East for a few days."

"I called your office. Some people hadn't even heard of you. I guess you didn't go there."

"No, I don't spend much time in the office," she said. "I'm usually on the road."

I glanced at her and smiled. "Hey, it's nice to catch a glimpse of you from time to time," I said. "So how have you been?"

"Fine. You?"

"Well, I'm not making any money at this meet yet, but it's okay. I'll turn it around."

"How are your friends doing?"

"About the same. It's always this way at the start of every meet, until we figure the track out and the horses have had a run over it. Meanwhile, we're busy enjoying Del Mar. I called your hotel."

"I had a sort of emergency situation, Lou. You must have done a lot of calling around. I'm sorry."

"It's okay. When did you get back?"

"Last night. I was going to call you."

"You were? When?"

"Today, maybe. Are you busy tonight?"

"Nothing I can't get out of. Where are you staying?"

"At the Doubletree."

"Where's that?"

"Just off the freeway, south of Del Mar. It's an okay place. You want to pick me up there around seven?"

"Sure." Superpatriot had now disappeared from view behind the tote board and I figured he must have begun his run. "You here to watch the workout?"

"You guessed it. Wayne's holding a little press conference afterwards."

"Really? Where?"

"Over at the barn. We're going to announce our plans for the colt."

"Is Wayne here yet?"

"Right down there."

I looked to my left. Wayne Copeland was sitting on a big white-and-brown Appaloosa just inside the gap. He had the reins in his right hand and in his left one a small pair of Zeiss binoculars through which he was watching Superpatriot move around the turn.

"Boy, this colt is something, isn't he?" Megan said.

"He may be one of the ones," I said. "No way of knowing yet, because he hasn't beaten anything. There may be a couple of real good colts in the East. I don't know."

"Wayne's lucky and you need luck in this game. My father spent his whole life around horses and never had one anywhere near this good." She walked away from me to check with the spotter, who was in touch with the clockers high up in the grandstand. "Forty-six and one," she said as she came back. "Come on, let's get to the stable. There'll be some press there."

Wayne Copeland came trotting up to the barn on his Appaloosa as Billy Bob Short and McRae brought Superpatriot back. His groom, a small, angry-looking blond woman of about forty, began to unsaddle the colt. She was obviously not happy with the presence of the half-dozen or so reporters, who were lounging about the tack room, waiting for the interview to begin. She was mumbling angrily to herself, even as she petted and fussed over her charge. The colt was still excited and full of himself after his run, so it was no easy job to calm him down. "What's she so angry about?" I asked Meg as we joined the group. "Is she his regular groom?"

"Yeah, that's Babs Harper," Megan said. "She's quite a character. She doesn't like human beings much, especially the press. She only likes horses. She just wants to get him settled down, and I guess she figures all this excitement isn't good for him. Horses are creatures of habit, you know."

"So are most men."

Wayne Copeland dismounted and Meg squeezed my arm. "I better get on over there and make sure Wayne keeps his foot out of his mouth. I'll see you later."

I lingered around the fringes of the interview, listening to the racing reporters ask their routine questions. How was the colt doing? When would he run again? Would he go in the Breeders' Cup at Santa Anita in early November? And so on and on. Wayne Copeland allowed Short to answer all the queries about the horse's health and fielded the ones having to do with generalities and hopes for the future. The sports sections of newspapers publish thousands of such interviews nationwide every month and I had long since stopped reading them. I walked over to look at Superpatriot, who was now being hot-walked in a circle around the central pens by Babs Harper. The colt had calmed down considerably by now and seemed to be enjoying a steady stream of soothing conversation pouring out of the little groom's mouth. "It's okay, it's all right," she was saying as I fell into step beside her, "it doesn't matter. They're a bunch of idiots and you don't need to pay any attention to them."

"You like talking to horses?" I asked.

She shot me a fierce, sidelong glance. "Who are you?" she asked. "What do you want?"

"Nothing, nothing," I assured her. "I'm not a reporter. I'm a friend of Meg's."

"Oh, all right, then. I can't stand all this bullshit."

"What bullshit?"

"The political crap and all these damn reporters, bunch of damn parasites, every one of them. What do you do?"

"I'm a magician."

"No shit. Well, why don't you fly away? I'm trying to get Junior here calmed down. He don't like people much either."

"Junior? That's what you call him?"

"Yep. Go away now. I got to keep talking to him. It's the only way he'll settle down. Beat it."

I stepped away from her and she went right back to conversing with the colt as they walked. The horse would bob his head up and down from time to time, as if he were indeed listening to her.

By the time I returned to the circle of people around Copeland, which had now grown to about a dozen, the actor, looking intensely serious, had launched one of his patriotic pitches. "My aim for this colt is to make him America's horse," he was saying. "We don't have enough heroes in this country, and we need them. Like I said before, every penny he earns is going to go toward helping my fellow Americans through the auspices of America One."

"Wayne," one of the reporters called out, "we've been hearing some rumors lately about you running for political office. Any truth to that?"

"Well, maybe, but nothing's been decided yet, folks."

"What for?"

"You mean, like for what?"

"Yeah, Wayne, that's it. You want to be president?" There was a ripple of laughter from the reporters.

"I never said I did," the actor replied, smiling uneasily, the same smile I'd seen him flash in those movie scenes where, for once, the hero is confronted by a woman, the sort of good woman who loves him but can't understand his manly ways. "We're not ready to talk about that, guys."

"When will you talk about it?"

Copeland shot Megan a quick look, as if asking for a cue, then shrugged and grinned, the sort of gesture he'd use in the movies to convey to the woman who loved him that he was what he was and she'd just have to grin and bear it. Like all Wayne Copeland heroes, he had a higher motive and was acting only on the noblest principles. "Folks, we're here to talk about this horse, not me," he said. "I don't know about politics yet. That's another world, isn't it? Anyway, we'll have some announcements to make, when and if the time comes."

"When might that be, Wayne?" another reporter called out.

Copeland hesitated and Megan took over. "Perhaps around the time of the Breeders' Cup, fellows," she said. "We'll make some sort of announcement then."

"If the colt gets there," the actor said, grinning.

"You mean your political aspirations depend on the success of this horse?" the reporter asked.

"No, of course not," Megan interjected quickly. "That's not what you mean, is it, Wayne?"

"Hell no," the actor replied. "It just seems like it might be a good time, that's all. It's halfway."

"Halfway? What do you mean, Wayne?"

"I'll let you boys figure that one out," Copeland said, starting to move away with Megan beside him. "Nice talking to you. See you at the races." They walked off together toward the line of cars parked along the fence beyond the last row of stables.

I headed back toward the cafeteria, along with two or three of the reporters. "You figured out what he meant by halfway yet?" one of the men asked.

"Sure," another one said. "It's halfway through Clinton's first term."

"You're kidding me. That's what he means?"

"What else?"

"I'd rather vote for the horse."

8
Versifying

♠

Why didn't you tell me you're a cop?" I asked as we drove down the freeway toward San Diego.

"What makes you think I'm a cop?"

"Come on, Meg. The other morning, when I spotted you in the Wells Fargo parking lot, that wasn't exactly PR, was it?"

She smiled. "No."

"Well?"

"Lou, there's something going on with Wayne that I don't quite understand," she said. "He thinks somebody's stealing from him."

"Stealing what? Cash?"

"Yes. But not from him, exactly. From his organization."

"America One?"

"Yes. Somebody's cooking the books."

"How?"

"Taking money out of the America One account in Wells Fargo and using it for something else. Wayne told Bill about it and Bill asked me to look into it, if I could."

"How could you look into it?" I asked. "Wouldn't you call in someone to audit the accounts? Why you?"

"I don't know why me," she said. "Bill told me Ed would be at the bank that morning. He asked me to show up there, try not to be seen, and to report to him what Ed was up to and if anybody was with him."

"Who was the other guy?"

"A man named Mark Clovis. I've only met him once before. He has something to do with America One at a pretty high level, heads a chapter or something back in upstate New York. Anyway, I was waiting for them to come out of the bank when you came along. I didn't want them to see me, so I shooed you away."

"Blew me away, you mean. And then you followed them."

"Just to see where they were going. Boy, are you nosy."

"And where did they go?"

"Back to Ed's house." She laughed. "It was kind of silly, really. I felt like an idiot. I think I overdid the gumshoe bit. You must have thought I was a real nut."

"That thought did occur to me," I admitted.

"Anyway, it's all pretty silly. Let's forget about it and have a good time, okay?" She leaned over and gave me a quick kiss on the cheek. "This is the first time off I've had in two weeks. Let's have some fun."

I had every intention of having fun. It was a balmy evening with a clear sky and I had put the top down on the Toyota so we could revel in it. I had picked Megan up at the Doubletree a little after seven and now we were speeding along the coast with Mission Bay on my right and the high-rise glass-and-steel towers of downtown ahead of me. Meg had not seemed enthusiastic about going anywhere with me in the Del Mar area, because, she said, she wanted to keep her personal life completely separate from her professional one, so I had suggested going into the city, only about twenty minutes away. "Great," she said. "I've never been downtown at night. Is it fun?"

"I don't know. We'll find out. I usually just hang around Del Mar."

Actually, I had worked a nightclub gig in downtown San Diego a few years earlier and had found it depressing. The town emptied out at night, with the white-collar middle class in full flight to the suburbs, abandoning what the natives call "the centre city," fancy spelling and all, to the homeless, the military on leave, and the adventurous. Since then, I'd been told, matters had improved. South of Broadway, historically San Diego's dividing line between affluence and despair, a badland of grand old buildings converted into flophouses, adult movie theaters, porn bookshops, massage parlors, and rescue missions had been redeveloped and restored to make the area attractive to the locals as well as to tourists. Once known as the Stingaree, which had flowered in the 1880s as the site of gambling dens, saloons, and so-called fancy houses, the district had prissily been rechristened the Gaslamp Quarter. Many of the old Victorian structures had been fixed up and revitalized as shops, office buildings, and trendy eateries. I told Megan all this, but added that I hadn't seen any of it with my own eyes or been down there at night since my earlier tour of duty.

"Why not?" she asked.

"I don't want to get too far away from the horses," I said. "Besides, Del Mar is such a nice place to be, why go looking elsewhere for fun at night?"

"How about your friends?"

"Arnie stays in a motel in Solana Beach, a mile away. He won't go anywhere that isn't within walking distance of a racetrack. Angles, he just hangs out in the bars and chases women. Jay sees no reason to inconvenience himself. Everything he needs is within a five-mile radius. Also, he spends six to seven hours a day handicapping, after which he has to spend time on the phone with his clients."

"His clients?"

"Yes. Jay picks horses for a living. When his clients win, he collects a percentage."

"He's a tout."

"Not exactly. He'll never give an opinion on a horse unless he's asked. He's a pro, that's all, but he also dispenses a lot of free advice to anyone who does ask."

"Wow," Megan said, "what's happened to the pioneer spirit? If it had been up to you guys, we'd have never crossed the Mississippi. We'd be negotiating with the Apaches for permission to get to California."

"It depends where the racetracks are," I said. "You know how we could have won the Vietnam War? Draft all the horseplayers, send them over there, and tell them that in Hanoi they have a track running twelve races a day, with no takeout, no taxes, and exotic wagering in every race. We'd have been in there in a matter of days."

"Very funny," Megan said as we drove past the airport and headed for downtown, with the harbor on our right. "Anyway, I like this town. It's pretty, don't you think?"

I had to agree with her. San Diego is basically an outdoor scene, a laid-back metropolis nestled up against a seemingly endless line of beaches—flat, white, broad, where the surf breaks in long, sweet, unbroken swells. All year round, the citizens picnic by the water or jog along the stretches of hard-packed sand or hurl themselves into the waves. The bay harbors yachts, tuna boats, the dark gray hulls of warships, a festival of life nourished by salt water, dark blue and sparkling under the sun. "You know, it calls itself America's finest city," I said. "Maybe it is."

"So why are you living in L.A.?"

"It's a little too relaxed down here," I explained. "I might go to sleep. Besides, I have to be in L.A. for my magic, and my agent's up there. Otherwise, I can't think of any reason not to live here."

Once off the freeway, it took me less than twenty minutes to find a restaurant we both liked the looks of. It was a small, unpretentious place on lower Fifth, in the heart of the old Stingaree. There was a long, dark wooden bar, with booths along the opposite wall, not unlike Dudley's, and the menu posted at the entrance looked adventurous, offering a variety of Oriental as well as Continental entrées. The walls were decorated with blowups of the district as it had looked in its scandalous heyday, as well as portraits of notables and sports heroes of the past. "My kind of joint," I said as we settled into the last open booth. "And it's not trendy."

"How do you know?"

"Look around, Meg. You see any loud kids in here, or Eurotrash? Just solid citizens out for a good feed. I'll bet you the food is terrific."

"I wouldn't bet you on the sun coming up," Megan said, smiling. "Okay, you're such an expert, I'll let you order for me, from drinks to dessert. Fish, preferably, and no hard booze. I can't handle it."

"All right, here we go," I said as I signaled for a waiter.

Luckily, I turned out to be right. I played it safe and ordered fairly traditional dishes, salmon for Megan and sole for me, which we washed down with a bottle of Sonoma County chardonnay. "An unpretentious but amusing vintage with a bit of *je ne sais quoi* about it," I said as I poured the first of it into her glass.

"What are you talking about?" she asked.

"French, for that indefinable something that makes for true pleasure."

"My God, Lou, where did you learn all this stuff?"

"Phony sophisticated chatter that impresses the boobs who don't know anything. Would you like to hear me on the subject of bouquet?"

"Flowers?"

"Taste, as in wine."

"Spare me. I'm one of the boobs and I'm impressed."

"You're neither. You're a country girl with a hidden agenda."

"Suit yourself. Now, can we talk about something else?"

We did. We talked mainly about magic and horses, my two obsessions. Every time I tried to steer the conversation toward her own life, she'd answer vaguely or in generalities, then ask me a specific question that would return the dialogue to my areas of interest. "Meg, what are you trying to hide from me?" I finally asked as we sipped a couple of cappuccinos.

"What do you mean?"

"All evening we've been talking about me," I said. "But I'd like to know more about you."

"I've just about told you all there is. I don't lead a very exciting life."

"I don't know why, but I don't believe you. You want to tell me some more about Copeland and the glamorous Hollywood scene?"

"No. That's just a job. And Wayne's a pretty dull customer, Lou. Most movie stars are."

"You want to tell me about America One?"

"What's there to tell? You read the papers, don't you? It's basically a charitable foundation to promote and funnel money into various good works that Wayne believes in."

"Come on, Megan. That's bullshit and you know it. Who are the people behind it and what's their real purpose?"

"Lou, I really can't talk about it, to you or to anyone."

"All right, then tell me about the Goldmans."

"What about them? You know the story, don't you? Bob Goldman shot his wife and children and then killed himself, poor bastard."

"But why?"

"I'm sure it was about money. But why are you asking me?"

"Because you were at the memorial service, I guess. I thought you might know a little more about it than was in the news."

"How do you know I was at the service?"

"You showed up on our TV screen."

"Oh. Well, I don't know much more about it," she said. "The only reason I was there is that Goldman was a friend of Wayne's. He was also one of the founders of America One two years ago. Bill, my boss, suggested I go, so I went. That's it. Why are you so interested?"

"I don't know. As you said, I'm nosy. I'm always butting in where I don't belong. Anyway, forget it. You want to walk around a bit, check out the Stingaree?"

"No, I don't," she said, leaning over the table to kiss me quickly on the mouth. "I want you to take me home and put me to bed."

"Now, that's the best suggestion I've heard all evening," I answered, gesturing for the waiter. "What else are we going to do?"

"I'm sure we'll think of something."

The phone woke us up. Megan reached for it, then sat on the edge of the bed to take the call as I staggered into the bathroom. When I returned, she was hunched over the receiver, listening intently and from time to time saying yes or no. It was still dark outside and the clock radio at my end of the bed showed 5:05 A.M. I lay down again beside her and put my hand on her bare shoulder blade, feeling the warmth of her soft skin and enjoying the firmness of her strong back. She ignored me, then said into the receiver, "I can't talk now, I'll call you back." Two or three more yeses and then she hung up. "You'll have to go," she said, turning toward me.

"Who was that?"

"Washington, and I've got to call them back," she said. "You'll have to go, Lou."

"What kind of PR work are you in? It's not even dawn."

"I can't talk about it. Anyway, it's after eight back East."

"You mean they always call you in the middle of the night? Great folks to work for."

"Lou . . ."

"Okay, I'm going, I'm going." I began to scramble into my clothes.

"I'm sorry," she said. "Anyway, thanks for a wonderful evening."

"It was, wasn't it?"

"Yes. I enjoy making love to you."

"The feeling is mutual." I sat down beside her on the bed to put on my shoes and she placed her arm around me and kissed me. "I could go downstairs, get us some coffee, and come back," I suggested.

"No. I have to get up and get on the road."

"Where are you going?"

"Up to L.A."

"For how long?"

"A few days. I'll call you."

"Sure you will."

"I promise, Lou. As soon as I can get free."

"Okay. And still no phone number?"

She shook her head. "I don't know where I'm going to be, honest." She kissed me again, this time a real one that brought back the smell and the feel and the warmth of the night we had just spent together in this sterile hotel room. "I'll miss you," she whispered.

"I want you to promise me something," I said.

"What?"

"That someday we'll have breakfast together."

"I promise."

Instead of going home, I drove straight from the Doubletree to the track, flashed my horse owner's license to get past the stable gate, and squeezed the Toyota into the last parking space in the main lot next to a row of barns. Inside the cafeteria, I bought a cup of coffee and a newspaper, then looked around for a quiet corner. Angles and Reginald Montrose were sitting across the room, conferring over the *Racing Form*. As I hesitated, wondering whether I should join them, Angles spotted me and waved me over. "Shifty, what the hell are you doing up so early?" he asked as I set my coffee down on the table. "You remember Reggie, don't you?"

"Sure, how are you?"

"I am giddy, expectation whirls me round," the actor said. "The imaginary relish is so sweet that it enchants my senses."

"I'm glad I asked," I said, sitting down.

"Reggie just got here yesterday for a week," Angles explained. "He thought we ought to come back here and talk to people, sniff out some winners. I told him it won't do any good. Most of the information you get from the backside of a racetrack ain't worth listening to. We should stick to the *Form*."

"There are more things in racing than are dreamt of in your *Form*, my lad," Montrose said. "We must converse with trainers."

"Why?" Angles asked. "The good ones will lie to you and the bad ones you don't want to hear from."

"Well, Angles, I suppose they know their own animals," I said.

"Precisely my point," Montrose declared. "There is a tide in the affairs of horses, which, when taken at the flood, leads on to fortune."

"The only trainer I ever trusted completely on horses was Charlie Pickard," I said. "I think Angles is right, Reggie. You'd do better just handicapping and not listening to tips."

"And where is this paragon of a conditioner? Forsooth, let us beard him in his lair."

"He retired a few months ago," I said. "His health hasn't been too good. I miss him. Do you own any horses now, Reggie?"

"There is a limit even to my folly," the actor said. "Nay, I would no longer yield my kingdom for a horse."

"Unlike your pal Copeland. What was he like to work with, Reggie?"

The old ham shook his head in pity. "Alas, poor Wayne," he said. "He struts and frets his hours upon the stage in most lamentable fashion. To be condemned to celluloid becomes him well."

"What kind of a guy was he to work with?"

"A fellow of infinite jest, of most excellent fancy," Montrose replied. "He hath borne the blather upon his tongue a thousand times, but nay, do not discourse with him upon world events. He maketh Genghis Khan to seem but a mere babe in sentiment. For all but Republicans encamped upon the slopes of incipient tyranny he has no eye but one of malice and contempt, though he dissembleth much and seems an easygoing sort."

"Do you understand any of this?" Angles asked. "Reggie, do you ever speak plain American?"

"An uncouth and barbarous tongue," the actor said, "fit only for uncivilized discourse."

"Okay, I give up," Angles said. "Let's talk horses. This is a card we can beat."

Montrose looked at me intently with his light blue eyes, as if actually seeing me for the first time. He was wearing black slacks, a buttoned-up black shirt, and a dark gray windbreaker with a ratty-looking fur collar. He suddenly reminded me of an old owl sitting on a tree branch, still alert but much too wise to commit himself to wasteful action. "Why do you inquire?" he asked me.

"A friend of mine is working for him," I answered. "She won't talk much about him, but I gather he's on some sort of political power trip."

Montrose nodded. "Then everything includes itself in power," he said. "Power into will, will into appetite, and appetite, a universal wolf, so doubly seconded with will and power, must make perforce a universal prey, and last eat up himself."

"What in the fuck are you guys talking about?" Angles asked in despair. "Can we get back to horses here? Reggie, we came here to get some inside angles on live horses, didn't we?"

Montrose ignored him. "Come feast with us this very eve upon the village green," he said, reaching into his pocket to hand me an invitation. "I received this but yesterday."

I glanced at the card. It was an engraved invitation to a party at Copeland's house in Rancho Santa Fe. Drinks, dinner, dancing. "Sounds like fun," I said. "What's the occasion?"

"The revels of summer. Is not the occasion timely?" The actor smiled and leaned toward me. "Doubtless you will find assembled there the chivalry of the true faith, gathered about their charismatic leader. But, my boy, beware the ideas of Mark."

"Mark who? Clovis?"

Montrose nodded. "The fountainhead," he said.

"I don't think I can take much more of this shit," Angles said.

"It's okay, I'm going to read the paper," I said, standing up and holding out the invitation. "Can I keep this? You don't need it?"

"Nay, lad, we shall gather there in the fullness of the hour," the actor said, "when time doth come round to meet merrily again."

"We were in the Turf Club yesterday and Reggie bumped into Copeland," Angles said. "He handed him the invitation."

"I instructed him in a few of the finer points of play," Montrose explained, "when he and I strutted and fretted our hours together upon the stage. He remains grateful, for look you, in acting, at least, he is not choked with ambition of the meaner sort."

"I look forward to it, Reggie. Thanks."

"Reggie—" Angles began.

The actor at last turned his attention to his personal counselor. "Ah, Angles," he said, "to tout, perchance to steam . . ."

9
Socializing

♥

After breakfast, I strolled over to Willie's barn, but he wasn't there. Pablo told me he'd gone to the track with a couple of horses out for a gallop, so I thanked him and moved on. It was a cool morning, but clear, and it wouldn't be long before the sun warmed things up. At the corner of Short's stable, Babs Harper, dressed in jeans, boots, and a soiled white cowboy shirt, was leaning against the wall and sipping from a large Styrofoam container of coffee. "Good morning," I called out. "How's the big colt doing?"

She didn't answer, but stared at me over the rim of the container as if I were a carrier of disease. I decided to ignore her hostility and kept on coming, with a big smile on my face. "He sure is a great-looking animal," I said, "and you're terrific with him. It is Babs, isn't it?"

"What do you want?"

"What do I want? Let's see," I said. "Okay, I want to be an inch or two taller and very good-looking, maybe like Tom Cruise. I want to be back in my mid-twenties, but knowing what I do now. And I want ten or twelve million bucks, so I could buy a few good two-year-olds and have one of them maybe turn out to be as good as Junior. How's he doing?"

"What do you care how he's doing?"

"Hey, Babs, ease up, will you? Remember me? I'm not the press. I'm just another track junkie." I reached into my pocket and pulled out a big colored handkerchief. "You like flowers?"

"Flowers? What kind of flowers?"

"Well, let's see what we've got here this morning." I snapped the cloth open and shook it out, then held it up by the corners and turned it back and forth, so she could see that nothing was concealed in it. Then I crumpled it up into a ball, removed it with my left hand, shook it open by the middle, and produced a tiny bouquet of fresh violets, which I removed with my right hand and proferred to her. "Here. For you."

Her jaw dropped open about an inch. "What the . . . How'd you do that?"

"It comes naturally to me. You like violets?"

She didn't answer, but she took the bouquet from me, smelled it, and looked up at me again. "So what do you want?"

"Boy, Babs, you're tough," I said. "Nothing. I'm just passing the time of day with you. I was looking for Willie Vernon, but he isn't around just now and I saw you standing here, so I came on over. I love this colt of yours and I like the way you feel about him. I guess you do like horses a lot."

"He's doing real good, if they'd just leave him alone."

"What do you mean?"

"Oh, all this bullshit about him being America's horse," she said, her green eyes narrowed in anger. "It ain't good for him. He ain't nobody's horse but his own. I hate to see him used this way."

"How are they using him?"

"They're lining up all these races he's supposed to be running in," she said, "like he's some kind of machine or something, instead of letting him tell them when he's ready. He's only a two-year-old. You can ruin just about any young horse if you rush him too much. That's what I mean, see?"

"Yeah, I understand," I said. "They're going to run him in the Balboa Stakes in a couple of weeks, right? And then the Futurity, and then maybe at Oak Tree, and then the Breeders' Cup."

"That's what I'm talking about," she said. "It's too much. He's still pretty green. You treat an animal like this gently, bring him along nice and slow, and maybe you've got yourself a Derby winner. But no, they got to nail it all down quick, like he's some kind of robot. And I don't like this political shit, either. What does politics got to do with racing? These goofy assholes are trying to use Junior to get his owner elected president. Now, that's a crock of shit and you know it."

"They haven't made a formal announcement yet. You sure Wayne's going to run?"

"Oh, hell yes," she said. "I don't think he gives a hoot, really, but all these other guys, they're talking like he's going to be the next Abe Lincoln, free the slaves and all that shit."

"What slaves?"

"The poor oppressed capitalists," she said, "who are fed up with paying taxes to give welfare and food stamps to the blacks and the Mexicans and the other bad races and the perverts and the bureaucrats, that's who."

"Is that the way you feel?"

"Not me, fella," she said, cocking a thumb back in the direction of the tack room, "them."

"Billy Bob?"

"He's one of 'em." She poured the last of her coffee on the ground, then crumpled up the container and tossed it into the trash bin a few feet away. "I got to get back to work. Now, about these flowers . . ."

"They're for you."

"Yeah? That's nice." She sniffed the little bouquet again. "How'd you do that?"

"Magic, Babs. I told you."

"Can you make all these assholes go away?"

"Unfortunately not," I admitted. "Only small objects, not people."

"Then what good are you?" She started to walk away, then stopped and glanced back at me. "You want to see Junior?"

"I sure would."

"Come on, then."

We went around the corner of the barn and walked down the shed row to Superpatriot's stall. The big colt was standing quietly with his back to us. "Every time I see a horse's ass, it reminds me of people I know," Babs Harper said. "Hey, Junior, come over here." The horse glanced behind him, then turned and walked up to us. "You can pet him if you want to," she said, "but watch out for him. He'll take a nip out of you."

"He's a little mean?"

"No way," she said. "He's just playing. I guess you don't know much about horses."

"A little, but not like you, Babs. I like to bet on them."

"Oh, you're one of those sickos," she said. "Well, you can bet on Junior anytime. He ain't never going to disappoint you."

I reached out and patted the colt on the neck. He pinned his ears back and lunged for me, but I managed to move away in time. "Thanks for the warning," I said. "He's just playing? I'd hate to be around him when he gets serious."

"Aw, he's just a big kid," Babs Harper said, grabbing the colt's upper lip and smacking him on the neck. "Ain't you, you big phony." She patted him and swung his big head back and forth as she talked to him, then reached into her pocket, brought out a carrot, and shoved the fat end of it into his mouth. "He's mad 'cause he ain't had his coffee this morning."

"He drinks coffee?"

"Loves it. With a little cream and three sugars. It ain't good for him, though, so I don't let him have it every day. Only when he's real good. And today he's been kind of feisty and all worked up, so I'm going to make him sweat a little for it. Maybe I'll give it to him later."

"Hey, what the hell are you doing there?"

I looked around. Billy Bob Short was standing outside his tack room, glaring at us. Babs gave the colt one last pat and left him munching on his carrot. "Nothing, Billy Bob," she said. "This here's a friend of mine. I was just showing him old Junior."

"Yeah? Well, we ain't got but about thirty horses to take care of here," Billy Bob said. "Can't you find something to do?"

"I'm just waiting for the filly to come back from the track," Babs said. "I'm all done with Junior."

"Well, find something to do, goddamn it," the trainer said. "Go help Lopez down there. We got two horses to put wraps on. Get busy, goddamn it."

Babs winked at me and went off to succor Lopez, a stocky little Mexican who was three stalls away and down on his knees in front of a big, bony roan who was refusing to stand still and be ministered to. "I'm sorry, Mr. Short, it was my fault," I said, strolling toward the trainer. "I'm a little bit in love with this colt of yours."

Before Short could say anything, a small fat man dressed in a dark business suit appeared in the doorway of the tack room behind him. "Any problems?" he asked.

"No problems," the trainer said. "I got a lot of lazy help, that's all. This ain't the social hour."

The small fat man looked at me. "Who are you?" he asked. He had a strangely high-pitched voice, like a man using falsetto, flat, devoid of color or resonance. His face was flat, too, with a tiny snub nose and a prim little mouth under the thin line of a mustache. His eyes were large, pale gray, and protruding.

"I'm a friend of Miss Harper's," I said.

"Yeah? That's nice. Now get lost."

"He's going, Vinnie," Short said. "Don't you worry about it."

The little fat man looked at me and smiled, revealing a row of tiny, perfectly matched white teeth. "I don't want to have to worry about it," he said. "Nobody we don't know gets near this horse. Is that clear?"

"I'll take care of it," Short said.

"Do that." The little fat man went back into the tack room and the trainer followed him.

I walked away past Babs Harper. She was holding the bony roan's bridle and talking softly to him while Lopez worked on his ankles. "Who's the little fat guy?" I asked.

"I don't know," she said. "He comes by every morning to talk to Billy Bob. He bets big money."

"Friend of Copeland's?"

"Who knows? Just another horse's ass," she said. "Beat it, will you, or I'll lose my job."

The first person I saw as I walked onto the grounds of the Copeland estate was Megan Starbuck. She was standing on the front lawn outside the main house, deep in conversation with several middle-aged men, among whom I recognized Ed Drumheller and Tom Greenwood. She saw me coming toward her and broke away from the group to meet me. "Lou, what are you doing here?" she asked, obviously astonished to see me.

"I was invited," I said. "Nice place."

"You were? By whom?"

"Reginald Montrose. You know him?"

She shook her head. "Who's he?"

"An old actor pal of Copeland's. I thought you were supposed to be in L.A.?"

"I was. Plans changed. Lou, be careful."

"Careful? What about?"

"What you say."

"It's okay, I'll pretend not to know you."

"That's not what I mean. I—"

"Hello, I'm Cheryl Copeland," the woman said, holding out her hand. She had come up behind Megan as we talked. "And you are?"

"Lou Anderson, nice to meet you." Her hand settled into mine like a small dead fish and allowed itself to be squeezed. She was tall and slender, in her middle or late forties, with pale blond hair going to gray and the delicate features of a porcelain doll. She was dressed in a bright, flowery frock that made me want to water her, and her eyes were as innocent as those of a child. "I'm a friend of Reggie Montrose."

"Oh, yes, how nice," Cheryl Copeland said, turning to Megan. "And you're . . ."

"Megan Starbuck," Megan said. "I work for Wayne."

"Oh, yes. How nice to see you all," Cheryl Copeland said, smiling sweetly. "Now you just make yourselves right at home. There's plenty to eat and drink, and you all have a real nice time." She squeezed my arm and giggled, then moved away to greet another group of recently arrived guests.

"I'd forgotten there was a Mrs. Copeland," I said.

"Oh, yes," Megan answered. "They've been married twenty-three years. She comes from an old New Orleans family. She doesn't have much to do with show business, stays in the background."

"How does she feel about Wayne's political ambitions?"

"Off the record?"

"Come on, Megan, I'm not a reporter."

"She hates it. She hates all of his public activities. That's why you never see her at any of them."

"She's going to love politics. Is she a little out of it or am I mistaking Southern charm for idiocy?"

"She's a secret drinker," Megan said. "Nips all day long, but rarely gets falling-down drunk. That's also off the record."

"How's that going to play in the White House?"

"Lou, stop talking like that, will you? That's what I mean about being careful. All these people here, a lot of them anyway, are involved with the possible campaign, but we're not talking about it. And neither will you, okay?"

"Okay. Let's get something to drink and then I want to look around. This is quite a spread."

"I can't hang out with you, Lou. I'm working, if you know what I mean."

"Great surroundings and great perks," I said, "but I don't think I'd like your job."

"No, you wouldn't. I'll see you, okay? Have a good time, but be careful."

"What kind of threat am I?"

She smiled. "Your mouth, Lou," she said. "It shoots off at the wrong moments. Go find somebody to talk horses or magic to, all right?"

"And any day now you'll call me."

"You can count on it."

"By the way . . ."

"What?"

"You look terrific." She did, too, in a sleek, black leather pants suit that showed off her tall, athletic figure and mop of red hair. "Is there an empty bedroom available?"

She blushed, smirked with mock anger, and left me. "Behave yourself," she called back.

The Copeland property occupied several partly wooded acres on the eastern outskirts of Rancho Santa Fe. The main house was a low-lying, one-story white brick structure that rambled eccentrically over the long sweep of a lawn leading down toward a high red brick wall and the road behind it. Armed with a beer I had procured from a bar set up inside the front entrance, I wandered through it. The original building, which had been a stable, had been remodeled and a series of rooms had been added onto it, each one impeccably furnished with American antiques and decorated with paintings and artifacts of the Old West, including a number of Remingtons. Although it was midsummer, fires burned in the fireplaces, an effect that made me think of a stage or a movie set. Either Cheryl Copeland had great taste in furnishings or some expensive decorator had cleaned up. I suspected the latter. Here and there in the social rooms I came across small groups of people, well dressed, mostly middle-aged, a golfing and tennis crowd, chatting with one another, but most of the action was outside, on the lawn between the house and a large swimming pool. About forty guests were milling about out there, while beyond the pool and below a small guest house a five-piece band was playing show tunes and themes from Wayne Copeland movies.

The star himself, wearing a white fringed buckskin jacket, was holding court at the far end of the pool, his big frame towering over the group around him. He looked very serious for the host of a festive occasion, so I wandered over to hear what he was saying. "We have a lot of problems in this country and the trouble is that the folks in Washington aren't dealing with any of them," was the first sentence I picked up. And for the next twenty minutes I listened to Wayne Copeland unload on the incompetent federal bureaucracy, the professional politicians who only care about being reelected, the tax-and-spend liberals around Clinton, the welfare cheats, the homeless who are homeless because they want to be, the need to erect an electrified Berlin Wall along the Mexican border, the misguided bleeding hearts opposing the death penalty for hardened criminals, the stupidity of sending our boys overseas to try and keep the peace in backward countries that hate us and have been fighting among themselves for centuries, and so on.

What struck me most forcibly was not what he was saying, which sounded very much like what a lot of establishment politicians on the right have been saying for years, but the soft-spoken, manly, aw-shucks manner of his delivery. He had none of Reagan's folksy charm and wit, but something equally effective going for him—a sort of home-on-the-range sincerity that made the message he was delivering sound heartfelt and utterly sincere. He was the good guy who had just ridden into town, didn't know much about local goings-on but could distinguish a villain from an honest citizen when he saw one and was going to see to it that the bad guys got taken care of so the good folks and their true-blue, all-American kids could take their towns back and pursue the American Dream. It was a Wayne Copeland production. I couldn't help it, I was impressed. I decided on the spot that if Wayne Copeland ran for office, any office at all, he might easily be elected. Voting against the man could be construed as being un-American. He was definitely a threat. All the people around him would have to do is control the media, not too hard to accomplish, really, as attested to by the Reagan presidency. Could Wayne get the Republican nomination? Why not? Whom did the Republicans have? Darth Vader Dole? Jolly Jack Kemp? Ross Perot, out there on the fringes and increasingly discredited? I began seriously to worry about the future of the country.

I left the group around Wayne Copeland to get myself another beer from the small bar set up behind the diving board, then strolled around the back of the house, where I came upon Angles Beltrami engaged in conversation with a small group of affluent-looking citizens, including Ed Drumheller and the other man Megan had been waiting for the morning I'd spotted her in the Wells Fargo parking lot. Angles was wearing his most formal outfit, a pair of black loafers, gray slacks, a shiny green sports coat that looked as if it might glow in the dark, and a black silk necktie decorated with pink horses' heads. I had only seen him this dressed up once before, when we had all attended his sister's wedding at the Beverly-Wilshire Hotel in L.A. two years ago. "Yeah, I got a PHD, too, but not in economics," Angles was saying as I came up beside him. "I got mine in poker, horses, and dice. Oh, hiya, Shifty. Folks, this is my pal Shifty Lou Anderson, a great magician. Shifty, meet the folks. I'm not good at names."

I introduced myself and began to shake hands all around. "Really? A magician? How sweet," the only woman in the group observed. "Are you here as part of the entertainment?"

"No, ma'am, I'm an honored guest," I said. "We're friends of Reginald Montrose, the actor."

"Oh, I see," she said, not seeing at all. She was a short, trim-looking brunette of about fifty with a deeply lined, tanned face and a brusque no-nonsense manner about her. "I'm Blythe Clovis. This is my husband, Mark. I'm afraid we don't know anything about magic."

"That's okay," I said. "It's not required."

Clovis was the thin, blond man I'd seen coming out of the Wells Fargo Bank with Drumheller. He had a firm, viselike grip and a pair of fierce dark eyes that never left my face as we shook hands. "Perhaps you'd enlighten us a little later," he said with a faint smile. "We're always willing to learn. We were talking about the economy. That would take some real magic to revive."

"I think that's a little beyond even my powers, Mr. Clovis," I said. "I deal in cards and small objects, mainly."

"How fascinating," Blythe Clovis said, not meaning it.

"Country's in a hell of a mess," Ed Drumheller said in a big, blustery baritone voice that suited his football player's frame. "Going right down the tubes if we don't get this bunch out of there and take charge of this country."

"You said it, Ed," another man agreed. "Mark, I know you and Ed are working hard to change things. What about NAFTA? What's your position on that? Everybody I know is split on it."

"Not at all," Clovis said. "I think we need this agreement. It'll create jobs, for one thing, and it'll help to put a stop to this tidal wave of illegal immigration. It's the one thing Clinton's right about."

"But we also have to get this border under control. Get that electrical fence up and bring in the National Guard, too," Ed Drumheller said. "We start shooting and frying a few of these people, maybe they'll think twice about sneaking in here."

"And we have to turn off the welfare juice and stop giving these illegals a free education and medical care," somebody else said.

"There are a lot of things we have to stop doing," Mark Clovis said. "This administration isn't going to fix any of them. If we don't get the deficit under control and stop squandering the taxpayers' money, the whole country, this America we real Americans love, is going to decay into one of history's corpses."

"Yeah," Angles said. "In New York the economy's so bad I heard the Mafia laid off six judges."

Somebody in the group snickered, but on the whole Angles's remark didn't go over as well as he had anticipated. We were dealing here with a group of committed true believers, and in the house of God, jokes about the deity generally don't charm the congregation. Angles sensed the hostility and decided to withdraw. "I guess I'll go find Reggie," he said. "See you, folks." And he moved away toward the crowd around the pool.

"Who was that extraordinary person?" Blythe Clovis asked.

"He's just a gambler and a horseplayer," I said. "He's harmless."

Blythe Clovis turned to her husband. "Really, Mark, that was a bit much. How did these people get in here?"

"They were invited, my dear," her husband replied. "It's Wayne's party, you know."

"Well, yes, but really . . ."

I smiled at her. "Forgive me, Mrs. Clovis," I said. "We didn't mean to contaminate your evening." I reached into my pocket, pulled out my big silk handkerchief, and repeated the effect I'd worked on Babs Harper earlier in the day. "A small token of apology," I said, proferring my tiny bouquet.

Blythe Clovis was unmoved by my action, but her husband proved to be a little more appreciative. He took the bouquet from me and smelled it. "They're real. Extraordinary, Anderson," he said, handing the flowers to his wife. "Violets, darling. You like them, don't you?"

She took the flowers from him, but her attitude remained unchanged. "Thank you," I said. "It's been enlightening to listen to you."

I started to leave, but Mark Clovis came after me. "Anderson," he asked, "do you have a business card?"

"Yes," I said, producing one from my wallet and handing it to him. "I do private parties, children and/or grown-ups."

"Good, just what I have in mind. Do you travel?"

"If the price is right and my expenses are paid."

"Good, we'll be in touch. And please forgive my wife's rudeness. You're not to blame for your friend's boorishness."

"He was just making a joke."

"Yes, but the world is becoming a very serious place."

"It always has been, Mr. Clovis, but—"

"Mark."

"Mark. But maybe that's what's wrong with it."

"What's wrong with it is what we at America One are trying to correct. Maybe we do lack a sense of humor."

I smiled. "It's never too late to acquire one."

"Yes, well, it was pleasant talking to you," he said, turning away from me.

Dinner was served on picnic tables set out under the stars, with the guests playing musical chairs until everyone was able to find a seat. Inevitably, Angles and I wound up at the out table, along with a handful of horse people and Reggie Montrose, who joined us at the last minute, looked about him before sitting down, and declared, "Ah, eating the bitter bread of banishment."

"Hello, Reggie," I said. "How are you?"

"A lunatic, lean-witted fool," he answered, "presuming on an ague's privilege."

"Aren't you glad you asked?" Angles said.

"I count myself in nothing else so happy," Reggie said, raising his wineglass in a toast, "as in a soul remembering my good friends."

"What play, Reggie?" I asked.

"*Richard II*, much maligned and underrated."

"Goodness me," Cheryl Copeland said, "how are you all doing?" She had come up behind me during the actor's last speech. "Is everything just fine?"

We chorused our approval as a small horde of youthful waiters fanned out from inside the house to tend to our needs. "Wisely and slow," Reggie said. "They stumble that run fast. *Romeo and Juliet*, Shifty."

"Well, isn't that nice," Cheryl Copeland said, smiling and seeming to waver in the dim light, her face a blur of slight confusion. "It's just wonderful to have you all here. You have a real good time now." She faded away from us like an image briefly recalled from an old movie.

"The very pink of courtesy," Reggie said. "She speaks, yet she says nothing."

"She's sweet," a woman sitting across from us observed. "I don't know how she puts up with Wayne and all his doings."

"Madam, she is past hope, past care, past help," the actor said.

"That's rude," the woman said. "She's so nice."

"To live a barren sister all her life," Montrose continued, "chanting faint hymns to the cold fruitless moon."

"What?"

"Shakespeare, madam."

"No kidding?"

"Lady, by yonder blessèd moon I swear."

All through dinner, during which Reginald Montrose kept our table entranced by an endless stream of appropriate quotes from the

Bard, I kept an eye out for Megan, but she seemed to have disappeared. I skipped dessert and went in search of her. She was inside the house, sitting at the main dining-room table with Copeland, the Clovises, the Greenwoods, Ed Drumheller, and several couples I hadn't met. She saw me, but made no effort either to acknowledge my presence or to come after me. Out on the front patio, the band was still playing, this time a medley from *The Sound of Music,* not one of my favorite shows. At my table, the actor had risen to his feet and was delivering Mark Antony's funeral oration to the Romans. Angles had detached himself from our party and gone back to the bar. I decided I'd had enough of life among the superwealthy for one night and headed back to my car. I was afraid that if I hung around too long, I might embarrass Megan. I couldn't figure out how she could stand to work for these people, but then I've never been either very poor or very rich. My friends are mostly horse-players or on the fringes of the big time in every field except magic. Maybe I envied Megan her success. What about that? I asked myself as I drove away from the party. Maybe that's why she didn't want me to call her or to mingle freely in her world. If she got to the White House, she'd have to let me in by the back door. Sad.

10
Dances

♦

With a regularity that I was beginning to find predictable, Megan Starbuck dropped out of my life again. This time I didn't try to get in touch with her, because I figured that eventually she would reappear. I told myself it didn't matter that she obviously wanted to keep her distance from me while she was working. She had her reasons and the least I could do was respect them. I even tried to make myself stop thinking about the people she was involved with. It would all sort itself out in the end, I promised myself. I also stopped worrying about the prospect of Wayne Copeland running for the White House. A nation that had survived the presidencies of Nixon and Reagan could obviously survive anything. And what could I have done about it, anyway? I was just another Joe Citizen, trying to make the most of my life while shutting my eyes and ears to the follies around me.

This was easier to do now, because we had begun to win. After a fairly dismal opening three weeks of the meet, the horses at Del Mar had started to follow form, at least as we interpreted the form. Jay and Arnie and Angles and I were cashing tickets every afternoon, some of them sizable. Jay, in fact, had embarked on one of those hot streaks that all dedicated horseplayers dream of, when the winners seem to leap up at you from the mass of statistics in the *Racing Form* and run around the track like little automated figures, as predictable as the falling of leaves in autumn. We were doing so well that even Angles stopped complaining and looking for an underhanded way to outwit fate. He kept feeding Reginald Montrose live horses and being duly rewarded in return, so that he actually invited all of us out for dinner one night at a good French bistro in Encinitas and picked up the check, a milestone so overwhelming that for once Arnie found himself speechless. At least until after dessert. "Angles, civilization has bestowed its benefits upon you," he then announced. "There's nothing like a few winners to enlighten the darkest soul." After which Angles ordered another bottle of getaway champagne and sent us dancing into the night.

"Where are we going?" Jay asked as we headed for our cars.

"I don't know about you," Arnie said, "but my motel is up the road here. You done any work yet, Jay?"

"Only the preliminaries," the Fox announced. "But it's a treacherous card tomorrow, with maybe only one or two solid possibilities."

"Well, don't shirk your responsibilities," Arnie said. "We don't want to rest on our laurels, do we? I'm going home to crack the *Form*."

"Come on, you guys," Angles said, "let's go to the Belly Up. There's a good blues band there tonight. There'll be lots of women."

"All the more reason to withdraw," Arnie observed. "In the great race of life, women constitute the only insuperable obstacle to freedom from care and want. I'll see you all on the field of dreams. Thanks for the splendid feed, Angles. I'm not going to endanger my contentment with an expensive pursuit of the stronger sex."

"What do you mean, expensive?" Angles said. "The Belly Up's cheap."

"Where women are the object, nothing is cheap," Arnie replied.

"Yeah, you're right," Angles said. "They're all bisexual, but think of the fun."

"What do you mean, bisexual?" I asked.

"They won't give you sex unless you buy them something."

"Precisely my point," Arnie agreed. "Good night, gents. I wish

Reggie were here to provide the appropriate parting quote. Where is he?"

"Still back in L.A.," Angles said. "He does voice-overs for these digestive pills, K-Brume. Reggie calls them Ka-Boom. Anyway, he's coming back. It's not enough we're winning, he wants to be in on the on-site action."

"Understandable," I said. "Being there is most of it."

Jay also dropped out in order to put in some fruitful hours on his numbers, but I decided to join Angles at the Belly Up, one of my favorite watering holes in the area. It's a large, soundproof, hangarlike building just east of the railroad tracks in Solana Beach. It's home to visiting rock, reggae, and blues bands, with several bars, a small eating area, a big dance floor, and a social alcove with a pool table. I hadn't been there since the previous summer, so I thought it might be fun to drop in and have a couple of beers before going home.

It was a few minutes after ten o'clock when we walked in, but the place was already crowded. A five-piece band was hammering hard on a rhythm-and-blues number, dancers were out on the floor, and people were lined up two and three deep along the bars. It was mostly a young crowd, but there were also plenty of folks in their late thirties, forties, and fifties. One of the most enjoyable aspects of the Belly Up is that it doesn't cater to the acid-rock or heavy-metal lost souls and is therefore accessible to establishment types as well. And then, of course, there are the available women, in all sizes and shapes, the objects of Angles Beltrami's fevered pursuits.

We pushed our way to the bar nearest the bandstand and settled at a corner from where we could observe the dancers and the flow of traffic to and from the floor. It was noisy and I had to shout to order us a couple of beers. By the time they arrived, Angles had moved out onto the dance floor to join a couple of girls in tight miniskirts who had been gyrating on their own. I took a swallow of beer and watched, while Angles put on quite a show. I wouldn't say he was a great dancer, but he was completely uninhibited and would try anything, including some near-acrobatic leaps and spins that would send him soaring into the air or plunging to the floor, from where he'd rise steadily upward like a demented limbo performer. His partners were stunned by him at first, but he was having such a terrific time and obviously enjoying himself so much that they soon yielded to the spirit of the occasion and tried to match him move for move. They cleared a small space around them and a few minutes later, when the band stopped for a short break, their performance drew a smattering of applause from the nearest onlookers. Angles bowed, kissed the girls' hands, and returned to our corner. I handed him his beer.

"That was great," he said. "Did you see those two?"

"I certainly did, Angles," I said. "You're an inspiration."

"Sisters," he said. "Bad scene. You can't get laid if you're with sisters. They're fun to dance with, though. You got any condoms?"

"No. Angles—"

"Shit. I forgot mine. I don't like to use them," he said, "but these days you got to be careful."

"It's a little early, isn't it? I mean, you don't even know if you're going to meet someone."

"Shifty, I always meet someone," he said. "That's the trouble. It's usually the wrong someone, but hey, why not try? I'll be back." He went off to make a tour of the premises and size up the available female contingent, while I stayed put and finished my beer. I turned back to order a second one.

"Hi, want to dance?" a familiar voice asked.

I looked around. Babs Harper, also holding a beer in her hand, was standing two feet away. She was dressed in boots, blue jeans, a blue long-sleeved shirt, and a straw cowboy hat. "Babs, what are you doing here?" I asked.

"I like to dance," she said. "I come here a lot."

"Aren't you working?"

"Sure. So what? I sleep three or four hours, get up, take care of the horses, and sleep some more in the late morning. Something wrong with that?"

"No, only I didn't think—"

"What? You think I'm too old? I just asked you to dance, not to screw me. What are you, queer or something?"

"No. Hey, I'd love to dance with you."

The band was about to start up again, so we set our beers down on the corner of the bar and went out on the floor. "How's Junior?" I asked as we waited.

"He's doing good," she said. "He breezed this morning in thirty-five flat."

"He's going in the Balboa in a couple of days, isn't he?"

"He's going to win by ten," she said. "Go bet your life savings on him."

"I don't have any life savings, Babs. I'm a magician, remember?"

"How could I forget?"

"You here by yourself?"

"Sure. I always come by myself."

The band now exploded into action and so did Babs. She went straight up in the air, came down with her boots stomping, and hammered on the floor in time to the beat, while her arms flailed about wildly. Her eyes assumed a glassy stare and her cheeks flushed a bright red from the effort. I managed somehow to stay out of range, while doing my best to keep up with her. We stayed out there for three numbers until I thought my legs would give way. Finally, unable to continue, I signaled that I was going back to the bar. She ignored me or didn't see me in her trancelike state, so I left her there, still stomping and flailing, and went back to the bar.

"What the hell is that?" Angles asked as I retrieved my beer.

"That's Babs Harper," I said. "She works for Billy Bob Short. She grooms Superpatriot."

"That's one crazy broad," Angles said. "The way she dances, she's going to strike oil any minute. Ain't she a little too old for you?"

"She's not that old," I said. "Anyway, we were just dancing."

"That's dancing? Man, she stomps on your foot you got a cracked instep. You did good to dump her."

"I didn't dump her. And anyway, she doesn't even know I'm gone. She's in some sort of quasi-religious trance, like a whirling dervish. How's the hunt proceeding?"

Angles shrugged. "There's a couple of Marine wives over there who need me," he said. "The angle is their husbands are off on training missions. Not bad. I may just have to console one of them, if you know what I mean."

"I guess you're good at that."

"I don't know, Shifty. Women, who understands them? It's like Arnie says, it's too much dead weight, but I need them. I'm going to get me a beer and go over and talk to them, feed them a little Beltrami horseshit, and see how far it gets me."

As Angles pushed his way in toward the bar, with Babs still out there stomping and flailing on her own, I saw the little fat man named Vinnie. He was standing to my left, thirty feet or so away from me, and looking at the dancers. He was dressed in dark gray slacks and a pink sports jacket. Even without a tie, he looked completely out of place; he wasn't drinking, he wasn't smiling, he clearly wasn't enjoying himself. He looked, I decided, like somebody's bodyguard, the only working guest at the party.

The music finally stopped and Babs came off the floor. "What the hell happened to you?" she asked, reaching for her beer.

"You didn't need me, Babs," I said. "You were doing great on your own."

"You're some kind of wuss," she said. "You don't really get into it. You got to get into it."

"Hey, Babs, your friend Vinnie's here."

"Who?"

"The little fat guy who was with Billy Bob the morning I saw you at the barn. Isn't his name Vinnie?"

"Yeah, he's a real creep. Where is he?"

"Over there," I said. I looked, but he had vanished. "He *was* there. Who is he?"

"I told you, he likes to bet," Babs said. "He works for one of those guys around the actor."

"Who? Do you know?"

"No. I told him to fuck off the other day. He didn't like it. He's always hanging around, getting in the way, asking a lot of dumb questions. I don't know what he wants from me."

"Maybe he wants to dance with you."

"Nah, he's some kind of security guy, I think. Billy Bob's scared of him."

"Really? He doesn't look all that menacing."

"You don't think so? Maybe not. You want to dance some more?"

"No, thanks, Babs. I'm going to go home in a couple of minutes."

"Okay, I'll see you. You're a wuss, Shifty. Stick to magic."

Babs went back out on the floor by herself and I lingered for another few minutes, just long enough to finish my beer. On my way out, I caught one last glimpse of Angles. He was dancing with a dark-haired woman of about thirty-five who was dressed in a purple miniskirt and a tight jersey that clung to her large, unfettered breasts like wet tissue paper. If she was one of the Marine wives, I figured Angles was odds-on to score. "Shifty," he explained the situation to me at the track the next day, "the lady's getting a divorce from this colonel at Pendleton. I landed on the shores of Tripoli, man, and explored the halls of Montezuma."

The next morning I finally heard from Megan Starbuck. She was in Los Angeles, but would be in Del Mar the following day for the running of the Balboa Stakes. I suggested we meet for dinner. "I don't know, Lou. I'm not sure I can get away," she said. "If Superpatriot wins, I'll probably have to go to some sort of celebration somewhere. But I'll be around for at least a few days. We'll see each other, I promise."

"I won't ask where you're staying."

"I'm not sure. Maybe the Doubletree again. I'll let you know."

"Nice of you to call."

"You knew I would."

"Yes, but it's still nice."

"How are the horses treating you?"

"I'm thinking of retiring from magic and allying myself permanently with Jay."

"In other words, you're winning."

"Steadily and sometimes spectacularly."

"Lou, it isn't going to last."

"I know that, Megan, but it's a lot of fun while it does."

"I'll see you, Lou."

"I'm counting on it."

Later in the day, I found myself wishing that she hadn't said anything about our winning streak, because it ended with that call. Jay and I went out to the track in the afternoon, prepared to continue riding our hot streak, but hit a small avalanche of losers instead. It began with being nosed out of the double, then losing a triple when our eleven-to-one winner was disqualified from first place and set down to last for impeding another horse on the turn into the stretch. We passed the fifth, an unbettable race for bad two-year-olds, then lost two more bets in the sixth and seventh, after which Arnie Wolfenden, whose long nose can sniff out any change in the wind faster than a roving hyena can scent a rotting kill, decided that our luck had turned. "It was bound to," he announced to the box at large. "It wasn't going to go on forever."

"The thing that pisses me off," Angles said, "is that we're losing these goddamn photos. I'd rather finish last. It's like having second-hand high in poker. You get trapped into betting too much."

"My suggestion to you, Angles," Arnie said, "is to bet more so you won't lose so much."

"Very funny, Arnie. Give me a break, will you?"

"We wrap up for the rest of the day," Jay said. "The only possible bet is in the ninth, Ducato's sprinter stretching out to a distance for the first time, but he'll be the favorite. No value there." He snapped his big black notebooks shut and stood up. "I'm heading for the beach. Shifty?"

"No, Jay, I think I'll stick it out," I answered. "I sort of like Duke Vernon's filly in the eighth. She'll enjoy the grass."

"Acapulco Gold?" Angles asked.

"Willie told me a couple of days ago she's kicking down the barn, she's so ready to run."

"Yeah, we'll have to ignore those real slow training moves," Arnie said sarcastically.

"You can do that, Arnie," I said. "She's never been a good work horse."

"I see nothing there to like," Jay said, picking up his notebooks and binoculars and heading out. "Arnie?"

"The beach?" Arnie said in horror. "All that sand and nothing to bet on? I'm staying put."

"Shifty, I heard she may be a little short for the mile on the grass," Angles said.

"They're always a work short," Arnie observed. "That's how trainers cover their ass."

I left them, still bickering over my selection's credentials, and went down to the paddock to look at Duke Vernon's filly, a big, awkward-looking three-year-old named Big Babe. The horses had already been saddled and several of them, including Duke's animal, were being walked around the ring to keep them calm. Duke himself, looking impeccable, as usual, in a well-tailored, tight-fitting gray suit and conventional dark blue necktie, was standing on the edge of the grass with the owners and a group of their friends. I looked at the board. Big Babe was eight to one, while the favorite, at six to five, was a roan mare named Traditionally, trained by Billy Bob Short. She was also being walked around. I recognized her groom, the young Latino named Lopez who worked next to Babs, and nodded to him. I decided that I liked the looks of Traditionally, but that at eight to one I couldn't afford to ignore Big Babe. I'd bet them both.

As the entries in the eighth moved out toward the track, I fell in next to Duke on our way back to the stands. "Your filly looks good, Duke," I said. "Willie claims she's ready to run."

"Oh, sure, Shifty," Duke said. "I think she'll run good. She's got to beat Billy Bob's filly."

Lopez came up on my other side, heading for the track where he'd wait by the scales for the race to be run and his filly to be returned to him. "Lopez, good luck," I said.

"Gracias, señor," he answered. "She run good."

"How's Babs?" I don't know what made me ask him, probably just curiosity; I'd left her at the Belly Up, still cutting up a storm, and I was wondering idly what sort of shape she was in.

"She's bad, *señor,"* Lopez said.

"I figured she would be. Hung over?"

"No, *señor,* she in the hospital," Lopez said. "She's bad."

"Hospital? What's wrong with her?"

"She get beat up."

"When? Last night?"

"I don't know," the groom called back as he hurried away from me. "I don't know nothing. But she's bad, *señor.*"

"What hospital?" I called after him, but he shook his head and kept on going.

I went back upstairs and bet twenty dollars to win on Big Babe and a ten-dollar exacta box on Big Babe and Traditionally, then looked around for Billy Bob Short. I couldn't find him, so I figured he'd gone up to the Turf Club with his owners. I was dressed in my usual Del Mar garb of shorts, sandals, and a short-sleeved shirt, so there was no way I could get in among the swells to track him down. I went back to our box and watched the race. Big Babe broke poorly out of the gate, fell back ten or twelve lengths behind the leaders, and made a big move turning for home but was carried too wide and finished third behind Traditionally and a thirty-to-one shot I had given no chance.

"That's nice," Arnie said. "I bet on your horse, Shifty. You didn't tell me the jock would try to bring her home through the parking lot."

"Fucking jocks," Angles said. "I'd rather have a trained monkey on my horse's back."

"Yeah, but who'd train the monkeys?" Arnie asked. "Think of that, Angles."

I left them and went in search of a public telephone.

11

Americans

♣

As soon as I arrived home that afternoon, I called up the sheriff's station in Solana Beach to inquire about Babs. The woman who answered the phone seemed to be suffering from a terminal case of disinterest, but eventually revealed that a woman answering my description had indeed been found unconscious and lying on the pavement about a block up the street from the Belly Up Tavern. "Do you know what hospital she was taken to?" I asked.

"Hold on," the woman said and left me hanging for several minutes, after which a man came on the phone. "Deputy Foster here," he said. "Can I help you?"

"Your voice has changed," I said.

"What?"

"Skip it. I was asking about a friend of mine who apparently was beaten up last night. I'm trying to find out what hospital she's in."

"Who's your friend?"

"A woman named Babs Harper."

"You want to come in and make a statement?"

"No, I just want to know where she is."

"You say you're a friend of hers?"

"That's right."

"May I have your name, sir, and where you're calling from?"

"Sure." I gave him the information he wanted. "She was at the Belly Up last night. I saw her there."

"Okay, we may be contacting you. You're a friend of hers?"

"Yeah, more of an acquaintance, really. I heard about it this afternoon from a guy named Lopez—"

"First name?"

"I don't know it. He works with her. They both groom horses for a trainer named Billy Bob Short."

"This at the racetrack?"

"Yes. Did she say anything about herself?"

"She was unconscious when they found her. We haven't been able to talk to her yet."

"You mind telling me where she is?"

"They took her to Scripps Memorial, the ER there," the deputy said.

"Thanks. Anything else?"

"No, not for now. We may be calling you."

I wondered for a moment whether I should mention the presence at the Belly Up of Vinnie, the little fat man, but decided not to. What did I know about him, anyway? Not much. I could always bring his name up later, if Babs didn't. I assumed all along that she'd eventually be able to tell us herself who had attacked her.

The hospital was located one freeway exit below Del Mar. It was a large red brick edifice flanked by subsidiary buildings containing medical offices and located in the low hills just east of the highway. At the front desk, a sprightly, blue-haired woman in her seventies informed me that there was a Miss Harper currently in the Intensive Care Unit on the ground floor. She gave me directions and then asked, "Are you a relative?"

"I'm her brother," I said.

"Oh, that's all right, then," the cheerful ancient said. "Have a nice day."

I wondered, as I made my way down the long corridors toward the ICU, whether "Have a nice day" was really the appropriate expression with which to speed hospital visitors on their way. But what the hell, in California it wouldn't surprise me to hear someone say "Have a nice day" to people about to undergo chemotherapy or entering the gas chamber. I'd been living in L.A. for over two decades, but I remained an Easterner at heart.

Babs did not look well when I found her. She was lying on a bed in a corner of the unit with all sorts of tubes sticking into her and hooked up to machines measuring her vital signs. Her head was heavily bandaged and she was very pale, but breathing on her own. Her eyes were closed and her mouth was open, which at least suited what I knew of her character. I stood by her bed for a few minutes, hoping vainly that she would open her eyes and start talking to me, then I went back to the nurses' station at the front of the room.

"Mr. Anderson, is it?" the middle-aged woman behind the counter asked me. "You're her brother?"

"Yes," I answered. "How's she doing?"

The woman produced a clipboard with a medical form on it and thrust it at me. "Would you mind giving us a history on your sister?" she said. "She's been unconscious ever since she was brought in here, and we don't know anything about her beyond what was on her driver's license and that at some time she had her appendix out. Does she have insurance? We didn't find anything in her purse."

"I don't know," I said. "And I'm afraid I can't be much help to you. I hadn't seen my sister in years and she's actually only my half sister. We were brought up separately and in different parts of the country. I met her again at the racetrack, where she works for a trainer named Short, Billy Bob Short. He's pretty well known. You could ask him, maybe he knows." Not bad, I thought, as I improvised our backgrounds; they'd never have let me in to see her if I hadn't succeeded in passing myself off as a close relative. "What's happened to her?"

"I'll let you speak to her nurse," the woman said. "Andy's with another patient now. Is there anything at all you can tell me about your sister's medical history? Childhood illnesses, that sort of thing? Is she allergic to anything?"

"I'm sorry to be such a washout," I said. "Babs and I were just getting to know each other after all these years."

"You can wait here, Mr. Anderson," the woman said, putting the clipboard away. "Oh, you can leave us your phone number, in case we need to call you."

I wrote my telephone number down on a piece of notebook paper and remained by the counter, waiting. All around me, in the curtained nooks where the ICU patients lay, desperate struggles to maintain life were being waged, but the atmosphere was curiously peaceful. The nurses and medical techs moved swiftly and silently about their tasks, as, here and there, groups of mostly anxious-looking relatives clustered about their fallen loved ones and talked to one another in hushed tones, as if in church. Through this scene, like white-robed chivalric knights in a dream landscape, doctors occasionally appeared, never seeming to be in a hurry or alarmed, moving with the confidence of those to whom has been entrusted the quest of the Holy Grail. I thought about Ed Hamner, my horse-playing doctor friend up in L.A., who once said to me, "Shifty, in life everything is six to five against." He was the only doctor I'd ever met who didn't believe in his heart that someday somebody would find a cure for natural causes.

"Hi," the young man said, coming around the corner of the station. "You're the brother? I'm sorry you had to wait. I was with another patient."

"That's okay. You're Andy?"

"Yes," he said. "Your sister's doing okay. She's holding her own." He was about thirty, thin, slightly built, obviously gay, with orange hair, a bristly little mustache, and the kindest soft brown eyes I'd ever seen. "Have you been in to see her?"

"Yes, I have. She doesn't look great to me."

"Well, no, of course not, but we're keeping a very close watch on her," he said. "Have you spoken to Doctor Filbrick?"

"No, I've spoken to no one," I said. "I heard she'd been beaten up and I came straight over."

"I see. Well, you mustn't worry," Andy said with a benevolent smile. "She's stable now. The next couple of days will be crucial."

"What happened to her?"

"Well, the biggest problem is her skull fracture," he said. "She was hit very hard several times with some sort of object, probably metal. There's been some hemorrhaging, but we don't know what the long-term effects might be. She also had a ruptured spleen, which had to be removed, and she has three broken ribs on the right side, luckily no puncture of the lung. She's had a rough time, but, like I said, she's doing okay now."

"Is she paralyzed?"

Andy shook his head. "No, thank goodness. The bleeding was pretty slight. She's got a very hard head."

"I guess I know that," I said.

"Do you want to speak to Doctor Filbrick? You could reach him at home."

"No, that won't be necessary. Thanks a lot, Andy. I left my phone number here. If she comes around, will somebody call me?"

"Oh, yes." He put his hand on my arm. "And don't worry, we'll take very good care of her."

I believed him. Scripps Memorial was located in North County, mostly a rich and middle-class area well out of reach of the dingier sections of San Diego. This meant a happier, not so overworked medical staff not having to deal daily with gunshot and knife wounds, drug overdoses, and swarms of the beleaguered poor. Poverty is a sin in this great nation of ours, an insult to the very concept of the American Dream the politicians all prattle about. We punish the sinful by neglect. It was lucky for Babs that she'd been assaulted among the well-to-do, or who knows what medical hellhole she might have been whisked off to. I said good night to Andy and left Babs Harper to his capable care.

I got up early the next morning and went straight to Short's barn, where I found the trainer standing outside his tack room and giving orders to his help. He saw me but displayed no hint of recognition. When he finished, he turned his back, went inside, and shut the door. I knocked on it. "What do you want?" he called.

I opened the door and looked in. Short was sitting behind his desk, looking over a chart that listed all the horses in his care and their training schedules. "Mr. Short, I'm Lou Anderson, Babs's friend," I said.

"Yeah? So what?"

"I guess you know about her."

"Yeah. Somebody called from the hospital. Then some cop came by this morning to talk to me. Who are you, anyway?"

"I'm just a friend, that's all."

"Well, it's too bad," the trainer said. "Goddamn perverts are everywhere these days."

"Do you have any idea who might have done this to her?"

"Hell no, how would I know? I don't know what she does when she ain't working for me."

"She worked for you a long time?"

"What the hell business is that of yours? And how come you don't know, if you're such a friend of hers?"

"You don't have to be an old friend of anybody's to be upset when they get beaten up, do you?" I asked. "She's in pretty bad shape."

"Yeah, so I heard. I don't know nothin' about it," Short said. "It's too bad. She's only been working for me since about halfway through Hollywood. She's good with horses, all right. She shouldn't have gone to one of them places alone."

"You mean the Belly Up? Lots of people go there alone," I said. "It's just a place to listen to music and dance. It's not some dive full of gang members and criminals."

"I wouldn't know about that," the trainer said, looking down at his chart. "It's got so you can't walk down the street in this country anymore without some pervert tries to kill you or steal your money or both. Hell of a thing, ain't it?"

"This guy Vinnie who was here the other day, when Babs was talking to me about Superpatriot—"

Short's head jerked upward. "What about him?"

"He was at the Belly Up that night."

"Yeah? So what? Maybe he likes to dance."

"He doesn't look the type, Mr. Short."

"Type? You got to be a type to want to dance?" He returned to his chart. "You mind, whatever your name is? I got things to do here."

"You know Babs told him to fuck off and chewed him out the other day," I said. "Who is he?"

The trainer looked up again and leaned back in his chair. "What are you implying, mister? Who the hell are you, anyway?"

"I told you, a friend. I thought you might want to know about this guy being there, that's all. He struck me as an unfriendly soul, if you know what I mean."

Short stood up and came around the side of his desk toward me. "Listen, you," he said, taking my arm and pushing me out the door, "I don't know who you are or what you want, but I don't give a shit. I got a stable to run, I got horses to take care of, I got calls to make, and I don't need to be wasting my time talking to you." He slammed the door shut behind me.

Lopez, who was two stalls away working on a horse, looked up in alarm. "Not a good audience," I said as I waved to him and walked away.

I spent the next half hour up in the guinea stand watching the workouts, then went over to the cafeteria at the break to have a cup of coffee before going home. The Vernon brothers were at their usual table out on the screened porch, along with several other trainers and a couple of owners. I pulled up a chair and joined them just as Willie was saying, "Now, you take Maxwell here, how long have we had horses together?"

"Too long," Maxwell said. He was a stocky citizen in his late sixties or early seventies, with an angular, good-humored face and the raspy voice of a man who has inhaled too much bad air in his lifetime. "Maybe twenty years, and I don't think we've ever had a winning year, have we, Willie?"

"What do you care?" Willie said. "You're a rich man. Owners aren't supposed to make money."

"That's right," Duke Vernon said. "We don't want to spoil you."

"Why don't you just give me a million dollars?" Willie suggested. "Every night you'd go to bed and think, Hey, I made Willie Vernon happy."

"I'd give you a million and you'd blow it on gambling and women," Maxwell said. "It would break up your marriage and ruin you. And I'd have to lie in bed awake at night, thinking, My God, I ruined Willie Vernon's life."

There was a lot more of this sort of banter, which I found relaxing after my hospital visit to Babs and tense little scene with Billy Bob Short that morning. "So, Shifty, how are the horses treating you?" Willie asked as we got up to leave about fifteen minutes later and headed for the Vernons' adjoining stables.

"Not bad, Willie," I said. "We're cashing a few tickets. Did you hear about Babs Harper?"

"Who's she?" Duke asked.

"She works for Short," I said. "She grooms Superpatriot."

"Oh, her," Duke said. "She's got a mouth on her."

"What happened to her?" Willie asked.

I told them. "Whoever did it must have been waiting for her, or someone alone, anyway. Didn't steal her purse, though," I concluded.

"Some punk just beat her up for the fun of it," Willie observed. "She probably said something to him."

"That's what's wrong with this country," Duke said. "These damn punks and perverts are taking over. We've got to put a stop to it."

"How are we going to do that?" Willie asked.

"I told you," Duke said. "We're going to put somebody in the White House who's going to do what has to be done. Call out the damn troops if we have to. This whole thing is out of control and you know it, Willie."

Willie grimaced and shrugged his shoulders. "Duke wants the government to get tough," he said. "Trouble is, the lawyers won't let them."

"We put the lawyers in jail first," Duke said. "Then we go after these gangs and drug dealers and freeloaders who are screwing the whole country up, that's what we do."

"We don't have enough jails for all these people," I said.

"We take over the empty military bases they've been closing down and we put 'em in there."

"Concentration camps, Duke?"

"I don't care what you call 'em," Duke said. "Let's get these criminals and punks and foreigners off of our streets and put 'em where we can keep an eye on them. Shoot a few if we have to. That'll get their attention, at least."

"Sounds like a good program to me," Willie said, "as long as they don't shut the racetracks down."

"Now, why in the hell would they do that?" Duke asked. "You just don't talk sense, Willie."

"I guess you're a Ross Perot man," I said. "Think he's going to run again?"

"Ross Perot's a good man, but he ain't got a chance," Duke said. "He blew it last time. And he ain't tough enough. We need a real two-fisted American to do this job."

"Somebody like Wayne Copeland," I suggested.

"Well, why not? He's got a good organization behind him. Those people know what has to be done. If Wayne runs, I'm sure as hell going to vote for him."

"As an independent?"

"I don't care, Shifty. The country can't go on this way. We got to take our country back."

"Who's 'we,' Duke?"

"The real Americans, that's who," Duke said, his face turning a fine pink color in the early-morning light. "Goddamn it, Shifty, you're like all the rest, a bunch of wishy-washy liberals and goofy bleeding hearts. Jesus, man, these fucking people are taking over everything under Clinton and his bunch, and we ain't never going to put the pieces back together."

"That's an interesting theory, Duke. Is that what America One is all about?"

"You're damn right it is."

"You a member?"

"Yeah, what of it?"

"Nothing, just asking. Do you have meetings and stuff like that?"

"Sure do."

"Listen, you two politicos, I got to get back to work," Willie said. We had reached the corner of his barn. "Shifty, you go to one of them meetings, they'll ask you for money."

"That's okay. It might be worth it."

"Sign him up, Duke," Willie said. "You rich, Shifty?"

"No, but I can spare a few bucks for a worthy cause."

"Get out of here, you guys," Willie said, heading for his tack room, where Pablo stood waiting for him. "Politics is just a bunch of horse-shit."

Duke turned left toward his own barn, one row nearer the parking lot. I tagged along after him. "You ain't kidding me, are you, Shifty?" he asked. "These people are trying to do good things."

"Duke, I agree with you about the shape the country's in," I answered him. "I'm interested, really."

"Come on over to the barn," Duke said. "I'll give you a number to call. The party gets together once a month, wherever there's a branch. They don't take in just everybody, though. I'll put in a word for you."

"Party? You mean it's a party already?"

"Not exactly. I just think of it that way. We got to do something, Shifty, and maybe Wayne's the man to do it."

"Duke, is Billy Bob a member, too?"

"Sure is. He don't come to the meetings much, though."

"What about this guy Vinnie?"

"Who?"

"Little fat guy who hangs around the stable in the morning. You know him?"

"I've seen him, but I don't know who he is," Duke said as we reached his stable. "He bets a lot, Billy Bob tells me. Come on in, I'll give you that number to call. You tell 'em I referred you, okay?" He suddenly stopped and looked at me in surprised admiration. "Damn, Shifty, if I didn't think you was just another goddamn liberal. I guess you can't tell about people just from their looks, can you?"

12
Pain

♠

I should write my autobiography," Arnie said, "but I can't remember the first forty years."

"Who's asking you?" Angles said.

"No one, but it would make a good story."

"I'd buy it, Arnie," Jay said.

"I could have a whole chapter just about the photos I've lost."

"I thought you said you couldn't remember the first forty years," Angles said.

"People, it's people I can't remember," Arnie answered. "Horses, I remember everything. Sometimes I wish I could forget."

We had just lost our third photo finish of the day and were now clearly embarked on a losing streak. Jay, as usual, knew exactly how to respond to it. He snapped his big notebooks shut, folded his arms, and relaxed. "The last three races are hopeless," he said. "And if things don't turn around tomorrow, I may stay home for a few days. At the beach I'm always a winner."

"Thank God Reggie didn't call me today," Angles said. "Yesterday was bad enough."

"He's still in L.A.?" I asked.

"Yeah, and he doesn't like to bet unless he can see the race," Angles explained. "It's lucky for me. We've had so many losers the past couple of days, Reggie could take his action elsewhere."

"I like that guy," Arnie said. "He's just crazy enough to be entertaining."

Angles stood up and stretched. "I guess I'll go put the make on this chick I met at the clubhouse bar," he said. "She's with some bozo, but she doesn't like him."

"How do you know?" Jay asked. "Did she tell you?"

"Nah. I got a built-in radar, Jay. It picks up the distress blips, if you know what I mean."

"What happened to your Marine wife?" I asked.

"She's history. That was a one-day campaign, Shifty. In, out, and roundabout. Too many complications. Colonels carry guns, don't they?"

"Everyone carries guns," Jay said. "It's our Constitutional right."

"Yeah, but military guys know how to use them." He stepped out of the box and winked at us. "Anyway, if I don't have a live horse today, at least I can find me a lively lady." And he bounced away in pursuit of his latest quarry.

"I get this feeling that his interest in women is only sin deep," Arnie said.

Jay, Arnie, and I sat through one more race, a dull affair on the turf course in which the odds-on favorite and the second choice finished one-two, then I went to the paddock for the feature, the Balboa Stakes. Superpatriot was expected to annihilate an undistinguished field of seven two-year-olds and had been installed as the overwhelming favorite in the morning line, at even money. I knew, however, that he'd go off at one to two or less, which made him an impossible betting proposition, even in some sort of exotic wagering combination, such as an exacta or a triple. Any one of his opponents in the race could finish second and third and the payoffs wouldn't justify the risk. The hardest discipline of all to master at the racetrack is knowing when not to bet and having the fortitude to stay away from the pari-mutuel windows. It was what distinguished the pros like Jay and Arnie from the great mass of the horse-playing public and made their survival in a tough game possible.

I had no betting interest in the race, either. I merely wanted to watch the big black colt run and, more important, see if I could spot Megan Starbuck.

I arrived at the paddock early enough to secure a good viewpoint at the rail by the corner of the gap leading out toward the track. To my surprise, no sooner had I taken up my position than I saw the little fat man. Nattily attired in a light blue suit with a dark red necktie, his face half hidden by large, dark sunglasses, he was standing almost directly across from me. I couldn't have failed to notice him, because in that sporty crowd of California summer revelers, most of them tanned and dressed casually and skimpily, he stood out like a priest at a convention of nudists. He took no notice of anyone or anything, but stayed intently focused on the goings-on in the walking ring.

When Wayne Copeland arrived, surrounded, as usual, by his entourage, Megan wasn't with him. I figured she had stayed upstairs in the Turf Club for some reason, so I didn't worry about it. Besides, my attention was suddenly galvanized by the erratic behavior of America One's favorite horse. Superpatriot had apparently decided that competing in the Balboa Stakes was not the way he wanted to spend his afternoon. After being saddled quietly enough in his stall, he had allowed himself to be led out into the walking ring before expressing his displeasure. Halfway around the circle the first time and in full sight of several hundred watchers, the colt suddenly reared up in the air and lashed out with his front hooves. Lopez, who had been leading him around, jumped to one side to avoid being kicked. Luckily, he held on to the lead shank and immediately began to try to calm the animal down. Superpatriot was not to be mollified. He kicked out with his hind legs this time, sending the spectators on the grass nearest to him scurrying away, then bobbed his head savagely up and down, neighing and snorting with rage.

Billy Bob Short came running across the ring to help Lopez, while the handlers of the other entries in the race did their best to keep their own charges as far away from Junior as possible. Between the two of them, the trainer and his groom were finally able to calm their horse down enough to enable Short to give Kelly McRae a leg up and send their champion out onto the main track along with the rest of the field. By that time, however, the colt had worked himself up into such a fine frenzy that sweat poured down his neck and between his hind legs. He looked as if a giant hand had picked him up and dipped him in a tub of suds.

As the crowd headed back into the stands, with people around me still murmuring about Junior's uncalled-for behavior, I looked for the little fat man, only to find him missing. "Did you see that?" a young dude in back of me said to his girlfriend as I went up the escalator toward our box. "Boy, I wouldn't bet on that one with your dad's money." His opinion was not shared by the majority, as indicated by the odds of one to two on the horse, but then most people hadn't seen the drama in the paddock.

"America's horse looks like shit," was the way Arnie put it to us as I returned to the box.

I filled him and Jay in on what had happened as I watched the post parade. Both McRae and the rider on the escort pony had their hands full trying to keep Superpatriot under control on their way to the starting gate. Instead of galloping easily and purposefully, the colt had his head draped over the pony's neck and was jumping about erratically, so that McRae had to stand up in the stirrups and fight him every step of the way.

"He's also washy," Jay said. "I don't like the looks of that."

The smart money in the stands had taken note of Junior's behavior and the odds on him had begun slowly to rise, although he still seemed sure to go off at no more than even money. With five minutes to go, Arnie stood up. "This horse is not going to win," he announced. "There's money to be made here."

"I'd be careful, Arnie," Jay said. "This is a bad field. Horrible as he looks, the horse could win just on class."

"I'm going to wheel three long shots on top of him in exactas," Arnie said. "He'll run second on talent alone, but today's not his day."

I had a strong feeling Arnie might be right, so I followed him inside, though I wasn't quite certain what I would do. Arnie stepped into a line of bettors, while I hesitated. The little fat man walked past me, heading for another line, this one in front of a "Large Transaction" window. I took my place in line behind him. Two minutes later I heard him bet five hundred dollars to win on Superpatriot, whose odds had risen by then to six to five. I decided not to bet, but tagged after the little fat man, who went to a corner of the nearest bar. He ordered a ginger ale, then took up a position under a TV monitor, removed his glasses, and waited calmly for the race to go off. I joined the small group around him.

When the gate opened, Superpatriot broke last, stumbling badly out of his post position on the rail, while McRae struggled to stay on his back. By the time he began to run, he was at least fifteen lengths behind the leaders, an almost impossible amount of ground to make up at the sprint distance of six and a half furlongs. Furthermore, the colt at first showed no inclination to compete at all. Then, after McRae stung him a couple of times with the whip, he finally began to run.

Stride by stride, he began to close ground. Jay was right: he was so much the best horse in the race that he was a threat to win it, no matter what. Still, talent and all, he could not overcome his disastrous start. McRae was forced to swing him very wide on the turn in order not to run up the heels of the tiring animals on the inside. He finished third, beaten by less than three lengths for the win and a neck for second money, which meant, of course, that Arnie had lost his bet, even though one of his long shots, at twelve to one, had won the race. "I should have known better," Arnie said later. "When you're in a slump and you play exactas, you're always going to lose the photo."

The little fat man displayed no visible sign of distress. He reached into his pocket, removed his glasses, carefully polished them with a white silk handkerchief, and placed them back on his nose. "Hey, Vinnie, that was a bad beat," I said, coming up beside him as the other people around us dispersed. "I was behind you at the window. Tough."

He turned to look at me. I couldn't see his eyes behind the shades, but his face remained expressionless. "Who are you?" he asked in that strange falsetto.

"Lou Anderson. I'm a friend of Babs's," I said. "We met at Short's barn one morning. You weren't too pleased to see me there."

"Beat it," he said, as if he were greeting me. "I don't want to see you around."

"What is it you don't like about me?" I asked. "Was it something I said? I'm sorry you lost your bet, but it's not my fault, is it? Say, wasn't that a terrible thing that happened to Babs? I mean, getting beat up like that the other night. You know anything about it, Vinnie?"

He didn't answer me right away, but continued to stare impassively at me for a few seconds, then stepped in close to me. "What makes you think I know anything about anything, fella?"

"Well, you were there, weren't you? I saw you, Vinnie. We were all there that night. I thought you might have noticed something, you know, some guy hassling Babs or something like that, or an altercation of some kind. By the way, what were you doing there? You don't look like a dancer. No offense, Vinnie."

He jabbed me so hard in the solar plexus, just under my rib cage, that I slumped over like a discarded marionette, gasping for air. I couldn't move or speak or even breathe. Then he leaned over and whispered in my ear. "You want more of this," he said, "just keep shooting your mouth off. Next time I'll break something. Get lost and stay lost." And he left me there, with my mouth open and both hands clasped to my belly.

By the time I could straighten up again and stop fighting for air, Vinnie had disappeared. Only the barman had noticed my distress. "You okay?" he asked when I approached him for a glass of water. "You got gas or something?"

"I'm all right," I said. "Something I ate, I guess."

"Well, don't eat the food here," he said, handing me a glass of water. "It'll kill you."

It occurred to me, as I sipped the liquid, that Vinnie had hit me with his fingers. He obviously knew how to hurt people badly. And I also realized that what I had taken for fat must have been pure muscle. As a close-up magician, one of my talents is being able to size up an audience. Obviously, I had miscalculated badly with this member of it.

♠ ♠ ♠

Deputy Jack Foster was a nice, clean-cut young man with pink cheeks and blue eyes, just the sort of professional policeman Middle America idolizes. He was kind, courteous, thoughtful, and about as intelligent as a chipmunk. After I'd concluded the account of my encounter that afternoon with Vinnie and followed it up with everything else I knew about him, Foster gazed at me benignly and said, "In what way does this relate to Miss Harper?"

I tried to explain it to him, step by step, and added, "Look, Harper has a mouth on her. This guy has a bad temper and he can really hurt people. You see the possibilities?"

Foster wrote something down in the small notebook that lay open on his desk, then again focused those big blue eyes on me. "She didn't say anything about him, Mr. Anderson."

"That's probably because she's unconscious," I said.

"Really? Again?"

"What do you mean, again?"

"I spoke to her this afternoon, a little after four," Foster said. "She doesn't remember anything about the incident. She remembers leaving the Belly Up and going to her car, that's all."

I stared at him in amazement. "Foster, you could have told me," I said.

"Told you what?"

"That she's regained consciousness."

"Oh, yes. They telephoned from the hospital. Brady, my partner, and I went over to talk to her."

I stood up. "Well, that's good news. That she's conscious, I mean."

"About this man Vinnie, Mr. Anderson. What do you think we ought to do about him?"

"That's up to you, isn't it? I was just trying to be helpful. I'm pretty sure he's the one who did it to her."

"But you don't know his last name or what he does?"

"No. I'm not a policeman. You are."

Foster smiled. "That's right, Mr. Anderson, I am." He stood up and stuck out his hand. "Thanks for coming by," he said as I shook it. "It's important for every citizen to step forward and do their level best to help fight crime and senseless violence. Even if, like in this case, it doesn't lead to anything."

"I could find out his last name for you. Would you like me to call it in?"

The blue eyes blinked in mild confusion. "Why would you do that?" he asked.

"In case Vinnie has a record," I suggested. "Wouldn't that help?"

"Well, sure, if you want to. That's real nice of you, Mr. Anderson, but don't go to any trouble. We're pretty much on top of this one."

"Yes, I can tell you are." I headed for the door.

"Have a real nice day now."

"It's mostly over," I said, "but thanks for the good thought."

"*No problema,*" Foster said.

How reassuring to know, I thought as I headed down the freeway toward the hospital, that the safety of our troubled society lay in the firm hands of Deputy Jack Foster, linguist and philosopher.

Babs Harper was sitting up in bed when I arrived at her corner of the ICU. Her eyes were alert, but she was still pale and her bandaged head lay against the pillows. "What are you doing here?" she asked as I approached her. "Who asked you to come here?"

"Nobody asked me," I said. "I heard you got beaten up, so I came by to see you. Last time I was here, which was last night, you were out of it. Then I heard from a cop named Foster that you were compos. So how are you?"

"How the hell should I be? What a dumb question," she said. "I got a broken head and I can't breathe 'cause my ribs hurt and they cut me open for some damn reason and you want to know how I am. Jesus!"

"You're doing okay, I can tell."

"Yeah, I guess I must be. They're moving me out of here."

"Where to?"

"How the hell do I know? Shifty, get me out of this place."

"You'll leave when they tell you you can leave. You got medical insurance?"

"Are you kidding? I've never been sick a day in my whole life."

"Then you'll be leaving very soon, don't worry about it," I said. "You're costing the hospital money."

"So what? I pay taxes, don't I? They owe me."

"That's not the way the medical establishment looks at things, Babs," I said. "The minute you can stand up, they'll throw you out into the street."

"So let them."

"You have someplace to go?"

"Don't worry about it, I'll be all right."

"You want me to call somebody for you? You got any relatives or anybody?"

"None of your damn business." She stared angrily at me, started to raise her head, then fell back against the pillows. "Boy, some son of a bitch did a job on me, Shifty."

"Yeah. The cops say you don't remember anything."

"No, I don't. I must have got hit from behind."

"You know that guy Vinnie, he was there that night, at the Belly Up."

"Yeah?"

"I saw him. Who is he, Babs?"

"I told you, I don't know. He comes around every morning to see Billy Bob. He bugs me all the time about the horse. He's a creep, some kind of sick citizen. He bets big. He's probably Mafia or something."

"What makes you think so?"

"He's Italian, ain't he? His last name's Noranda. I heard Billy Bob call him that. Ain't most Italians Mafia?"

"No, Babs, they aren't," I said. "You made him mad and he's got a bad temper. I think he likes to hurt people."

"Yeah, he's a creep. But I didn't see anything, Shifty, and I don't remember anything." She propped herself up on one elbow. "Oh, my God," she said. "What day is this?"

I told her.

"What happened?"

"You were beaten up—"

"No, you idiot, the race. Did Junior win?"

"He ran third." I filled her in on all the pre-race shenanigans. "He was a mess, Babs. He finished third on class alone."

She lay back against the pillows, looking exhausted. "I knew he'd blow his top one day," she said. "They're pushing him too hard, too fast."

"Wayne apologized to the public afterward," I continued, "at a press conference. He compared the horse's setback to the sort of thing the country's been experiencing lately. And he donated what would have amounted to a winner's share of the purse to America One, anyway."

"He ought to apologize to the horse," Babs said. "What a jerk. Is he okay?"

"Who, Wayne?"

"The horse, you dummy."

"Oh, yeah. So far as I know."

She closed her eyes. "If I'd been there, he'd have been okay," she said. "I could have handled him. Jeez, Shifty, my head hurts. . . ."

I leaned over and took her hand. "Listen, Babs, I left my phone number at the nurses' station. Have them call me if you need anything. And you can stay at my place, okay?"

She didn't answer and her hand lay limply in mine. I thought for a moment she might have relapsed into a coma, but Andy, who luckily happened to be on duty again, reassured me when I went in search of help. "Oh, no," he said, putting a hand on my arm. "We gave her a sedative about twenty minutes ago. She's such an active one! It was all we could do to keep her in bed. She wanted to get up and go home the minute she woke up. What a personality! You know we're moving her out of ICU into a room, don't you?"

I nodded. "Andy, I don't think she has a place to go—"

"Oh, it's all right," Andy said. "Joe's coming to pick her up when she's ready to leave."

"Joe?"

"Yes, she gave us his number and we called him up. He was at the ranch."

I tried not to look surprised. "Oh, that's good," I said. "Then he can get here in time."

"Oh, yes. He was wondering where she was, you know? They must have had a terrible fight."

"Yes, I can imagine. What's he doing now? On his ranch, you said?"

"Yes, he's between rodeos." Andy giggled and sort of hugged himself. "My goodness, what it must be like, riding all those big, mean bulls. What a life! No wonder she left him! I would have, too!"

13
Encounters

♥

Wayne Copeland stood at the front of the room facing us and smiled. It was the same shy, slightly embarrassed smile he'd used in forty-seven movies to charm us into loving him. He was wearing spotless designer jeans, a broad, brown leather belt with a big silver buckle, brown boots, a plaid cowboy shirt with a black string tie, and a tan buckskin jacket. All that was missing were a couple of silver-plated six-shooters and his familiar black Stetson. Otherwise this could have been the scene in so many of his movies where the hero addresses the townsfolk, urging them to rally to the cause of justice and right. From time to time he ran his fingers through his thick head of spiky black hair, now fashionably gray at the temples. His voice, that reassuring voice out of American legends, spoke to us with the utter selfless integrity that had enshrined him in our collective memory and imagination as the incarnation of all that was true and upstanding and fine about this great country of ours. "It sure is nice of you folks to be here for me tonight," he began. "You know I really appreciate everything you've done, not for me, but for America One. We're all in this great effort together, and if we keep pulling together, we're going to make a difference, you bet we are."

After the applause, he launched into pretty much the same speech I'd heard him give the night of his party, full of those broad generalities about the American scene that so many of us wanted so desperately to believe. We were the good guys and we were in a battle now to save the whole country from the bad guys. That's why he had founded America One in the first place, to provide an organization through which we could all make our influence felt, not only by helping the needy, the trustworthy, and the virtuous, but, more important, by helping those who believed in the American Dream and everything it stood for. If we all lined up shoulder to shoulder with him in this struggle, we'd win the nation back from its wasteful, corrupt ways and restore the land to what our forefathers had intended it to be when they opted for freedom and drafted the Constitution. "It's the American way we're committed to, folks," Wayne Copeland said. "Is that so hard to understand? No, not if you're a real American and know what this country is all about, who its dreamers are and what the dream is." On and on he went, spouting these lines as if they really meant something significant and revelatory, confident in himself and his message, preaching the gospel of a vanished America the Beautiful to his rapt, already converted congregation. Sitting next to me, Duke Vernon leaned forward in his chair, his hands clasped under his chin, his face flushed from the concentration of listening to what he clearly considered a message from above.

I looked around me. We were about fifty strong, predominantly middle-aged, well-dressed, mostly married white couples. We sat on folding chairs that had been set in parallel rows reaching almost wall to wall in this small meeting room, rented for the occasion at the local Holiday Inn. Everyone there listened in rapt attention to everything Wayne Copeland said, with the same sort of intensity I'd witnessed in Duke Vernon. I began to listen again with renewed concentration, hoping to discern in Copeland's outpouring of clichés either a specific recommendation or a program that could serve to bolster his theme. I heard nothing except a flow of funny-sounding phrases that, I realized, clearly served a dual purpose. One was to reinforce a concept, however mistaken, of a vanished, virtuous way of life that we all mourned, a vision of an idealized America that had existed only in song and story.

The second, more interesting and more sinister, was a subtle but persistent propagation of the idea that the economic and social mess we were in was somebody else's fault, the work of socialists, subversives, and outsiders bent on the overthrow of our cherished rights and freedoms.

Wayne Copeland spoke for thirty-five minutes. At the end of his speech, we all stood up and applauded, including me. I wasn't going to be the only person in that gathering of true believers to remain seated. I was afraid somebody might kick the chair out from under me. There was a lot of belief in that room, but not much compassion or charity.

"Thanks, folks, I sure appreciate your coming here tonight," Wayne Copeland said as we all sat down again. "Now here's my pal Ed Drumheller to tell you exactly what you can do in your community to make America One strong, to bring back the American Dream into our lives and make it real and not just a dream."

More applause as big Ed rose up out of his seat against the far wall and replaced Copeland, who grinned, gave Ed a hug, and sat down behind him. Ed now proceeded to tell us what it was America One expected of us. First of all, for those of us who had not yet joined, a one-hundred-dollar membership fee, which would put us on the mailing list, alert us to monthly and other meetings, and essentially establish us as bona fide members of a great movement. Secondly, Ed wanted us to go out and recruit more members, get people to become active in the cause. There was literature to be distributed, there were phone calls to be made. The word *crusade* cropped up in his exhortations. His speech had none of Wayne Copeland's easy charm, but it had the appropriate fervor. It reminded me of Pat Buchanan in New Hampshire, tramping about the countryside in search of votes with which to derail George Bush. It was a hard sell, but it played well to the assembled faithful. And it removed the last vestiges of doubt I had about whether Wayne Copeland would be running for office against Bill Clinton in 1996.

After a number of questions from the floor, mostly regarding practical matters such as how to organize a local branch of America One and how to finance it, the meeting concluded with all of us rising to our feet again, this time to sing "America the Beautiful." Even Duke sang, in a flat monotone so spectacularly out of key that a woman in front of him turned angrily around, convinced that he was parodying the moment. One look at Duke's fierce expression, however, convinced her of his commitment, and we bellowed our way tunelessly through to the end of the hymn without being challenged. "I didn't know you could sing," I said to Duke when it was over.

"I can't," he said, "but I ain't going to just sit there when everybody else is singing."

"You could lip-synch," I suggested.

"Don't be a damn smart-ass," Duke said. "There's only two songs that'll get me to sing, that one and our national anthem. You understand that, don't you?"

"Sure do, Duke," I said. "It's the spirit that counts."

"You said it. Now, you going to join?"

"I'm thinking about it, Duke, but I need a little time."

"We ain't got a lot of time," he said. "We ain't got but about two years now to get these damn socialists and do-gooders out of Washington. Aw, you're probably a damn liberal after all."

"Give me a break, Duke," I said. "I came here tonight with you, didn't I? It was very interesting. I'm going to go up and lay in some of this literature they're hustling, read it, think about it, and then maybe I will join."

"You don't have to read anything," Duke said. "You ought to know by now what the hell's going on, Shifty."

"Is Willie a member?"

"You're damn right. I made him join."

"Why isn't he here?"

"He don't come to meetings. But he puts his money where his mouth is."

"If they had a pari-mutuel window here, he'd come."

"Damn you, Shifty, don't you take anything serious?"

"Sure I do, Duke. I take this very seriously."

"Then go do something about it."

"I'm planning to."

Duke snorted his displeasure at my equivocating and left me to talk to a couple of other horsemen he knew. The formal part of the meeting had broken up, but most of the people lingered, either talking to one another in small groups or milling about the front of the room, where Wayne Copeland and Ed Drumheller were holding court. Behind them and off to one side, several dedicated-looking young people were passing out pamphlets and other literature to the faithful. I stopped by their table to pick up everything they were handing out, including a membership application, then I turned my attention to Wayne and Ed.

"Ma'am, one thing we do know," I heard Wayne say, "the last election proved that Bill Clinton is going to be out of office two years from now. Whether it's me running against him or Ross or a good Republican candidate won't matter. The important thing is to turn this country around, get to believe in ourselves again."

I waited through two more such evasive answers to specific questions about his possible candidacy, then found an opening and popped my own query. "Wayne, what about Superpatriot?" I asked. "That was a disappointing race he just ran. What's going on with him?"

"That *was* a bad race," the actor replied, "but I guess you could say that in horse racing, like in life, you can't win all the time. The colt will be back, don't you worry about it."

"Some people seem to think you're rushing him a little," I said. "You've fixed him into a tough schedule that maybe, as a two-year-old, he's still too green to handle. What about that?"

"Well, I leave those decisions to my trainer," Wayne Copeland said. "Last thing I'd ever want to do is hurt this horse. He's become kind of a symbol for America One, and I'd sure hate to see anything go wrong with him."

"I heard his regular groom was badly beaten up last week and isn't with him anymore, so that's why he blew his top in the paddock the other day," I continued. "Do you know anything about that?"

Copeland looked surprised. "I sure don't," he said. "Where'd you hear that?"

"She's a friend of mine," I said. "I went to see her in the hospital."

"Well, I guess horses get attached to certain people, that's true,"

Copeland said, "but I'm sure Billy Bob—that's his trainer, folks, Billy Bob Short, a fine gentleman—I'm sure he's on top of things and he'll know what to do."

"But what if he runs badly in the Futurity here, Wayne?" I went on, determined not to be put off by evasive generalities. "Would you drop him out of the rest of his schedule, the Norfolk at Santa Anita and then the Breeders' Cup, or will you continue, regardless of what happens?"

Wayne Copeland hesitated, the shy grin frozen on his face, as if at some crucial point in the dialogue he had forgotten his lines and was waiting for some supporting player to bail him out of his difficulty. Ed Drumheller, who had become aware of my persistent questioning, rose to the occasion. "It isn't up to Wayne to decide about the horse," he said. "That's why we have trainers."

"Sure, I understand," I said, "but if he can't run, how's that going to affect the campaign plans?"

"We don't have any campaign plans," Ed Drumheller snapped. "Where'd you get that idea? We just want to get the country on the right track again."

"That's right," Wayne said.

"Whether it's Ross Perot or the right Republican doesn't matter a damn to us at America One," Drumheller continued. "And this great horse is just a symbol to us, that's all. Wayne loves this horse."

"I sure do," Wayne said. "He's a great horse."

"And he's not going to allow the horse's life to be endangered for anybody's sake. Is that clear now?"

I had a few more questions I wanted to ask, but big Ed had other ideas. He cut me off with a wave of his hand and then informed the crowd that he and Wayne had to mosey along now, but urged us to hang around and get to know one another better so we could really put America One on the map and do our country a great service.

Duke and I left the meeting together a few minutes later. "Shifty, damn you," Duke said as we headed for the parking lot. "What the hell are you asking all those dumb questions for? Don't you know he don't know nothin' about horses? And that ain't what's important. What's important is what's wrong with the damn country."

"And you think Wayne Copeland can fix it?"

"Well, who can if he can't?"

"You got me there, Duke," I said. "I haven't a clue."

It was about ten o'clock when I walked into our condo to find Jay still busily at work. The notebooks were spread out in front of him, along with the *Form,* on the dining-room table, and he was feeling optimistic. "It's always too good to be true," he said as I fished a beer out of the fridge. "I'm only on the seventh race and already I've got three solid bets for tomorrow."

"Good. Maybe we'll come out of our slump."

"I've got to do a little more checking," Jay said. "It's dangerous in this game to be too optimistic. If I find another live horse in here, Shifty, I must be doing something wrong. I'll go back over my stats number by number."

"You know something I've never understood, Jay?"

"What?"

"Why it is that whenever I'm losing, all the people I dislike at the track are winning."

"Sounds to me like the paranoids are after you."

"Yeah, maybe. Another thing I've never understood is why bills always arrive on a losing day."

"You need help, Shifty. Oh, by the way, your girlfriend called."

"When?"

"About an hour ago. Her number's next to the phone in your room. She said she wasn't going anywhere and for you to call anytime." I got up and started for the bedroom. "What about this lady, Shifty?" Jay asked. "How come she disappears on you all the time?"

"I don't know, Jay," I said. "She follows this guy Copeland around."

"What a job," Jay said. "I'd rather clean toilets."

"No, you wouldn't."

"You know," Jay said, "I met one man in my life who understood women."

"Yeah? Who was that?"

"He died before he could explain it to me."

Megan Starbuck answered on the first ring. "I knew it was you," she said. "How are you?"

"I'm fine. I thought we were going to have some time together this week."

"I had to rush up to L.A. again and I've been busy. What are you doing?"

"I just came back from an America One meeting."

"You're kidding me."

"No, it was very interesting. Wayne was there."

"I know."

"Where were you?"

"I got back two hours ago. I suppose you've had dinner."

"Yeah. You haven't?"

"No. I was just going to order something in my room. I was kind of waiting for you to call."

"What do you feel like eating? I'll bring something over."

"Great idea. Something light. And a bottle of wine, preferably white. Do you mind? It's kind of late to go out."

"Mind? I'll be right over. Where are you?"

"The Doubletree, Room Five Ninety-three. Lou?"

"Yes?"

"I've missed you."

"I'm glad to know that. I've missed you, too. In fact, I think about you a lot."

"Then get your lean little butt over here."

I said good night to Jay, who was too immersed in his numbers even to look up, and sped out the door. I stopped at the California Pizza in Solana Beach to pick up a big Oriental chicken salad, then at a nearby deli for a bottle of chilled chardonnay, and showed up outside Megan's room about half an hour after I'd hung up the telephone. "That was quick," she said, opening the door.

"Faster than room service. And you don't have to tip me, either."

I walked inside and she shut the door behind me. I put the salad and the wine down on the table by the window, then turned to look at her. She was barefoot and dressed only in a pair of scuffed jeans and a blue Dodgers sweatshirt. She had no makeup on and her red curls looked tousled. "You look wonderful," I said.

"Sure I do."

"No, I mean it."

She stepped into my arms and kissed me. "Are you hungry?" she asked.

"Only for you. You want to eat?"

"Maybe later. I've sort of stopped thinking about food."

"Want me to show you a few moves?"

"I was hoping you would."

We made love for nearly an hour all over the room except the bed. It wasn't so much that we were trying to be creative; it's just that we didn't have time to bother with geography. We sank to the floor together and coupled first on the rug next to the table, then moved onto the couch, from there back to the floor again, then into the closet, where she'd gone to hunt for a handkerchief, then finally into the shower, where we soaped each other down and let the hot water cascade over us as we embraced. After we finally emerged, tired but spotless and renewed, Megan fell back naked onto the bed. "Oh, God, Lou, that was so great," she said. "I love you."

"That's a big four-letter word, Megan," I said. "Put something on or I'll assault you again."

"I don't want to put anything on," she said. "I want the two of us to stay here forever and be naked all the time."

"We'll frighten the maids."

"They'll adore us," she said. "They'll never have seen such love before. Come here."

"Again?"

"No, stupid, just hold me."

We lay together on the bed for a while, then at last Megan sat up. "I guess I could eat now," she said. "You?"

"No. I'll have a glass of wine, though."

I opened the wine and we sat side by side on the bed, sipping it. After a few minutes, Megan put on a robe and moved to the table, where she proceeded to devour the chicken salad. I joined her there, drank the wine, and watched her. I couldn't get enough of looking at her. She sensed this feeling in me and suddenly leaned across the table to kiss me. Her mouth tasted of ginger and I laughed. "That's a good salad," I said. "I wish I were hungry."

And the phone rang.

Megan picked it up and I knew immediately that our evening was over. She sat cross-legged on the bed, her back toward me, and talked into the receiver in a low voice that I couldn't overhear. When she hung up a couple of minutes later, she swung around toward me and said, "Lou, I have to go."

"Now? It's nearly midnight."

"I know. I can't help it." She stood up, dropped her robe on the floor, and began to dress. "Come on, Lou, you can see me out."

"I could stay here," I suggested. "How long will you be gone?"

"No, I can't let you do that," she said. "Please, Lou. I'm sorry."

"What kind of a PR job is this?" I asked as I scrambled into my pants and looked about for my shoes. "Don't they ever keep regular office hours? Is Copeland a night owl or something?"

"Don't ask. You don't want to know."

We finished dressing and went out the door together. Megan had put on sneakers, dark gray slacks, a white shirt, and a blue windbreaker. "So this is good-bye again," I said as we waited for the elevator. "Yes, I know, you'll call me, right?"

She kissed me quickly as the elevator door opened. "Don't be grumpy," she said. "Be thankful for what we have."

"What do we have?" I asked as we stepped into the elevator and it started down.

"You have me and I have you," Megan said. "That's not so bad, is it? You know I'll call, don't you?"

"We have to find you a better job," I said. "One with regular hours."

"You don't keep regular hours, do you?"

"Compared to you, I'm a model of predictability."

We walked out through the empty lobby to the parking lot. It was a dark, moonless night, with a light mist drifting in off the ocean. The only illumination came from the orange glow of the street lamps and from the hotel itself. "I'm over around the side," Megan said. "Where are you?"

"Right over there." I'd found a spot almost directly in front of the main entrance.

"Good-bye, Lou. I'll call you." She kissed me, very quickly this time, and walked swiftly away from me. I watched her go, then strolled toward my car.

I think I must have sensed the danger even before I heard her cry out. I remember turning even as she called my name. She was running across the lot between rows of cars. At first I couldn't make out from what, but then I saw a compact, dark form in pursuit and I heard the muffled sound of a shot, then a second one. "Hey!" I shouted. "What the hell are you doing?" I began running toward her. "Hey, police! Help! Look out, there!"

At least I think that's what I shouted. My object was to make as much noise as possible. I kept shouting and running, but crouching low, trying to keep the rows of cars between me and the gunman. "Lou!" I heard her call. "Lou! Stay away! Go get help!"

I stopped and peered up over the roof of a car. I saw nothing. Then Megan suddenly burst into the clear, sprinting across the lot toward the highway. The dark shape rose up above another car not ten yards away from me. The long barrel of a gun rested on the roof, aimed at Megan. "Hey!" I shouted again. "Police! Help! Help!"

The weapon swung in my direction and fired. I felt something crack and a sharp pain in my left side. I remember falling and then nothing, only an enveloping silence as dark as the night itself.

14
Cooling

♦

The first familiar face I saw when I came out of surgery was that of Deputy Jack Foster. He walked into my hospital room and took up a position at the foot of my bed with a pad in his hand. He looked unconcerned and quite pleased to see me again, as if, like old friends, we might have just bumped into each other on the street. "Hi," he said. "They told me you'd be out of the recovery room by now, so I thought I'd come by. How are you feeling?"

"Not great," I said. "They told me I'd feel better tomorrow."

"Sure you will," Foster said. "You were lucky."

"I guess I was. I don't feel very lucky right now, though. I feel like somebody hit me over the head and my side hurts."

"Well, this is one fine hospital," Foster said. "Sure you hurt. They just took a bullet out of you."

"So they tell me." I looked around, even though it hurt to turn my head. I was in a small double room with a single window between the beds. It looked like morning outside, with a damp gray cast to the daylight filtering into the room through the half-drawn blinds. A very old man was lying on his back in the other bed. He was either asleep or in a coma. His mouth was open and he was plugged into various tubes that were either draining fluids out of him or pumping them in, perhaps both. His skin was gray and his cheekbones seemed to be all that were keeping his face from collapsing. "At least I'm better off than my roommate."

"That's for sure. You feel like talking?"

"No, but I will."

Foster took a ballpoint pen out of his breast pocket and aimed it at his pad. Before he could ask me a question, however, a doctor in a white lab coat with a stethoscope strung around his neck walked into the room. He was in his early thirties, with a full black beard, a short haircut, and dark, glittery eyes. "Ah, you're awake again," he said. "How are you feeling?"

"Like hell," I said. "Who are you? And why don't you tell me how I am?"

"I'm Doctor Chamberlain," he said. "I'm the resident on duty. Just thought I'd check on you."

"I appreciate it. So how am I?"

"You'll feel a lot better by tomorrow," he said. "We may even be able to send you home."

"I certainly hope so," I said. "I can't afford this place."

"You have insurance, don't you?"

"Not for the first two grand," I said. "So get me out of here, Doc."

He smiled briefly. "Forget it, you've already met your deductible," he said, "but we'll do our best." He picked up the chart at the foot of my bed and glanced at it. "It was a simple procedure and there shouldn't be any complications. You were lucky."

"That's what everybody keeps saying."

"It could have been a lot worse," the doctor said. "The bullet entered your left side near the kidney area and lodged in the muscle. You'll be pretty sore there for a while, but you'll be okay. There won't even be much of a scar. That's what Doctor Kell told me."

"The surgeon?"

"Yes, he'll be in to see you later this afternoon." He put the chart back in place. "Anyway, if not tomorrow, you'll be home the day after. And you'll start walking in about twenty minutes."

"You're kidding."

"No, I'm not. The sooner we get you up, the faster you'll start healing."

"Why does my head hurt?"

"You either fell or were knocked backwards by the force of the bullet," he explained. "I gather it was pretty short range. You must have hit the pavement or a car going down. You've got a bad bruise above and behind your right temple, but there's no internal bleeding. Do you remember falling?"

"Yes," I said, "but not much after that. I thought I was dying, and that tends to concentrate you wonderfully on yourself."

"Yes," Chamberlain said. "Well, I'll leave you now. I gather the officer here wants to ask you some questions."

"What about Miss Starbuck?"

"Who?"

"The lady I was with. The gunman was shooting at her," I explained. "I just got in the middle. Is she okay?"

"I wouldn't know," Chamberlain said. "You were the only victim of the shooting, as far as I know. Nobody else was brought into the ER with you."

I looked at Foster, but his cheerful face remained as blank as ever. "First I've heard of anybody else," he said. "That's why I need to get a statement from you, Anderson."

"Take it slow, Mr. Anderson," Chamberlain said, easing himself out the door. "I'll be in again later."

"Doctor, can this man here hear us?" Foster asked, indicating my comatose roomie.

"I'm afraid not," the doctor said.

"Well, that's good," Foster said cheerfully. "This is private police business."

Chamberlain looked at him in mild surprise, then shrugged his shoulders and left the room. Foster drew the curtains shut around the other bed, then turned back to me. "Okay, Mr. Anderson," he said, "you want to tell me now exactly what happened, please?"

"I'm not sure," I said. "The lady I was with and I were headed for our cars in the Doubletree parking lot. I was near the front of the hotel and she was around the side. I was just about to get into my car when I heard her shout. Then I saw a guy running after her. I went after him—"

"That was not a good idea," Foster said, glancing up from his pad.

"What was I supposed to do, let him attack her?"

"You should have tried to get help."

"How? I was making as much noise as I could, hoping to distract him, and I was calling for help."

"So then what happened?"

"My friend was running away from him between the rows of parked cars," I continued. "She's an athlete and she can run pretty fast. I was coming toward the guy from the other direction. When she broke into the clear and headed for the main road, he had dead aim on her, so I made a big hullabaloo. I couldn't have been more than ten yards from him. Megan must have gotten away."

"Did you recognize him?"

"No. But he was a short, stocky guy dressed all in black," I said. "He was wearing a cap, I think, and he might have been masked or had something covering his face. I couldn't make out any features. You remember that guy Vinnie I told you about? The man who was in the Belly Up the night that woman, Babs Harper, was beaten up?"

"Oh, yeah, I remember. You think it was him?"

"Same size," I said.

"Why would this guy want to kill your girlfriend?"

"I don't know. Maybe he gets off on maiming and killing women."

"You think that's it?"

"No, it doesn't make a hell of a lot of sense," I admitted. "But there are a lot of weird guys on the loose these days, right? By the way, I know the guy's last name now. It's Noranda." I spelled it for him. "You might look him up, see if he has a record or something."

"Now, this gal you were with, what's her name?"

"Megan Starbuck." I spelled her name out for him as well.

"What does she do?"

"She's in PR," I said. "She works for Wayne Copeland, the movie actor."

"No kidding." Foster's eyes widened; he was clearly impressed. "He's great. I love his movies, never miss a one. She works for him, huh? What's her address and phone number? I guess we need to talk to her, too."

"She was staying at the Doubletree," I said. "She lives back East, in Virginia, works out of Washington."

"Okay, we'll call the hotel. You got a number for her somewhere?"

"Not really. We just met. The firm she works for is Flaherty and McDame, in D.C." I spelled those names out for him as well. "But she may be hard to get to through them. You could contact Copeland. He has a house here in Rancho Santa Fe. The rest of the time, when he isn't filming, I think he lives in Palm Desert."

"Boy, I love his movies. I'd sure like to meet him," Foster said. "Wouldn't that be great? What's he working on now? Is he shooting a movie here?"

"No, he's got a bigger production in mind."

"No shit? Gee, that's great! Have you met him?"

"Yes."

"What's he like? A real nice guy, I bet. Boy, I've seen all his movies. Him and Clint Eastwood, what a couple of great guys! It'd make my day if I could meet Wayne Copeland. Boy, wait'll I tell Janie. That's my wife. She'll flip!"

"I can imagine."

"You know, I got a great story for him. There's this case I know about—everybody says I ought to write it down, it would make such a great script. Only I'm not a writer and I don't have the time. But if I could just talk it to somebody, you know, it's perfect for Wayne. You think you could get me to him?"

"Megan could," I said. "Why don't you ask her, if you can find her?"

"That's a great idea. I may just do that." He snapped his pad shut and stuck his ballpoint back in his pocket. "Okay, Mr. Anderson, I'll let you know what happens, okay? You know, Copeland would love my story, if I can just get it to him. It's perfect for him. He'd play this San Diego County sheriff's deputy whose daughter's hamster is stolen and he—"

I shut my eyes. "Excuse me, Foster, I'm feeling a little woozy," I said. "Do you mind?"

"Oh. Yeah. Sorry. Well, I'll be seeing you, right? Take it easy now. Boy, Wayne Copeland! What a guy!" And when I opened my eyes, he was gone. Christ, I thought, the whole country is nuts, one giant movie screen. What if Jack Foster did have a story Wayne Copeland would want to make a movie out of? I should have asked for a finder's fee. It's all Cloud Cuckooland—every movie star a real-life hero, every criminal with an agent to peddle his story, every cop a potential screenwriter. It's show time everywhere, let the docudramas roll. I slept—I don't know how long—until they woke me up to take a little walk down the corridor outside my room. With the help of a small, sturdy Irish nurse named Lucy something or other, I made it to the corner and back, then slept some more. One thing about being shot, it tends to drain the energy out of you.

While I was sleeping away the morning, Cheryl Copeland's body was found by the gardener, a Chicano named Alberto Morelos, who worked at the Rancho Santa Fe property three days a week—Mondays, Wednesdays, and Fridays. He always showed up for work at 9:00 A.M. sharp and rarely ever stopped at the house to get instructions; he knew what he was supposed to do. He had only met Wayne Copeland once, shortly after he was first hired, and he reported, every two or three weeks, to Mrs. Copeland, who also paid his salary. He liked Mrs. Copeland, although, as he told the police later, he also felt sorry for her. "She was alone a lot of the time, I figured," he said. "And I guess she was pretty shy. But she always paid me good and on time and she let me kind of take care of things on the grounds. I don't think she cared about the garden, if you want to know the truth. She liked the desert better, I guess. Anyway, that's why I couldn't believe it when I found her out there in them woods. I mean, she never went out there before, far as I know, you know what I mean?"

She could have been missing for several days, if on that particular Friday Alberto Morelos hadn't decided to clear out the underbrush in the glade behind the main house. It had rained heavily the previous winter and the undergrowth on the slope had become heavy, a potential fire hazard as the summer drew nearer to fall, the months of dry heat and Santa Ana winds. "I almost didn't go up there that morning," Morelos said. "I was going to wait till Monday, you know, but then I thought, geez, I better start doing something about the brush up there and not wait, on account of I didn't want no fires. So that's how I found her, you know? I guess she was alone in the house and Mr. Copeland wasn't due back, either."

Wayne Copeland hadn't been around since late the previous evening, when he had left in his private jet to attend an America One function the next morning in Chicago. The minute he heard the news, of course, he hurried back home, after telling reporters he would have a statement to make later. His spokesman in Chicago was Bill McDame, of Flaherty and McDame, the Washington PR firm. "Wayne's very upset, as we all are," Bill McDame informed the media. "None of us can imagine what could have motivated the person who did this terrible thing. Cheryl Copeland was a lovely lady who never did harm to anyone and was devoted to her family." There would be a private funeral service for family and friends in the Del Mar–Rancho Santa Fe area, McDame went on to say. He also asked the press not to turn the event into a media circus and to respect Wayne's desire to mourn his wife in privacy until such time as he felt he could confront the issue publicly, which he would surely do. Two of the Copelands' three grown daughters lived in the Chicago area and attended the press conference with their husbands, both businessmen. The third daughter was due home that evening on a flight from Germany, where she lived with her husband, a high-ranking military officer attached to NATO. None of the family had much to say to reporters except to express their grief in a general way, and both daughters dabbed at their eyes during Bill McDame's statement.

♦ ♦ ♦

Alberto Morelos had found the body about an hour after going to work. Cheryl Copeland was lying on her back under a clump of bushes about halfway up the slope. She had been wearing a dressing gown, which had been torn off her and discarded under a pine tree a few feet away. She was naked, her hands were tied behind her back, and her mouth was taped shut. She had probably been raped, though a final determination would depend on the results of the forensic examination then under way. She had been shot once at point-blank range in the left temple by a small-caliber handgun, probably a .25.

The police had taken Alberto Morelos to the sheriff's substation in Solana Beach, where he had been questioned for nearly four hours by local deputies and a special investigative homicide unit dispatched to the scene. "I guess they thought I did it," Morelos declared after his release. "Some of the questions they asked me were really dumb, but I guess they had to do it, you know? So I guess they figured I was guilty, even though it was me that called them. She was a nice lady. I'm really sorry for her."

I didn't hear the story until later that afternoon, when I was sitting up in bed, watching the news on the TV monitor in my room and trying to force myself to eat at least some of what the hospital kitchen had served up to me in the guise of food. The first thing I found myself wondering was whether Deputy Jack Foster had taken part in the interrogation of Morelos. If he had, that would surely account for the obtuseness of some of the questions. But now, at least, Foster might get his chance to meet his hero, Wayne Copeland. Maybe he'd even be able to sell him his screenplay idea. In this great country of ours, grief is rarely allowed to interfere seriously with deal-making, though I doubted that Foster's story about a missing hamster would prove to be a suitable vehicle for a movie star gearing up to run for president.

"So what the hell's going on, Shifty?" Angles asked as he and Jay walked into the room about an hour later. I was sitting on the edge of the bed, about to ease myself back into it after my third walk of the day. "Who shot you? What's the angle here? What did you do, stiff some guy on a horse?"

"Another victim of random violence, I guess," I said. "Sit down, guys. What's going on?"

Jay eased himself into the chair on my side of the room, while Angles looked about for another one. He peeked around the drawn curtains across the way and saw my comatose roomie, presumably still lying there with his mouth open and plugged into his bags of fluids. Angles cocked a finger at him, looked at me, and arched his eyebrows. I shook my head. "It's okay," I said. "I don't think he can hear you, if he's still out."

"Out? He's all but gone." Angles disappeared briefly behind the curtain and returned with a second chair.

"You're looking pretty good," Jay said, "for a guy with a bullet in him."

"They took it out this morning," I said. "Everyone keeps telling me how lucky I am. I don't feel lucky."

"You look strong as a horse," Jay said.

"Don't say that," Angles objected. "Somebody tells you that, I figure you got about a month to live."

"I see there's a double carryover in the Pick Six," I said, "so what are you doing here, Jay? Why aren't you home handicapping?"

"All in good time."

"He's worried about the double carryover?" Angles said. "Come on, Jay, let's go. He'll be all right."

"They're going to discharge me tomorrow, I think."

"See?" Angles insisted. "He's okay."

"Where's Arnie?" I asked.

"He was going to come with us," Jay said, "but we've been going so bad Arnie had to go up to Oceanside to pick up some loot."

"What's up there? A pool hall?"

"Yeah. And a card club. The pool hall is full of Marines who think they can shoot pool, and the card club is full of citizens who think they can play poker. You know Arnie whenever he needs a little infusion of capital." Jay sighed. "Boy, there's nothing like a hospital to cheer you up, especially when you're losing. Who decorated this place, Morticia Addams?"

Angles cocked a finger again at the other side of the room. "You think you got troubles, figure the angle on this guy. I make him eight to five to cool by morning."

"Charmingly put, Angles," I said.

"What's wrong with him?"

"I haven't a clue, poor bastard. Does it matter?"

"No. So anyway, you're okay?" Angles asked. He looked at Jay. "Let's blow. Shifty's worried about the double carryover. He ain't wounded, he's sick."

"What happened, exactly?" Jay asked. "You have no idea who shot you?"

"Yeah, I do, but I don't know why," I said. "It's somebody who hangs around Short's barn and bets big money. He may work in some capacity for Wayne Copeland or the people around him, I don't know. But he wasn't after me. He was trying to kill Megan. His name's Noranda. I just got in the middle. It was late, Meg was going somewhere and I was heading home."

"Ah, after a little bangie-bangie," Angles interrupted. "Boy, would I like to have those gams wrapped around my back for an hour or so."

"Knock it off, Angles," I said.

"Sorry, Shifty. You care for this lady, huh?"

I ignored him. "Noranda was waiting for her in the parking lot," I continued. "She'd just gotten a phone call that lured her out of her room, but not from him, from somebody else."

"You're sure it was Noranda?"

"Pretty sure. I didn't see his face, but I think it was him."

"Where's Megan now?"

"I don't know. She must have gotten away. I sure hope she did. At least she hasn't turned up."

"But she hasn't called you or anything?"

"No, and that worries me. I mean, she must have heard the shot and seen me go down, though she was running pretty fast. Did she call the house?"

Jay shook his head. "No, but if she does, I'll sure tell her where you are."

"She probably knows, though I guess she has no way of knowing how badly I'm hurt."

"You're worried about her, aren't you?" Jay said.

"Sure I'm worried. I don't like this silence, even though it's become a pattern with her."

"Don't worry about her," Angles said. "Women know how to take care of themselves. They're smarter than we are. She's okay, I'm telling you. You don't want to worry about no woman, Shifty. Think about getting out of here, right?"

"You are going to get out tomorrow?" Jay asked. "What time?"

"After the surgeon comes by and checks me out, probably midday or early afternoon."

"You want me to pick you up? Where's your car?"

"In the Doubletree lot, I guess," I said. "You could go by there on your way home and check that out for me."

"Okay, Shifty," Jay said, standing up. "I'll call you."

"And don't pick me up. I'll call a taxi and go get my car. Pick the Pick Six and cut me in for twenty percent of your ticket, okay?"

"Done." Jay stood up. "I'm glad you're all right. Come on, Angles."

Angles bounced to his feet and headed out the door. "I'm going to check the nurses' station. There was a real cute one out there, with eyes like limpid cesspools." He disappeared.

"That's what I like about Angles," Jay said. "He's an incurable romantic. Anything else I can do for you, Shifty? Want me to make some calls?"

"No, Jay. I'll be home tomorrow."

"Yeah. I'll see you. Obviously, you aren't going to make the races."

"You never know, Jay," I said. "I may show up for the feature. Handicap, make us rich."

After they'd gone, I lay back in bed and watched television for a while, then went to sleep. I was awakened sometime in the very early morning hours by a bustle of coming and going across the room. Angles would have cashed his ticket; my silent roommate couldn't make it to the starting gate by dawn.

15
Reunion

♣

I went home the next afternoon, as the doctors had promised, but I did not make the races. The wound in my side was healing quickly, but I was in a fair amount of pain, which I refused to dull with the pills the hospital had given me. I have an aversion to not being in control of my life, which meant essentially that I was more prepared to put up with some pain than with a share of oblivion. So I sat out on our balcony in the late-afternoon sunlight and watched the last two races through my binoculars. I had a view of the entire track and beyond to the ocean, but I couldn't hear the call or see the finish line, which was hidden by the tote board. I did, however, have a head-on view of the horses breaking out of the gate in sprints. I could see the riders compete for position on the turn, hear the roar of the crowd in the stands, follow the flash of the silks as the field swept around the far turn. Watching the racing while divorced from the betting action was not unlike attending an exhibition of abstract art, where, as a guileless spectator, you can be seduced by color and line alone. I found the spectacle so soothing that I forgot all about Jay's Pick Six action and everything, in fact, but Megan Starbuck, who remained implanted in my consciousness like another small, aching wound.

Between races, I made myself get up to go back inside to the telephone, but none of my calls yielded much information. My first effort to contact Megan had been that morning from the hospital, when I had phoned the Washington office of Flaherty and McDame. No one there knew anything, as usual, and once again I had to repeat Megan's name and credentials several times before anyone, in this case an account executive named Ted Shannon, admitted even to knowing her. "I'm sorry, Mr. Anderson, I haven't seen her in several months," this man had said to me, "not since she went to work for Bill McDame on the Copeland account. He's out in California. Have you tried to contact him?" And he gave me McDame's number.

I called McDame first, but was shunted off to a voice-mail recording instructing me to leave my name and number, which I did, to no avail, at least so far. I also tried to contact the Greenwoods and even tried to find a number for Ed Drumheller, but nothing worked. The Greenwoods were out of town and there was no Ed Drumheller listed in the North County area or in San Diego itself. Finally, right after the ninth race, I tracked down a telephone number in the Hemet area for a J. L. Starbuck.

A woman's voice answered on the third ring, sounding as if a telephone call at that hour was an unheard-of intrusion. "Yes?" she said. "Who is this?"

"Mrs. Starbuck?"

"Yes."

I introduced myself. "I know you don't know me," I continued, "but I'm a friend of Megan's and I'm looking for her. I've been in the hospital and I've misplaced her phone number."

"Oh. Just a minute, please." She put the receiver down and I heard her calling her husband.

He must have been outside, because it was several minutes before he was able to get to the phone. "Hello? Who is this?" he asked as soon as he came on.

I introduced myself a second time and paraded my friendship credentials. "I'm trying to get hold of Megan," I said. "It's kind of important, but she's been traveling around and I don't know how to reach her. I called her office in Washington, but nobody there seemed to know much about her whereabouts, either. I was wondering if you'd heard from her recently or might know how to get in touch with her."

"You're a friend of hers, you said? Funny, she's never talked about you," James Starbuck said. He had a dark, rumbly sort of voice, which went with the mental picture I had of him as an old retired horseman and outdoors type. "Who are you, anyway?"

"I haven't known Megan very long," I admitted. "I met her through some friends of mine, Willie and Duke Vernon, and we've gone out a couple of times."

"I know those two boys," James Starbuck said, chuckling. "Hell, if you know those two rascals, you got to be in the horse business. Is that it?"

"Not exactly, Mr. Starbuck. I used to own a horse and I go to the races a lot. Charlie Pickard trained for me, till he retired last year."

"Aw, hell, he's one damn fine horseman. I heard he hung it up a few months ago. That was a damn shame about that colt of his. How's he doing? I heard he had a heart attack a while back."

"He did, but he's fine last I heard. He's living up around Napa."

"Now, you say you've been trying to reach Megan and nobody knows where she is?"

"Yes, that's right. I have to talk to her. It's important."

"What kind of friend are you, Mr. Anderson?" James Starbuck asked. "You say you went out with Meg a few times?"

"Yes, we dated. In fact, I was out with her the other night and some guy was waiting for us in the parking lot," I said. "He tried to kill your daughter."

"What do you mean, kill her? What is this, a joke?"

"Just what I said. This guy had a gun and he tried to shoot her. He shot me instead. I'm just out of the hospital, Mr. Starbuck. I think Megan's okay. Last I saw her she was running away from this bozo, and I was the only one to get hurt, when I tried to help her. I'm all right now. I was shot in the side, but luckily it wasn't serious. I came home today and I'm trying to track Megan down. The police don't know who this guy was, but there haven't been any reports around here of anyone else getting shot the last couple of days, so I assume your daughter's safe. Only I haven't heard from her and that worries me, you see." I was wondering whether I'd left anything crucial out of this bare-bones account and whether James Starbuck would figure out that Megan and I had been together in a hotel room, but I didn't much care. I thought it was more important to find out where she was and if she was, in fact, beyond danger.

"Where are you calling from?" James Starbuck asked.

"Del Mar. This happened here the night before last, Thursday."

"Del Mar? What was she doing in Del Mar? Last we heard from her she was back East. How long has she been there?"

"Off and on since the meet opened in late July," I said. "She comes and goes. She's been up to L.A. a few times and back to Washington, too, I think, but I'm not positive. She's kind of secretive about her professional life. But when she comes to town we usually get together for dinner or something. I think she would have called me this time, Mr. Starbuck. I mean, she knows I was shot and I think she'd have called me. That's why I'm calling you. I thought you might have heard from her."

There was a long silence at the other end, so long that I wondered whether the line had gone dead. "Mr. Starbuck?" I said. "Are you there?"

"Yeah," he answered. "Listen, you want to talk to me some more, you better come on out here. It's about an hour-and-a-half drive. I'll tell you how to get here. You got something to write on?"

"Yeah."

He gave me the instructions. "When can you come?"

"Depends on how I'm feeling. Right now, I'd say Monday," I told him, "but if I'm feeling okay, I'll come tomorrow."

"Just give me a holler and let me know. And meanwhile, I'll see what I can find out on my own. You got that?"

"Yes. I'm sorry to trouble you, Mr. Starbuck, but I think your daughter's in some danger. This wasn't just some mugger who wanted to rob the first person who came along. He was waiting for her."

"Yeah, it wouldn't surprise me none," James Starbuck said. "Matty and I can't figure why she would want to be in this business."

"What business, Mr. Starbuck? PR?"

"You come on out here and maybe we'll talk. And hey—"

"Yes?"

"Don't you go to the police about this, okay? I did that one time a couple of years ago when we didn't hear from her, and Meg got real upset about it. Anyway, thanks for calling."

I didn't have much time to think about this conversation, with its odd implications, because no sooner had I hung up than the door opened and Jay strolled in. He was wearing his usual summer racing outfit of running shoes, shorts, and a flowery blue-and-yellow Hawaiian shirt, the costume of a man on a sweet swing through life. "Hello, Shifty. How are you feeling?" he asked.

"Not too bad. I'll be much better by tomorrow. How'd it go?"

I could tell he'd had a good day, because of the purposeful, self-satisfied look on his face. As I watched from my chair next to the kitchen counter where the phone sat, he put his blue canvas tote bag down, extracted his notebooks, and piled them all up at the far end of the dining-room table. "They ran like little trained piglets today," he said, trying to keep the canary feathers from sticking too far out of his mouth. "Everything happened exactly the way the numbers ordained they should. You feel up to going out?"

"I don't think so, Jay. That good, huh?"

"I figured you wouldn't be, so I dispatched Angles and Arnie to lay in some serious party goodies, including the obligatory champagne," he said. "They should be along within the hour."

My heart began to beat faster. "The Pick Six, I almost forgot," I said. "You hit it?"

"Not the biggest one in history," he said, grinning, "but how does eighty-two hundred bucks sing to you? That's net, Shifty, after the Feds have taken their undeserved cut."

"It sings like a Verdi aria," I said. "Details, please."

"You're in for a little over sixteen hundred of it, minus your twenty percent cut of the ticket, which was six hundred and forty-eight dollars," Jay said, "so your net's about fourteen hundred. We got unsalted fast."

"That'll help with the two grand I'm going to have to pay for my medical costs," I said. "Nice hit, Jay."

"Like little trained piglets," he said, "and not one Dummy God favorite in the bunch. Actually, I thought it would pay more."

"I'm not complaining. Was Angles in on it?"

"For only ten percent and he almost didn't do it. Arnie came in for twenty, like you." He reached into his pocket, pulled out a wad of hundred-dollar bills, peeled off fourteen, and dropped them in my lap. "So who's the greatest handicapper in the world?"

"I am," I said. "You're the luckiest."

"Envious bastard. It was genius and hard work, nothing less."

The Starbuck ranch consisted of about twenty acres of flat rangeland surrounded by low hills, between Temecula and Hemet. The area had once been desert, but the advent of water and irrigation projects back in the sixties and seventies had converted much of it into farming country, the rest into open range on which people with modest incomes had built small horse ranches and private retreats. Some of the roads had yet to be paved, and the houses themselves were mostly one-story affairs that lay flat against the ground, as if recoiling from the ever-present sun and the heat of the desert sky. The Starbuck spread included a main house built low to the ground, with a sloping roof that projected out from the walls for several feet, providing a narrow measure of shade; a second, much smaller building, more of a bungalow, next to two rows of canopied pens containing six or seven horses; and beyond the pens, a large stable, a stone building with a tall, conical roof supported by pillars, allowing air to circulate within. Beyond the barn lay a fenced meadow containing seven or eight mares with foals by their sides. The main house sat just off the road behind a strip of lawn and a row of pepper trees that partly shielded it from view.

I turned into the driveway and parked in front of the house, then sat there for a minute or two to collect myself. I had waited until

Monday morning to come, but the last half hour of the drive had taken a toll. I was hurting a bit from having to shift gears from time to time and I probably should have given myself another day or two to heal, but I'm nothing if not impetuous and I still hadn't heard from Megan. The silence had become ominous.

Before I could get out of the car, a large, ham-handed citizen stepped out of the house and stood in the driveway looking at me. He was six feet four or five inches tall, with a paunch that protruded over his belt, and big hands and feet. He wore scuffed working jeans, boots, and a red plaid shirt with the sleeves rolled halfway up to his elbows. A straw cowboy hat too small for his head perched on his skull like an overturned canoe on a boulder, and his face was pink from the heat, with a pair of bright blue eyes and a long, slightly hooked nose. He had none of Megan's grace or beauty, but I could tell he was her father. "How was the drive?" he said, making no move to come toward me.

"You look like Megan's dad," I said, easing myself slowly out of the car. "The drive was fine and your directions were perfect."

"You hurting some?"

"A little," I admitted. "I've felt better."

"Well, come on in," he said. "We'll get you something cool to drink. Beer all right or would you like a soda?"

"A beer would be great." I glanced at my watch. "It's about eleven," I said. "Is this as hot as it gets?"

"Hell no," Jim Starbuck said. "It's only about ninety-five right now. It'll be at least a hundred by noon, and some days in the summer it gets up to a hundred and ten. Come on in."

We shook hands and he ushered me inside into the living room. The house was cool and dark, with perpendicular slats drawn half shut across the picture window that looked out on the meadow and the horses. A short, fragile-looking woman of about sixty with graying copper-colored hair appeared in the kitchen doorway. She had large brown eyes set in a round pale face and wore rimless eyeglasses that sat on the tip of her nose. "Hello," she said, "I'm Matilda Starbuck, Megan's mother." We shook hands.

"Sit down, Anderson, take a load off," Starbuck said, pointing me toward an armchair.

The furnishings were plain and serviceable—a couple of large armchairs, a sofa, end tables, with floor lamps in two corners of the room. Magazines and newspapers were neatly laid out on a long coffee table in front of the couch and the walls were decorated with reproductions of early-American landscapes. I had the feeling I'd stepped into one of these paintings, an interior of the ideal older American family house. "Matty, get us a couple of beers, will you?" Jim Starbuck said. "How are you feeling, Anderson? You going to be okay?"

"Sure. I'm just a little sore."

"And lucky, I guess."

"You said it."

After his wife returned with two ice-cold bottles of Coors, Jim Starbuck sat down on the sofa facing me and asked for another detailed accounting of the night of the shooting, while Matty Starbuck hovered anxiously in the background. "Oh, my goodness," she said when I'd finished. "I just can't stand it." She went back into the kitchen, where I could hear her rattling about with dishes and pots and pans, as if to drown out the sound of her own distress.

"Matty doesn't like it when she hears about Meg's doings," Jim Starbuck said. "I wanted her to listen to this latest business from you, because she thinks I always try to soften it for her."

"I don't think she liked what she heard."

"No, but it isn't all that bad, either. Anyways, we talked to Meg last night."

"You did? Then she's okay? Where is she?"

"I can't tell you," he said, "but she's all right. She wanted me to let you know that much."

"Well, I'm relieved. I wish she'd called me, too."

"I got this special number for her, which is how I got a hold of her. Would you like to see the ranch? You feel up to it?"

"I guess. Isn't there anything else you can tell me about Megan?"

"Not right this minute," he said, standing up. "Come on. I'll get you a hat against this sun we got out here and I'll show you around. Then we can have some lunch. How does that sound?"

"Fine," I said, not meaning it. I wanted to hear more about Megan, but Jim Starbuck didn't look like the sort of man who could be pushed in any way. Maybe if I stuck it out through lunch, I'd find out more about what was going on, so I reluctantly rose to my feet, clapped one of Starbuck's straw cowboy hats on my head, and followed him out into the brutal desert sunshine.

It took about an hour to complete the tour. Jim Starbuck introduced me to every one of his horses and gave me a little background talk on each of them, especially his two California-bred stallions, both of whom had won a couple of small stakes races in their time and who stood at his ranch for breeding fees of a thousand dollars a pop for a live foal. "They each cover about twenty mares a year," he said, "and we've produced a few winners. Only four of them mares out there today belong to me, so we're just getting along, given the way this game is kind of falling apart on us. It's just too costly and people can't afford to get into owning Thoroughbreds anymore." He chatted on about his stock and the state of the industry in general, the sort of conversation I often find myself listening to in the barn areas of racetracks and which I ordinarily find interesting. That day, however, my only real concern was Megan, but every time I tried to steer the talk around to her, Jim Starbuck would put me off. "All in good time," he'd say. "Now look over here, Anderson, this here's a real nice filly by . . ." And so I finally gave up and went along with him.

As we came out of the stable and started back between the rows of pens toward the house, a blue Pontiac sedan came speeding up the road beside the property, slowed down, and turned into the driveway. Jim Starbuck glanced at his wristwatch. "Just about on time," he said.

Megan emerged from the car and stood beside it, watching us come toward her. She was wearing a dark gray business suit and low heels, with her short red curls gleaming in the hard light. She had a hand raised to shield her eyes against the sun and she was smiling. "Hi, Lou," she said. "Surprised?"

"Amazed," I admitted, not knowing whether to kiss her, a problem she solved by putting her arms around me and pulling me to her. "You want to explain this to me now?" I asked. "Or are you going to make me guess?"

She didn't answer, but went over and kissed her father. "Hi, Daddy," she said. "You're looking great. Where's Mom?"

As if on cue, Matty Starbuck came out of the house and threw her arms around her daughter. "Oh, Megan," she said, "I'm so glad to see you. We worried so."

"Well, let's go on inside," Jim Starbuck said. "No sense baking to death out here."

"Lou, that hat is not becoming to you," Megan said.

"I can't help it. Your dad made me wear it. I guess I'll never make it as a cowboy."

No sooner were we inside the house than Megan disappeared into the kitchen to help her mother with the lunch. Jim Starbuck and I remained in the living room, but I was too excited to sit down. I paced about the room, pretending to look at the prints on the walls, while I tried to figure out what was going on. "Sit down," Starbuck said, "you're making me nervous."

"Mr. Starbuck—"

"Jim, please."

"Okay, Jim. Is somebody going to explain to me what's going on?"

"I'm not sure," he said. "This is the way Meg wanted it. She said not to tell you anything till she got here. You want another beer?"

"Maybe with lunch."

"That ought to be in two or three minutes. You hungry?"

"Not really."

"That's too bad, because Matty's a damn fine cook. 'Course, in this heat, you don't want to eat too much," Jim Starbuck said. "We'll probably just have a salad and some cold cuts. That all right with you?"

He looked very pleased with himself and I realized he was enjoying my discomfiture, as if he and his daughter had planned a surprise party for me and it was working out just the way they had intended it to. "Of course it's all right with me," I said. "Everything's all right with me. I get shot and I'm worried sick about your daughter, whether she's even alive or not, and she's playing hide-and-seek with me, and then you plot a little surprise reunion for me and act as if nothing has happened, but I'm not complaining, am I? Shifty Lou Anderson, boy magician, butt of family jokes, everything's all right with me. Nothing happened the other night in the Doubletree parking lot, it was all in fun, or maybe it was an accident. Or am I dreaming it all up? I didn't get shot at all. Maybe Megan Starbuck doesn't even exist. I'm a professional magician, Jim, but compared to your daughter I'm small-time. She's the real article. She can make herself disappear and reappear whenever and wherever she wants. She can make you question your own senses. Now, that's real magic. The girl has talent. If she isn't in show biz, she's missed her true calling."

"Aw, shit, Anderson," Jim Starbuck said, heaving himself up out of his chair and stomping off toward the kitchen. "Meg, get the hell in here!" he called out. "Your boyfriend's blowing his stack. Are you going to tell him or am I?"

Megan appeared in the doorway. She had removed her jacket and rolled up her sleeves. She was holding a platter of cold cuts in one hand and a bowl of potato salad in the other. "Oh, damn," she said. "I was hoping we could have lunch first and then talk about it."

"Well, he's getting pretty antsy," Jim Starbuck said.

"Hey, don't worry about me," I said. "Megan, I'm glad you're okay, you don't know how glad, but don't you think you owe me some sort of an explanation?"

"Sure I do," she said. "I was going to tell you all about it later."

"Well, that would be okay, I suppose. I'm sorry I shot my mouth off. I'll try to keep quiet."

"You don't have to," she said. She walked into the dining alcove adjoining the living room, put the plates down, and turned back to me. "Lou, maybe I ought to start just by telling you who I am and what I do."

"I'd like that."

"Okay, I'm a cop," she said. "You guessed it that day you saw me in the Wells Fargo parking lot in Del Mar."

"You're a private investigator?"

"No, I work for the FBI."

"No shit."

She nodded. "Yeah. Does that bother you?"

"*Bother* isn't the word," I said. "I'm stunned. I never thought I'd fall for a cop, certainly not an FBI agent. You going to tell me about it or is that it?"

"A lot of what I do I can't even talk to my folks about," she said. "I'll tell you what I can, Lou, but not right now."

"I'm sure happy to hear that," Jim Starbuck said as his wife appeared from the kitchen carrying a tray with a pitcher of iced tea, two beers, and frosted glasses. "I'm starved."

I looked at Megan and smiled. "What a conjuror you'd have made," I said. "You could have taught Houdini a few tricks."

16
Revelations

♠

You know, they can do brain transplants now," Angles volunteered between the second and third races on Friday.

"What are you talking about, Angles?" Arnie asked. "Have you lost your mind?"

"No, but if I had, I could get another one," Angles said.

"All right, Angles," Jay said, looking up from one of his notebooks and leaning back in his seat, "let's have the punch line." He put his hands behind his head and grinned at us. "We don't have anything to bet on until the fifth. Tell us the joke, Angles."

"Arnie doesn't believe me," Angles said.

"Sure I believe you," Arnie said. "At least I believe you believe. How's that?"

"It'll do," Angles said. "Okay, so let's say you need a brain transplant and you've got three choices—the brain of a lawyer, a doctor, or a horse trainer. Which brain would you choose to have?"

"None of them," Arnie said. "I'd rather die dumb than venal."

"No, come on, Arnie—choose one."

"Pass."

"Okay, Angles," I said, "I'd choose the lawyer's. I could work real magic—I could make the truth disappear."

"That's funny," Arnie said. "I like that, Shifty."

"And you, Jay?" Angles asked.

"I don't know. Maybe the doctor's. That way I could make big bucks doing those operations."

"Not me," Angles said triumphantly. "I'd pick the trainer's."

"Why?" Arnie asked. "You like making wrong decisions about everything?"

"No," Angles replied, "I'd pick it because it's never been used."

"You know, for you, Angles, that's an outstanding joke," Arnie said. "At least it doesn't reek of vulgarity."

"Oh, from the William Buckley of the frontside, I guess that's a compliment," Angles said. "Want to hear another one, about this Irish guy who walks into a bar in a Polish neighborhood in Chicago?"

"No," Arnie said. "Quit while you're ahead, Angles. Do yourself a service."

Angles told the joke anyway, which I'd already heard and not found funny, thus wiping out whatever credit he'd acquired from Arnie with his previous effort. "That's enough for me," I said, rising to my feet. "I'm going to stretch my legs and go down to the paddock. Anybody want to come?"

Nobody answered, so I left my friends there, bickering with one another and telling bad jokes to pass the time until the fifth race, when we all agreed Jay had come up with a live horse, a long shot who figured to run no worse than second. I needed a little time to myself anyway, because in the aftermath of my reunion with Megan Starbuck I wanted to think about what she'd told me the previous Monday at her parents' ranch, especially now, given the announcement I'd read that day in the *San Diego Union.* There would be a memorial service on Sunday morning for Cheryl Copeland at the small Roman Catholic church in Fairbanks Ranch, after which, the media had been informed, Wayne Copeland would have a statement to make during a press conference at his summer home in Rancho Santa Fe. I guessed that Megan's client was about to officially launch his presidential political campaign; out of personal tragedy there was always political capital to be made. "Remember, Lou, it isn't what Wayne wants that we have to consider here," Megan had told me on the phone the night before. "It's the people behind him who are really running this show."

"What about our friend Vinnie?"

"He's just a hired hand, somebody's goon. We're not sure whose yet, but somebody high up in America One."

"Are you going to have him picked up?"

"No, not yet. The idea is to let whoever it is think nothing much has happened, that we think the attack in the parking lot was a robbery attempt. But watch yourself, Lou. Call me tomorrow again at the same time, okay?"

"When am I going to see you?"

"I don't know."

"And you don't know where you're going to be, either?"

"Probably here in L.A. for a day or two, but we'll be in touch now that you have my number. Call me tomorrow, same time."

"Megan, I don't know how good I'm going to be at this."

"I'm trying to keep you out of it, Lou."

"You think that's possible now?"

"I'm not sure."

"I don't think so."

"I don't want you to do anything, Lou. I'd like you out of it."

"What about you?"

"I've called in sick to McDame's office," she said. "I've got a bad flu, I said. Now I'm waiting to hear from my people in Washington. Where are you calling from, by the way?"

"A pay phone in Solana Beach. Isn't that what you wanted me to do?"

"Yes. Lou, I miss you."

"You know what I'd like?"

"What?"

"To go away somewhere, just the two of us. Do you ever get a vacation?"

"Not till January. Can you wait?"

"I don't know. That's the opening of Santa Anita."

"We are not going to spend my vacation at Santa Anita."

"Why not? It's a great track and great racing that time of year."

"You're diseased."

"Then afterwards, if we break up, like Ingrid Bergman and Humphrey Bogart, we can say to each other that we'll always have Pasadena."

"Paris, they always had Paris, Lou."

"Well, we could go there, but they don't race in the winter."

"Oh, boy. Good-bye, Lou."

"Here's looking at you, kid."

It was hard getting used to this kind of relationship, I reflected as I stood by the paddock rail and watched the contenders in the third race being led around the ring by their grooms. Falling in love with a cop was bad enough, but an undercover one was worse. In the past, I'd always tried to stay away from geographically undesirable women, which, in my case, meant anyone not connected in some way either to magic or to the racetrack. Even though Megan Starbuck had the right track connections, she was a woman who was not only a federal law enforcer, but an undercover operator working out of Washington, D.C. It occurred to me that my luck with women these past few years seemed to have remained consistently poor. Still, what could I do about it now? Nothing. I was involved with Megan Starbuck. I hungered for her physically and I wanted to get to know her a lot better. After all, we hadn't spent any time together, really. A couple of dates, some terrific sexual romps, but hardly enough to build a relationship on. Just thinking about her excited me, made me want to be around her and with her. Her voice on the phone turned me on. My trouble is, I tend to fall in love too easily and too often with the wrong people.

The horses and riders filed out past me toward the track, and the crowd began to move back toward the stands and the betting windows.

I lingered in their wake. I had no interest in the race itself, a sprint for mediocre allowance fillies, so I stayed behind. I found a seat on a bench in the sun, with a soft breeze blowing in my face off the ocean, and I shut my eyes. Megan Starbuck, FBI agent. Great. So where do we go from here?

"You know, Megan, it might have been better if you'd told me a little sooner," I had said to her as we strolled out after lunch into the searing sunshine of the desert midafternoon. "And why are we out here now, getting baked, when we should be talking quietly inside, where it's cool and relaxed?"

"Because there are some things I don't want my folks to know about, either," she had replied as we headed between the corrals toward the stable. "They know quite a lot about what I do and they accept it, but if I go into details about my work, my mom freaks out. I want to spare her as much as I can. She's had a lot of physical problems and she isn't very strong. That's why my dad retired from the racetrack. Mom couldn't take the stress."

"What's wrong with her?"

"She had cancer, Lou. She's had a double mastectomy and also two heart attacks. She may need heart surgery, too, if she's strong enough. I don't know how much time she has."

"I'm sorry, Megan, I had no idea."

"It's okay. She's doing all right now and she's happy. I just don't want her worrying too much about me. I can't stop her from worrying at all. She's a professional worrier."

"I understand."

"Put your hat on," she said, taking my hand. "This sun is really strong. I know Mom's watching us from the kitchen window, so I'm going to pretend to be visiting the horses while we talk."

"I hope nobody ever sees me in this hat," I said. "I feel like Mortimer Snerd."

"Come on, we'll get to the barn and then you can take it off."

So we strolled under the hot sun from pen to pen, feeding carrots and lumps of sugar to the horses, while Megan told me that she had been with the FBI since 1987. "They had me nailed to a desk in Washington for nearly three years in front of a computer screen," she said. "I almost quit. I wanted to be out in the field."

"What were you doing?"

"Pretty much routine investigative work. A lot of the people I went through training with got assigned to outside bureaus all over the country, but, of course, they were men. And I happened to have some computer skills, from when I was working and married to Dick. The bureau has had its problems with sexism in the past."

"Haven't most police agencies?"

"Sure, and how about racing? Any profession dominated by men, right? What about magicians?"

"Mostly men," I admitted. "I don't know why. Maybe women aren't that interested, Megan. There's no other reason I can think of."

"Anyway, Lou, I pushed and pushed and finally they let me out of my cage," she said. "I worked on a couple of kidnapping cases and then several investigations involving cults. You remember Waco, Texas?"

"When all those people died in that fire? You were involved in that mess?"

"Yes. I was there, Lou. I saw it. That was a totally botched operation, but it wasn't the bureau's fault."

"It wasn't law enforcement's finest hour."

"No, I was pretty down after that one. I expected to be part of the follow-up investigation, but they pulled me off the case—"

"You're better off."

"—and they assigned me to America One. I've been on that for the past year."

"Working out of Washington?"

"I'm still based there, but I spend more time in L.A. than at home."

"Why America One and why you?"

"I have the right background. I know the horse business inside and out and I know the people and the area. A PR job is a natural way in, right? Also, I'm a fresh face on the local scene. No one's going to wonder too much about me, and I guess I don't look like your average cop."

"No, you certainly don't. But why Copeland? What's going on, Megan?"

"It's not so much Copeland, it's the people around him, the ones backing him. We've had reports of fiscal irregularities, money siphoned off through charities and poured into the organization's political campaign, maybe into people's pockets. We think Wayne's pretty much an innocent figurehead. The real players are these guys like Drumheller and Greenwood and Clovis. And there are half a dozen others, back in New York and Texas, mainly."

"So it's people using a tax-exempt, supposedly charitable organization to steal money across state borders, is that it? A big enough deal to involve the FBI?"

"Millions of dollars have been raised for America One. That's big enough, and that's why the bureau got involved. But there's something more."

"Like people dying."

"Yes."

"You mean the Goldman family?"

"There are others. Two local chapter heads back East and the secretary of a branch in Dallas, all gunned down in their homes within the past eighteen months."

"And then there's Cheryl Copeland."

"Yes."

"All killed the same way?"

"Not exactly, but there are similarities."

"Like what?"

"Small-caliber gunshot wounds. No signs of forced entry or excessive violence. Mrs. Copeland was raped by a metal object, probably a gun barrel—"

"Nice."

"—but almost certainly only after she was dead."

"I'm glad you shared that with me."

"We think the idea was to make it look as if it were a crime of random violence, which it probably wasn't."

"Is the press going to be informed?"

"No, definitely not. Nobody's strung all these crimes together yet and we don't want to tip our hand. We want whoever is doing this stuff to think we don't see a pattern."

"And what about you?"

"What about me?"

"Why you, the other night in the parking lot?"

"That's a good question. Somebody's on to me, Lou. I don't know who."

"Whoever called you out of your hotel room that night."

"It was somebody from the bureau, who said that McDame had been trying to reach me. He passed on the message, but it couldn't have been McDame."

"Why not?"

"Because he's the one who hired me. He agreed to work with the bureau on this. And it's too obvious, isn't it? He'd be nailed for it within days. No, somebody else knows or suspects. And knew enough about my movements to be out there waiting for me."

"I know all about your movements. They're sensational."

"You're funny, Lou. Maybe that's what I like about you."

"What are you going to do now, Megan? You can't go back to work for Copeland as if nothing happened. They'll try again, won't they?"

"I don't know. Obviously, I'd like to stay with it. I'm waiting to hear. If they're convinced that I believe it was a casual parking-lot assault, then I can still be useful."

"Useful? Is it useful to be dead? Why don't you have this guy Noranda arrested? You know he was the guy that night. What do you really have on him?"

"He's a professional thug out of New York who used to work for the mob. He's supposed to have had a falling-out with Gotti and his bunch. When the boys went off to prison, he moved to

Miami and set up on his own. Noranda's one of several aliases. His real name's Portello, Vincent Portello, also known as Spats."

"Spats?"

"He likes two-tone shoes and he's a natty dresser."

"I never looked at his shoes."

"Maybe he doesn't wear them anymore. He's changed his ways and also his looks. He's had a couple of operations on his face."

"That accounts for his having no nose. But I'll bet you one thing hasn't changed about him. He's a horse junkie."

"You think so?"

"I know so. You can change a guy's name, everything about him, but you can't change his essence, Megan," I said. "Once a horseplayer, always a horseplayer. Why else would he hang around Billy Bob Short? To protect the animal? No way."

"We're not going to pick him up yet, Lou," Megan said.

"Why not? He's a menace and he may try again."

"We don't want to do anything to jeopardize the investigation," she said. "It's bigger than just a simple murder case. We want the people behind him. Anyway, I doubt he'll be around much from now on."

"Why not?"

"He's just a hired gun. He's brought in to do a job and then he leaves."

"He may have done several, Megan. And what if he isn't through? I mean, you're still alive."

"He has to think we might be on to him. I'd bet he's already long gone."

"If he isn't, I guarantee you he'll show up at the track one day."

"I don't want you involved in this, Lou."

"It's a little late, isn't it? I'm already involved. Say, can we go in now? My head is baking inside this hat."

I took her hand and led her into the big barn, which was dark and surprisingly cool. A light breeze blew through the building under the elevated roof and a couple of horses stirred restlessly at the far end. Otherwise, the building was empty, most of the stalls unoccupied.

"Daddy likes to leave the horses outside most of the time," Megan explained. "They come in at night and when it rains."

"You know, I still can't believe this," I said. "I mean, your being a cop. I've never much liked cops in general, though I've got a friend who's a homicide detective up in L.A."

"Does it turn you off?"

"I don't know. Want to find out?"

"Now?"

"Why not? Look, here's a nice empty stall, nice and clean, fresh straw, perfect privacy."

She looked at me and smiled. "Okay, you first."

"Me first what?"

"Take your clothes off."

"Hey, Megan—"

She suddenly pushed me inside. I grabbed her and we lowered ourselves onto the soft straw together. "Lie down," she said. "You're walking wounded. I'll take care of this." I lay on my back and she straddled me, pulled her shirt off, then leaned over and kissed me.

"What if your father shows up?"

"He won't," she whispered, unclasping my belt. "Oh, I can tell now I don't exactly disgust you."

"Not exactly."

And so—another first—we made love in a horse stall. Someday, maybe, I'm going to find a woman who likes to make love conventionally in a bed and who will either stay for breakfast or allow me to do so. Perhaps we might even have a loving, thoughtful conversation afterward, with the morning newspapers scattered on the bed around us and hot cups of coffee in our hands. But then in life you have to seize the moment when it comes and not expect perfection. Megan and I were still in that dangerous stage of furious carnal infatuation that tends to blot out reality.

Before starting back to the house twenty minutes later, we carefully plucked straw out of each other's hair and dusted each other off. I don't think we fooled Jim Starbuck, who was sitting in his living room with a cup of coffee in his hand as we walked in, but he never said anything.

Several hundred people, including a sizable media contingent, showed up for Cheryl Copeland's memorial service on Sunday morning, and some mourners couldn't get into the church itself, but had to follow the service from outside in the courtyard. It was a cool, clear morning, with a light breeze blowing in off the ocean and rustling the fronds of the tall palm trees lining the country road beside the church. I arrived about halfway through the service, which lasted more than an hour, and waited on the fringes of the crowd for the main body of mourners to appear. I was curious about who might or might not be there, but mainly I was hoping to catch a glimpse of Megan. We hadn't spoken since the previous Thursday night, and once again I had no idea where she was. She had not returned my phone calls.

Wayne Copeland himself was the first to emerge from the church after the ceremony. He was dressed in what looked like his Tombstone outfit, all in black with a long jacket that reached nearly to his knees and a string tie with a silver buckle that lay flat against the gleaming white of his shirtfront. The only thing missing was his six-shooter. As he came out, he clapped a large black Stetson on his head and moved purposefully through the mostly silent onlookers, including the press photographers and a cluster of video cameramen, toward the road, where a line of black limousines awaited him. In the group around him I picked out Drumheller, the Greenwoods, the Clovises, and Bill McDame, plus a few other faces I recognized from the party, but no sign of Megan. There was a sprinkling of horse people, too, including Billy Bob Short, Kelly McRae, and the Vernon brothers. I immediately fell in with the latter, feeling as if I had joined Wyatt Earp's posse on the way to the O.K. Corral. "Terrible thing, wasn't it?" I said as we headed back to our cars.

"I just can't get over it," Duke said. "She was such a nice lady, never hurt nobody, and some son of a bitch just walks into her home and shoots her. Goddamn, but this country's in one hell of a fix."

"Are you going back to Wayne's house?" I asked.

"Duke is, I ain't," Willie said. "I'm running a horse in the first and I got to get back to the barn."

"You looking for a ride? You can come with me, Shifty," Duke said. "Unless you got a sticker for your car to get in there. You need a pass."

"I don't have one, but I'd like to go and hear what Wayne has to say."

"Well, get in, then. I'll bring you back here when it's over."

It was a short drive of less than two miles to the Copeland rancho. Duke parked outside the main entrance, past the security guards who had checked us through at the corner of the street, and we walked onto the grounds to join the crowd assembled on the sloping lawn in front of the main house. A small bank of microphones had been set up by a corner of the patio and the press had been assigned a section to the left, separated from the main body of the star's family, friends, well-wishers, and colleagues from show business and America One. Duke and I took up a position toward the rear, where most of the horse people had clustered.

No sooner had I taken my place than Ed Drumheller, Bill McDame, and Megan, who was carrying a large sheaf of papers, came out of the house together, with McDame going right to the microphones. "Ladies and gentlemen, thank you for coming and for being so supportive on this sad occasion," he said. "Wayne wants to thank each and every one of you for being here. He has a short statement he wants to make personally, after which he will answer no questions. He asks that you respect his privacy in this time of mourning. Sometime in the next two or three weeks, we'll be holding a formal press conference on some of the statements you will hear today. For those of you who want to have copies of the statement, Miss Starbuck will be passing them out afterwards."

Ed Drumheller turned toward the house and nodded. Wayne Copeland now walked briskly out and took McDame's spot at the microphones, as the video cameras focused on him and the stillness was punctuated by the clicking of the cameras and the shuffling sounds of the photographers jostling one another for position. The star's face was grim, his jaw set as he positioned himself to read the statement prepared for him. He had removed his hat and the breeze ruffled his dark hair. He looked down at the sheet of paper in his hand, then up, his gaze ranging grimly over the assembly gathered on his lawn. "Folks," he said, "this is a dark time not only for me and for my family, but for our country. This is a dark time of mourning, not only for the loved ones we have lost, but for the virtues that made this country great—honor, decency, honesty, truthfulness, compassion, mercy, and generosity of spirit. We have lost our way, we are wandering in darkness, and we're haunted by the demons of violence and crime who stalk us and who cut us down when we least expect it. Folks, this is a dark time of the soul for the America we love. And so I ask you, are we going to put up with it forever? How many innocent victims are going to have to die before we wake up? Are we going to give in to the murderers, thieves, and rapists who pollute our land? How long, folks, are we going to stand for it? When are we—you and I and all the right-thinking folks who are the backbone of the real America, the true Land of the Free and the Home of the Brave—when are we going to take our country back? Tomorrow? The day after? The day after that? When? This is a dark time . . ."

After a while, I stopped listening to the words themselves, because I'd heard this sort of speech so often before on screen. I began to feel as though we were all in this movie that Wayne Copeland was living as he spoke. He was asking us, the good people, to arm ourselves and get behind him and help him get rid of the bad people. The town was rotten, the country was rotten, only the good citizens, with him at their head, would be able to restore decency and honesty to public life. The posse would form in the courthouse square and ride off behind him to gun down the heavies and watch the rebirth of society take place. "You betcha," I heard Duke Vernon murmur beside me every time Wayne made what Duke considered a great point, mainly in the form of calls for more police, more prisons, tougher laws, and a new government of honest citizens recruited from parts of the country that had nothing to do with Washington, D.C. Duke Vernon, his jaw set in an angry line, his face red with righteous indignation, believed, and there were others present who believed as he did, and all over the country there would be millions who also would believe. Was it conceivable that Wayne Wyatt Earp Copeland could fail? Not likely, folks. The man was in the race to stay and this was his formal kickoff speech, the one that told the world at large that Wayne Copeland was riding to the rescue. I figured it would be remembered and referred to in the media as the "dark-time speech." "I'm not going to let you down, folks, nor any of the good people in this country, because at the end of every dark time in this nation's history there has come the dawn," Wayne Copeland concluded. "And toward that light, folks, you and I are going to make the long ride together."

"You betcha," Duke Vernon said.

Wayne Copeland looked up at the silent gathering and nodded grimly, his mouth set in a tight line below narrowed eyes that always signified in his movies that the bad guys were about to be demolished. Then he folded up his speech, thrust it into his inside jacket pocket, turned, and walked quickly back into his house as the video cameras kept on rolling and the photographers kept on shooting. A surge of reporters now surrounded Bill McDame and Megan, who was handing out copies of the speech to anyone who wanted one. I tried to get her eye and wave to her, but she was much too busy to notice me. I walked out of the grounds with Duke.

"Hell of a speech, wasn't it?" Duke said as we drove away.

"Terrific," I agreed.

"We need somebody like him. We got to get all these damn liberals out of Washington, Shifty. You joined up yet?"

"No, but I'm thinking about it."

"Well, do it. We got to survive two more years of Clinton, and I'm not sure we can do it. You listen to me, if we all get behind Wayne, we got a chance."

"Ask not for whom the bell tolls, Duke," I said, "it tolls for thee."

"What the hell is that, Shifty?"

"Literature, Duke."

"You know, sometimes I wonder about you," he said.

"Why?"

"You read too damn much."

17
Mysteries

♥

I saw Megan twice more before the end of the meet. Each time we got together at the bar in Tracton's, a popular restaurant across the street from the backside and a couple of hundred yards from our condo. We had drinks and a quick dinner at the bar, then drove back to the Ramada Inn on the Pacific Coast Highway in Solana Beach, where I had rented a room for the night. It wasn't an ideal lovers' tryst, since the Ramada Inn is not exactly the Ritz, but at least we weren't interrupted there by phone calls. On our second night together I lucked into a suite that had a Jacuzzi in the middle of the living room. We sat in it for nearly an hour before and after making love, which handed us a few laughs but also proved to be relaxing. We had our first long conversation about life in it, during which I discovered that prior to meeting me, Megan had had a long relationship during her first year and a half in the bureau with another woman agent. "I was pretty angry at men in general after my marriage to Dick," she explained, "and Jane was very comforting and kind and loving to me. She was a few years older and very wise. It was a tough time in my life. Not only was I angry, but I was frustrated in my job. Jane was there for me. I was very grateful. Does this upset you?"

"No. I don't care who people go to bed with, Megan, as long as they don't frighten the horses."

Megan laughed. "That's funny."

"I stole the line from somebody else. Dorothy Parker, I think."

"Who's she?"

"You haven't read anything of Dorothy Parker's?" I asked. "She was a very witty lady who wrote funny poems and some nice short stories, mostly back in the twenties and thirties."

"I guess I have a lot of catching up to do," she said. "I didn't grow up in a cultured background, but I guess you know that."

"Neither did I, but I had a teacher in grade school back on Long Island who turned me on to books and showed me how to use the library. I spent a lot of my childhood reading, when I wasn't holed up in my room practicing magic."

"Jane was pretty well read. She used to read aloud to me sometimes."

"You said she was also a cop?"

"Yeah, one of the few in the bureau, and she befriended me when I came on board." She laughed. "She pretended to be very feminine and had a phony boyfriend she trotted out for the guys from time to time so they'd think she was straight. Otherwise she'd have been fired. The boyfriend was a stockbroker. He was gay, but he was also in the closet and they covered for each other. Anyway, our thing went on for a year and a half, but then it stopped."

"Why?"

"I'm not inclined much that way, Lou, or haven't you noticed? It was more of a loving friendship than anything else. Not for her, though. She got serious about me and I had to break it off. It was easy, after she arranged to get herself transferred. She works out of Atlanta now."

"And these days she can come out of the closet."

Megan laughed again. "She won't have to," she said. "She married a doctor she met there. He's gay, too, so it's another mutual cover-up."

"I find that sad."

"Yeah, it is. We're still in touch, but it's over."

I put my arm around her and we kissed. "Want to get back in bed," I asked, "or splash around some more?"

"Up to you, lover. We have until morning."

We also managed to have breakfast together, though not in bed, because Megan had to get back to L.A. She had work to do there she didn't want to discuss with me, but I also gathered she had been, at least temporarily, reassigned by McDame to PR work that didn't involve close contact with Wayne Copeland. "They're trying to keep you from getting killed," I said. "That's thoughtful of them."

"I'm pissed," she said. "I'm so close to breaking this thing wide open and there isn't anybody else inside America One."

"Will they send you back to Washington?"

"I'm fighting it. In L.A. I can at least stay on top of some of it. Bill's worried sick. He thinks they may suspect him, too, so we have him protected when he's not on the scene with the America One crowd."

"I don't blame him for being frightened. Where's our favorite hit man?"

"I don't know," she said. "We've lost him. Probably back in Florida."

"You've lost him. That's great," I said. "Now I remember what worried me about your employers. The FBI couldn't find Patty Hearst."

"Who's she?"

"Oh, my God, Megan, you don't read history, either? Look up the case, will you? She was a celebrity who was kidnapped by a terrorist group, which she then joined. She was about as visible as Madonna and they couldn't find her. Anyway, who's protecting you?"

"I am."

"Oh, that's comforting."

"Listen, Lou, you're a great magician, I'm a good cop. I have a .38 I know how to fire. I also know how to use an M-16 and a shotgun if I have to. I can take care of myself."

"Where was all this artillery the night I got winged?"

She blushed. "My gun was in the car. Dumb, huh?"

"Dumb enough to get you fired, I'll bet."

"They don't know. And nobody's going to tell them."

"Megan, who called you that night?"

"We don't know. The voice was disguised, but it came through Bill's office. The message was relayed to me."

"Noranda or Portello or whatever the hell his name is."

"We don't know, Lou."

"It seems to me there's a lot of heavy stuff going down with these people, considering it's only bucks we're talking about."

"What do you mean?"

"All these killings, Megan, just over money?"

"Everybody kills for money, Lou," she said. "We're talking about millions of dollars here."

"It still feels fishy to me," I said. "I can't put my finger on it, but there's a connection I'm not making."

"Don't worry your pretty head about it," she said. "Take me back to bed."

The last few days of the meet I didn't hear from her at all, but she showed up on getaway day for the running of the Futurity. I had gone down to the paddock to look at the two-year-olds in the walking ring. Superpatriot seemed fairly calm. He was fidgeting about in his stall, but allowing himself to be saddled; unless he blew his top again, I figured he was a cinch to bring home the money. Then, just as Lopez led him out into the ring, Wayne Copeland and his party, about twenty strong, showed up. Megan was walking right next to him and he had his hand on her arm just above the elbow as they crossed the dirt onto the lawn. A smattering of applause and cries of "Go get 'em, Wayne!" came from the onlookers. Copeland let go of Megan and turned to grin and wave to his supporters.

Instead of remaining by the rail, I walked into the paddock and took up a position a few feet away from Copeland's party so Megan would be sure to see me. She did, but managed to ignore me until the horses and riders headed toward the track. She lingered behind her group just long enough for me to come up beside her. "Like anything in this race?" I asked.

"Superpatriot's going to win," she said.

"Big deal. He's four to five here. Got any other hot tips?"

"When are you going back to L.A.?"

"Not till Friday morning. How about dinner that night?"

"I don't know. I'll call you at home." She started to follow her party toward the Turf Club and I strolled along beside her, keeping it distant and casual.

"How come you're so chummy with Wayne these days?" I asked. "The bureau changed its mind?"

"He asked for me," she said. "He wants me close to him. How could we refuse?"

"Watch yourself, Megan."

"Don't worry about me, lover. Put some money on Wayne's horse."

"I wouldn't bet Secretariat at four to five. I love you."

She glanced at me in alarm as we separated, then hurried after her party. As they neared the Turf Club elevators, I saw Wayne Copeland look around for her, then take her arm again. Had she told him she was blind and couldn't see where she was going? I doubted it.

Superpatriot seemed a bit nervous on the track and had some kidney sweat, but he was so much the class of the eight-horse field that it didn't matter. He broke first out of the gate, dropped back to midpack before the turn, then came on the outside with a huge rush that brought him home four lengths ahead of his closest pursuer in near record time for the seven furlongs. "The gorilla's back," Jay said afterward. "All they have to do now is keep him sound for the Breeders' Cup."

Junior must have stopped missing Babs Harper, but then horses have short memories. It's one of their many saving graces.

Jay and I were in no rush to get back to L.A. We had until Saturday to clear out of the condo, so we packed up our stuff on Thursday morning and spent the rest of the day on the sands. September and October are the best months in Del Mar. The horses and their retinues have departed, the kids are back in school, and the tourists have gone home. Walk a hundred yards north or south of the main lifeguard station at the public beach and you can enjoy a private communion with sun and surf.

That Thursday, Jay and I took our towels, folding chairs, and a cooler full of beer south toward the bluffs of Torrey Pines and settled comfortably just out of reach of the waves, then retreating toward low tide. The sky overhead was a flawless blue and the sand warm underneath us. We spread our towels, set up our chairs, and ran into the water. Twenty minutes later, sitting with newly opened bottles of Bohemia in our hands and facing the ocean, we let the sun dry us off as we looked back over our curious summer. "I can't remember one exactly like it," Jay said, rubbing sunblock into his face. "Usually, at Del Mar, we start off slow and then gradually build to a winning season. This year was a roller coaster, feast or famine, very inconsistent. How'd you come out?"

"Your Pick Six saved me, Jay," I said. "It paid for my medical costs, most of them. Otherwise I'd have taken a beating. Time to go back to work."

"It saved my ass, too," Jay admitted. "I made just enough to break even on my expenses. I've had better years than this one."

"And getting shot, that was a first," I said. "And a last, I hope."

"What about this lady?" Jay asked. "What's the story there?"

"What about her?"

"I mean, you really care about her or what?"

"I don't know. I certainly enjoy our time together. The sex is great. Apart from that, I'm not sure. Sometimes I think I love her."

"I think she's trouble."

"How would you know?"

"She's not worth getting shot for, Shifty, that's what I mean."

I didn't answer him right away. For one thing, I had to admit that deep down in my soul I thought he might be right. It seemed to me, as I looked back over the past few years, that I had been singularly unlucky in my choice of partners. I always picked women who were either married or involved with somebody else or were in some sort of desperate trouble. On several occasions I'd fallen for ladies as lethal as coral snakes. And the good women in my life, the ones who might have made me happy, usually dropped me. Who could blame them? I wasn't exactly a great catch. Close-up magicians and horseplayers don't make it to within sniffing distance of the allure engendered by money and status. I was a fringe performer, dancing on a tightrope for the delectation of the happy few, while all around me people were hammering out huge careers for themselves. I had to think there was something wrong with me, some vital ingredient missing from my character that kept me from achieving fame and fortune, the happiness we Americans pursue so relentlessly and is right there for us to seize—just around the next corner, over the neighboring hill, beyond that last line of trees, across that open stretch of prairie. If I could just get there, make that one big score, what woman could fail to appreciate all my fine qualities? Take Megan Starbuck, for instance. What could I offer her but my wiry body, a few good moves, a handful of winning horses, and some laughs? How did that compare to the excitement of being an undercover agent packing enough weaponry to blow away a whole host of evildoers? To her I must seem an amusing toy, someone to dally the summer away with between bouts of serious drama. I shut my eyes, sank back in my chair, and tried not to think about her.

Jay wouldn't let me off the hook. "So what are you going to do now, Shifty?" he asked. "She doesn't even live in this part of the country, right? Forget about her."

"You sound like Arnie. The mere sight of a woman terrifies him."

"He's been there, Shifty. He's been married, he has a daughter. His whole family hates him."

"He doesn't like them, either. He can't bet on them. I'm not Arnie, Jay, and neither are you. Though it occurs to me you're becoming a little like him." I sat up a bit straighter, cocked my tennis hat back off my forehead, and looked at him. "What about you, Jay? You didn't have a date all summer. You giving up women, too?"

"Let's say I'm on hiatus," he answered. "The last lady I took out gave me a long lecture on how I've been wasting my time at the track. This was after a day when I'd picked nothing but winners for her. She said she had a friend who owned a shoe store. She said she could get me a job there, selling shoes, men's shoes."

I laughed. "She was serious?"

"Oh, yeah. She said it was a start. I was a smart guy, I could work up to become assistant manager there in a year or two, maybe have a store of my own someday. She'd help me. She worked in retail, in Nordstrom's on Pico, so she'd come in with me eventually. Maybe we could have a chain of shoe stores one day."

"That's exciting."

"That's not what I told her. I told her I'd rather be buried alive than work in a shoe store. I told her I could make more money in one day at the track than she could make in a year in retail. I told her that I didn't believe in life after death, either, and that even if I lost at the track, I was having a better time than she was selling underwear at Nordstrom's. And then I put on my clothes and went home and I haven't seen her since."

"Jay, we're not considered good risks in the mating game."

"You know, Shifty, I look around from time to time and what do I see? I see a whole lot of people leading absolutely terrible lives, slaving at jobs they detest. I could have done that. I graduated from UCLA with a degree in economics and I could play tennis well enough to become a teaching pro and spend my time coaching kids or giving lessons to rich assholes. Luckily, I found the track instead. It's not easy, but I work hard at it. I've learned how to manage my money and survive doing what I love to do. I don't owe anybody any money and I'm having a hell of a lot of fun. So what's the beef? Who says I have to become a model citizen and feed society my soul? I wouldn't trade my life for anyone else's, would you?"

"I have my moments of doubt, Jay," I admitted, "but no, you're right, I wouldn't."

"So now you're involved with some woman who has some kind of nutty secret agenda. What is she, a cop?"

"Sort of," I said. "Don't ask me more, because I can't tell you."

"She hangs around with jerks like Wayne Copeland and all those right-wing pricks in America One, she doesn't even live in this part of the country, she almost gets you killed, and you're serious about her? What's next on the program, Shifty, impalement?"

"I can't help the way I feel about her," I said. "I really like her, Jay."

"Try to overcome it."

"Easier said than done."

"Your problem is you fall in love with every woman you get the hots for," he said. "Shifty, every day I see at least ten women I'd like to spend an hour with in a motel. I get a diamond-cutter of a hard-on, but it doesn't mean I want a life with them. Grow up, man. Sex is sex. You don't have to make a commitment to every lady who strikes your fancy. By the way, she cropped up on our TV set last night."

"Really? Where was she?"

"I meant to tell you. You were asleep already and I forgot about it till now."

"So?"

"So I was watching the late news and they had a rerun of the Futurity, then a little interview up in the Directors' Room at the track. Wayne was even more serious than usual. Made his little speech about the colt being America's horse and all that. Dedicated the race to his wife. Very touching."

"And Megan was there."

"Right. She was standing behind him, a little off to the side. When Wayne finished his interview, he turned away and the camera stayed on him for a couple of seconds. She took his hand."

"So what? The guy's just lost his wife. She works for him. She's offering him a little comfort. There's nothing wrong with that."

"No, I guess not," Jay said. "Just thought I'd mention it."

I rolled off my chair onto the warm sand and stretched out on my back, with my tennis hat over my face. I remembered Wayne's proprietary hand above Megan's elbow Wednesday afternoon, before the race. And now they were holding hands. Ridiculous, I told myself. Megan wasn't going to become involved with Wayne Copeland. She thought he was a bubblehead, basically. I closed my eyes and fell asleep.

Usually, the end of the Del Mar meet leaves me feeling wistful and a bit melancholy. I hate to see the horse people disperse and depart for L.A., where they'll become merely a small detail in a much larger panorama. I'm saddened by the rows of vacant barns, the shuttered cafeteria, the small clouds of dust blowing along between the shed rows, the lingering aroma in the air of the horses themselves, the yawning emptiness of the grandstand, the silence. Nor is there much immediately to look forward to. The cheaper animals have moved on to race at Fairplex Park, on the grounds of the L.A. County Fair in Pomona, where for the next three weeks they'll compete around the tight turns of what the horsemen call the bullring, any track less than a mile in circumference. I'm usually ready for a breather by this time of year, so I rarely get to Pomona, but still the end of Del Mar is always the end of an adventure. Less so this time, I had to admit to myself as I drove north up the freeway the next morning. I needed to get back to my other life, the world of magic and entertainment that had nourished me since my childhood. And I wanted to see Megan.

I had been in the house only about half an hour and hadn't even begun to unpack when my phone rang. It was Happy Hal Mancuso, my intrepid agent. As usual, he wasted no time on the minor niceties. "So you're busted and want to get back to work," was his opening line. "It's about time you got back."

"Hello, Hal, how are you?" I said. "I'm fine, thank you very much for asking. It was a very nice summer except for getting shot."

"What? You were shot? What did you do, forget to pay your bookie?"

"I bet on the wrong horse and tried to kill myself."

"Cut the crap. What happened?"

"Some guy tried to hold me up in a parking lot. When the girl I was with ran away from him, I shouted at him and he shot me."

"Jesus, in Del Mar? I thought that was a safe neighborhood. Are you okay? Where did he shoot you?"

"I told you, in the parking lot."

"Goddamn it, Shifty—"

"In the side, Hal. The bullet lodged in the muscle. I'm okay. I was in the hospital a couple of days and I've got another scar, but I'm all right."

"If you'd give up the goddamn horses, you wouldn't get shot."

"Maybe I ought to give up women."

"That's harder to do," he said. "Shifty, can you work?"

"Sure. I'm ready."

"Yeah, well, I turned down two nightclub gigs for you while you were gone, you bum."

"I know it's hard on you, Hal. What's up?"

"Okay, I got a call from some production company I never heard of called Old Glory. They want to film you in a two-minute or three-minute commercial, maybe two of them."

"Who are they?"

"I told you, I don't know. I checked them out with the Guild, but nobody's heard of them. They're brand new, just opened an office out here in Century City. The guy I talked to there, somebody named Jonathan Small, says they're set up to film commercials for TV and promotional short films. You know this guy?"

"Never heard of him."

"Me neither. Very tony East Coast accent. I told him we couldn't work for him unless his company signed a Guild contract. He assured me that was all being taken care of. They want you for two days. I asked for ten thousand, knowing I wouldn't get it. I lied. I told him you were the greatest close-up artist in the world, but he wouldn't buy it. I got you twenty-five hundred a day. That okay?"

"It's great. What do I have to do?"

"I don't think they have a script yet, just a scenario. They want to see you tomorrow morning at eleven o'clock." He gave me Old Glory's address and phone number. "They seem to know all about you."

"Really? I wonder how. Maybe Vince told them."

"They could have hired him. No, this guy asked specifically for you. I didn't try to pry too much. I bluffed. I acted like you were famous and of course they'd know about you. What kind of dumb schmuck do you think I am?"

"Not dumb at all, Hal. I guess I'll find out more tomorrow."

"One thing the guy did say is something about your doing a trick that makes money disappear. You can do that, right?"

"Sure. There are several moves I can do—"

"Yeah. What I should have told him is to just film you at the track, you miserable degenerate." And he hung up on me.

18
Risks

◆

The offices of Old Glory were located in one of the twin steel-and-glass towers between Pico and Olympic that dominate the skyline in West L.A. I parked in the underground garage below the structures, took an elevator up to the seventeenth floor, and found the production company about halfway down a long corridor between the offices of two legal firms. A plump young woman looked up from behind the reception desk as I entered and smiled at me. There were no pictures on the walls and the only decorative touch was a small tree standing alone in a corner to my left. "You must be Mr. Anderson," she said. "Mr. Small is expecting you." She stood up to escort me inside.

"I gather you've just moved in," I said.

"Oh, yes, only last Monday. Most of the furniture, including my desk, arrived yesterday. This way, please."

I followed her down a short hallway between rows of empty offices to a large one at the end, where Mr. Jonathan Small was waiting for me. He was a trim-looking citizen of about thirty-five with a cherubic Anglo-Saxon face under an already-receding hairline. He had a prim little mouth and his cheeks dimpled when he smiled. He was dressed in black loafers, dark gray slacks, a striped button-down shirt, blue-and-gray-striped necktie, and a gray herringbone sports jacket. He looked as if he had just stepped out of a Brooks Brothers ad. "Mr. Anderson, how superb of you to come," he said, standing up to shake my hand. "I've heard so much about you." He had a light baritone voice blocked by a potato embedded in his sinuses.

"Really? From whom?" I asked.

"Your agent, for one," he said, "but also from Mr. Clovis. Please sit down."

I lowered myself into one of the two padded leather chairs facing his desk. From where we sat we had an uninterrupted view south over the smoggy landscape of the city toward a ridge of low-lying hills bristling with the derricks and pumps of a working oil field. "Interesting view," I said.

"Yes, a little bit of America at work," he said. "I find it comforting."

"In what way?"

"I love to be reminded that we still have our own sources of energy, don't you?" he answered. "That's one of the things that's made this country superb, don't you think?"

"Oh, sure, I understand. You're connected with America One, I gather."

"Yes, I thought you knew that."

"Not till you mentioned Mr. Clovis."

"He was going to call you himself to let you know we'd be getting in touch with you, but then he thought it would be more professional to have us do it. He was very impressed with your magic."

"I didn't do much for him, but it's what I do best."

I should have known from the moment I walked into Small's office. The walls in here had been fully decorated, mainly with patriotic photographs, including a huge blowup of the famous one of our Marines raising the flag on Iwo Jima. There were portraits of Lincoln and Eisenhower and Douglas MacArthur and Ronald Reagan. There were group shots of Small himself at various America One functions, and directly behind him, over his desk, a large, brooding head shot of Wayne Copeland under his black Stetson. It was a publicity shot from one of Wayne's early epics, filmed in Spain, in which he single-handedly demolishes an entire army of evildoers. "I remember that movie," I said, indicating the photograph. "*The Hanging Tree,* right?"

"Right," Jonathan Small said with a laugh. "Everyone remembers that movie. It's the one that made Wayne a star, I was told. I grew up watching his old flicks on television, much to the despair of my parents. Wayne has always been my sort of hero, and now here I am working for him."

"Exclusively for him, or are you under contract?"

"We're privately financed," Small explained, "but we're pretty much set up to work for Wayne and America One." He smiled again, showing me the dimples at their most beguiling. "As you can see, we're just starting up here. Right now it's me and Becky, our receptionist, but we'll be adding more staff very soon."

"As the campaign heats up."

"Yes, I suppose so," he agreed, suddenly a bit ill at ease. "Of course, Wayne hasn't said he's a candidate, you know. It's much too soon."

"That last statement of his left little doubt," I said. "I also see where the *L.A. Times* has come out with a big spread on him and America One. I have it at home, but I haven't read it yet."

"You won't get an unbiased account from that left-wing rag, but it's all just about to explode," Small said. "Still, there are rules and forms for the process."

"Sort of like a mating dance, don't you think?" I said. "You put yourself forward and preen and bob up and down and show your colors and wait to be tapped for the big job."

"I never thought of it that way, but I can see your point," Jonathan Small said. "Perhaps we should talk about your magic."

"That's what I'm here for."

"We want to shoot a three-minute spot, Mr. Anderson, in which you make money disappear."

"You don't have a script yet, do you?"

"No, sort of a scenario, if you like," Small said. "In fact, we've discussed several possibilities. In one of them, you appear onstage as a traditional magician, you know, all dressed up in tails and top hat and with a little table and so on, and you do a very old-fashioned routine in which you make money disappear. Another approach would be to focus on your hands alone, with voice-over narration accompanying it. We might shoot two versions."

"And you'd like me to show you a couple of appropriate moves."

"Exactly, Mr. Anderson. None of us knows anything about magic. We just know what we want to see on screen. We could trick it up with the camera, special effects and so on, but we'd rather our audience see the stunt performed in a very straightforward, recognizable way. We're not out to fool anybody. One of the secrets of America One's success and the reason people trust Wayne Copeland is that we don't try to fool people. We say, 'Look, here's what it's like and what's happening and what are you going to do about it?' Does that make sense to you, Mr. Anderson?"

"It does. Okay, let me describe some possible moves to you. I can't actually perform them for you on the spot, because I haven't anything with me except a deck of cards. But I can talk the effect to you and you can tell me if it's right or not."

"Superb. Go ahead."

I described a trick I'd seen performed years ago by a close-up artist named Johnny Paul, in which he produced a tiny dollar bill from a change purse in his pocket and converted it before the audience's eyes into a huge one. "I can work a variation on that one, if you like," I said. "I can go from large to small and I can change the denomination of the bill as well."

"That sounds perfect," Small said.

"With coins there are all kinds of moves," I continued. "I can work up several routines moving coins around, changing denominations, making them disappear, whatever you want. I'll need a couple of days to work these routines out. When do you want to see them?"

"As soon as possible. Early next week?"

"That would be fine. Shall I call you?"

"I'll have Becky contact you." He stood up and shook my hand. "I can't wait to see what you can do. Please leave your phone number with Becky on your way out, would you? This is very exciting. People can really respond to money, you know."

"I respond to money myself. Are you a dues-paying member of America One, Mr. Small?"

"Oh, yes," he said. "If we don't take this country back from the people who are ruining it, we're as doomed as the ancient Romans, don't you think?"

"I don't know."

"Do you know about America One?"

"I attended a meeting this summer."

"Then please join us. We need everyone to get into this fight."

"I guess I'm in it already," I said. "I'm working for you."

Jonathan Small laughed. "By golly, that's right, you are." He stood up and stuck out his hand. "See you next week. Once we actually see the routines, we can adapt a text to it. Is that all clear now?"

"Perfectly," I said, shaking his hand.

"And remember, America for Americans."

"Is that the slogan?"

"One of our central themes, Mr. Anderson," Jonathan Small said. "At America One we're not ashamed to be patriotic."

I spent the rest of that day poring through magic catalogs and visiting magic stores in the Valley and on Hollywood Boulevard. By late afternoon I had a pretty clear vision of the routines I'd perform for Old Glory, and I planned to spend the next couple of days working on them. I wouldn't be able to perfect them, but I thought I could come in with a polished enough presentation to please the patriots of America One. A few minutes after seven, while I was drying myself off after my shower and preparing to go out, my telephone rang. "Jonathan Small here," the voice in my ear announced. "Mr. Anderson?"

"Yes."

"I'm glad I caught you," Small said. "I hope this isn't too short notice."

"For what, Mr. Small?"

"Oh, call me Jonathan, won't you? Now that you're on board, so to speak."

"Okay, Jonathan, what's up?"

"Well, I was talking to Mark Clovis this morning, after you left," Small said. "I explained to him what you had in mind and he was extremely enthusiastic. He said that's exactly the sort of thing he wants. I told him you'd have something to show us by midweek, at the latest, but he was wondering if you could have something by tomorrow night."

"I don't know. That's pretty short notice, Jonathan."

"I know it is, but you see, Mark's hosting a big private party for some of our people tomorrow night and he wants you there to provide the entertainment."

"That's okay, but I get paid for this kind of thing."

"Oh, of course, whatever your usual fee . . . . Shall I call Mr. Mancuso?"

"He won't be in his office, but I can tell you what it will be—five hundred dollars."

"That's no problem," Small said. "Of course we'll pay you your fee. But the key element is being able to do those tricks you told me about."

"They'll be pretty rough, but I'll come up with something. What time and where?"

"The party's in Malibu, at Buck Tender's place. The actor."

"I know who he is. He's been in a lot of Wayne's movies."

"Yes, they're great friends. And Buck's with America One, too."

"What's the occasion?"

"It's the second anniversary of the founding of America One. It's a celebration. There will be no press there, it's a private affair. Mark's in town and he wanted to do this. It should be fun."

"I'm sure it will be."

Small gave me the address. "It's a mile or so beyond Zuma Beach. You'll pass a fire hydrant on the right and then there's a driveway, also on the right, leading to a big white iron gate. Just give your name after you push the bell and you'll be admitted."

"How big is the party?"

"I'm not sure, actually. It was arranged rather hurriedly. Fifty or sixty people, I should think. Can we count on you?"

"I'll do the best I can. I might not have all the right props, but I can give you a pretty good idea of what the final thing will look like."

"Superb. See you there. Eight o'clock."

With only twenty-four hours left before Clovis's party, I should have gone right to work and I intended to. I had yet to hear from Megan. I was planning to go out, grab a bite at Dudley's, and come back within the hour. I could begin putting the moves together and plot a little patter to accompany them, then get up early the next morning to spend the rest of the day on them. If I flopped at Clovis's party, Old Glory would almost certainly not proceed with me, and I needed the money. I hadn't even finished dressing, however, when my phone rang again. This time it was Megan. "Lou, I need to talk to you," she said. "Are you free?"

"I've been waiting for you to call me," I said. "How are you?"

"I'm okay, but I have to see you."

"Well, I'm here. Have you had dinner?"

"No."

"Want to meet at Dudley's?"

"I'd rather meet somewhere where nobody knows us."

I suggested a small Japanese restaurant on Sawtelle in West L.A. It was dimly lit and patronized mainly by local Nisei and young people. "Best of all, the food is good and inexpensive," I added. "Megan, what's wrong?"

"It's nothing serious, Lou. I'll tell you when I see you."

I thought it was serious enough when she told me, half an hour later in the privacy of our booth toward the rear of the room. "We're going to have to stop seeing each other for a while," she said.

"How long?"

"I don't know, Lou. Maybe weeks, maybe a few months."

"Why?"

"I can't tell you. This is difficult for me, Lou. There are just so many things you don't know and that I can't talk about."

"Why not? I'm some sort of security risk? You think I'm a menace to the success of your mission?"

She smiled wanly. "You make it sound silly," she said.

"It is silly. Look, Megan, I know what you do. I know how hard it is to mix business, especially police business, with pleasure, but aren't you overdoing it a bit? I mean, in what way does seeing me occasionally pose a threat to your investigation?"

"If you knew what was involved here, you'd understand," she said. "I can't talk about it to you. You're going to have to accept it on faith."

"Faith?"

"In me, Lou. Please believe me, I'm as unhappy about this as you are."

I had to admit that she looked it. Her face was pale and her eyes seemed haunted. I thought she might cry if I spoke the wrong words to her. And because I had never seen her in such a state before and it was uncharacteristic of her, it alarmed me. I leaned over the table and took her hand. She allowed me to, but failed to respond; her fingers lay limply against my palm. "What's going on, Megan? Don't you trust me at all?"

She withdrew her hand from mine and leaned back in her chair. I had the feeling that we were separated by some sort of invisible barrier, as if she were a picture on a screen and someone had turned the sound off. The waitress came to take our orders, but neither of us was ready. I told her to give us a few more minutes. "Look, Megan, you don't have to tell me anything," I said, "and I'm not going to ask you anything more about what you're doing, okay? Just tell me this, are you going to spend some time with me later tonight or not?"

"I don't think we should."

"Okay, then are you going to stay in touch with me, at least? I mean, the occasional phone call?"

"Yes, I'll do that, Lou."

"Want to eat something?"

She shook her head. "Let's order some saki," I suggested. "It'll make you feel better. Then we can eat something." She nodded and I signaled for the waitress to come back.

Eventually, Megan did eat some dinner. She picked listlessly at her chicken teriyaki and listened while I did most of the talking. I didn't discuss anything having to do with her investigation or America One in general. I also didn't tell her about my interview at Old Glory or the invitation to Mark Clovis's party. I had a feeling that if I had, she would have objected, perhaps even made a move to prevent me from taking the gig. I knew that she'd find out about it and I also felt certain that I'd see her the next night at Buck Tender's place. After that, if she still wanted to derail me, she'd be free to try her best. I was not going to give up the job for her. Not only because I needed the money after a lean Del Mar season, but also because I wanted to find out what exactly was going on. Megan may have thought she could go on dictating the terms of our involvement, but I have an ornery streak in me, along with this unfortunate curiosity about life that so frequently plunges me into scalding water. I had my own suspicions about what might be going on here and I thought, by this time in our relationship, I had a right to find out.

So I talked to Megan all through dinner about the Del Mar season and horse racing in general and told her anecdotes about Arnie and Angles and Jay and the other characters who I hang out with at the track. Once or twice I even made her laugh, but most of the time she listened in silence, wrapped inside her sadness like a larva in its cocoon. When it came time to leave, she insisted on splitting the check with me. I didn't argue. We walked out into the night together. "I'm parked up toward the end of the block," she said. "Where are you?"

"Right here." We were standing by my car. "I lucked out. Somebody pulled out as I arrived. I'll walk you to yours."

"No, it's okay, Lou. I'm not exactly helpless."

"Which reminds me," I said. "Have we heard anything about our assailant?"

"No. I don't think we have to worry about him anymore."

"They found him?"

"No, but don't worry about it."

"Be careful."

"Of course I will."

She allowed me to kiss her, but her mouth was lifeless and she broke quickly away from me. I watched her walk away, her long legs moving in that purposeful, athletic stride I'd admired from the beginning. Then I climbed into my Toyota and drove home. It was lucky I had something to look forward to, I thought. I had work to do and soon, to my relief, I'd be able to lose myself in magic.

19
Partying

♣

Buck Tender's house was an insult to nature. My first impression, as I rounded the curve of the mountain road leading up to it, was that something from Las Vegas had been picked up intact and dropped into place by a fleet of giant helicopters. The house sat on the crest of a hill looking down over the Pacific Ocean as if it owned it. Its architectural style seemed to have been borrowed from several Italian models that did not blend into any sort of harmonious whole. It was the kind of retreat Liberace might have built for himself, and it should have been covered in rhinestones.

I arrived about half an hour late. As I pulled to a stop in front of the main entrance, I noted a fleet of cars parked along the road curving toward the rear of the house. A uniformed parking attendant whisked my Toyota away, leaving me to confront a massive front door that looked as if it might have been peeled off the face of a Spanish castle. I wouldn't have been surprised by a portcullis. Holding my small bag of magic paraphernalia, I rang the front doorbell and waited.

A minute or so later, a tiny Latino maid, dressed in a black-and-white uniform, ushered me into a front reception hall that reminded me of the apse of an Italian cathedral. Military banners and pennants fluttered from sconces embedded into the whitewashed stone walls, and an enormous Confederate flag hung like a tapestry facing me. On a balcony over my head a small orchestra was playing American folk tunes. "*Señor,* this way, please," the maid said, smiling timidly and pointing toward the corridor on my right, which led to a living room where I could see a main body of invited guests. Before I could move, however, Jonathan Small popped into view from the hallway to my left. He was holding a drink and sweating slightly, probably because it was a warm day and he was wearing one of his Brooks Brothers outfits, complete with an old-school striped necktie in red and gray. "There you are," he said. "Superb! Did you have trouble finding it?"

"No. I didn't want to come too early," I said.

"Excellent, excellent!" he said, bouncing lightly on his feet. "We can't wait to see what you can do."

"I haven't had much time, but I hope I won't disappoint you."

"I'm sure we'll take that into consideration, Anderson," he said. "Would you like a drink?"

"Never before I work," I said, "but I'd like to find a place for my bag."

"Of course. This way." He led me down the corridor to my left, past a bar where a young man in a white jacket was serving drinks to a cluster of middle-aged couples, then a formal dining room that could seat at least forty and where a lavish buffet was in the process of being laid out by two other servants, a game room with a pool table and several old-fashioned jukeboxes, a library of floor-to-ceiling books where more people were gathered around an hors d'oeuvres table, and finally through a doorway at the very end that led to a wing containing several bedrooms.

"You can use any one of these," Jonathan Small said. "Will you need to change?"

"No, I don't wear a costume in my act," I said. "I usually wear just what I have on—plain black pants, a white shirt, and a black vest. I take off my jacket and I roll my sleeves up above my wrists so people don't think I'm hiding anything. If you want to film me in a costume, that's up to you. Tonight I'm merely going to show you the basic moves. Isn't that what you wanted?"

"Oh, yes. Superb!" Small said, bouncing again.

"Whose bedrooms are these?" I asked as we entered the nearest one. It was fully furnished and the single bed was made up, but it had an air of being unlived in.

"No one's," Small said. "Nobody lives here but Buck."

"You're kidding? What does he need all these rooms for?"

"Guests, mainly. His children and grandchildren by three ex-wives," Jonathan Small explained. "Most of the time the house is empty. Buck has a condominium in town."

"And he built this extravaganza for himself? He must be working out some elaborate private fantasy."

"No, he bought it from a dentist who speculated in Malibu real estate in the eighties and made a fortune," Small said. "Then the dentist overreached himself and went broke when the recession hit a couple of years ago. I understand Buck picked this place up for a song. It's worth at least fifteen million and my understanding is he paid six point seven."

"That's a song, all right," I said, "but not one I can sing. It must be expensive as hell to keep up. And all the servants."

"Oh, Buck has money, you know. He made lots of it in the movies and he also inherited quite a bit. His family was in oil back in Texas. He's tons of fun. Have you met him yet?"

"No." I dropped my bag on the bed. "What time do I do my stuff?"

"After the buffet, I expect. Come on, let me introduce you around."

Small accompanied me back into the main body of the party, which was centered between the living room and an enormous patio area, partly supported by steel girders, that thrust out over the mountainside toward the ocean several miles below. The view was magnificent, but none of the guests seemed to be paying much attention to it. Mostly middle-aged and more formally dressed than usual for Southern California, with at least half of the men wearing suits and neckties, they were gathered in small groups and talking seriously to one another. A notable exception was our host, who was holding court for several male guests in a corner of the patio terrace and was laughing uproariously at something he himself had apparently just said. He was wearing a purple shirt, a gigantic black bow tie, and a knee-length flaming red plantation jacket. Buck Tender, with his red face, gap-toothed smile, and long gray hair, seemed to be playing in real life the sort of roles he portrayed on screen—scruffy confidence men, gamblers, drunks, shiftless cowboys, crooked dealers of one sort or another. I must have seen him in dozens of those parts; he'd been a fixture on Hollywood screens for forty years, and his best roles had been in Westerns with Wayne Copeland. "Great, great to see you," he said when Small introduced me to him. "Get yourself a drink and join the party. Or you can hang around here and listen to me tell racist jokes, how does that strike you?" And he cocked his head back to let loose another whinnying guffaw.

"Buck, tell the one about the niggers tied hand and foot and set floating out to sea on a raft," one of his listeners suggested.

"Aw hell, that's an old one," Buck Tender said. "You probably all heard it. Here's one you haven't. You all know about the difference between Hillary Rodass Clinton and a razorback sow?"

I decided I didn't need to know and left the group. "He's a card, isn't he?" Jonathan Small said, coming up beside me.

"He's a class act and a million laughs," I said. "Listen, Jonathan, you don't have to worry about me. I'll get myself a soft drink and sort of hang out. Just let me know when it's time to do my stuff."

"Sure thing. You know where the bar is?"

"Yes. By the way, is Wayne here yet? I haven't seen him."

"Not yet, but he'll be along, don't worry. Have you met?"

"Yes. I was at a party he gave this past summer at his place in Rancho Santa Fe."

"Superb!" Jonathan Small said, bouncing as he cased the premises. "I'll just go see some people. Enjoy yourself, Anderson."

"I always try to do that," I assured him, but he'd already flitted away from me toward more important guests.

I wandered about the premises for the next half hour or so, during which I mingled with what I assumed was the cream of America One.

Ed Drumheller was out on the patio with some people I'd never seen before. Janet and Tom Greenwood were in the living room. I also spotted Bill McDame, off in a corner in earnest conversation with two of the younger couples in the crowd. Then, on my way back to the bar for a second ginger ale, I came face to face with Blythe and Mark Clovis. "Hello there, Anderson," he said. "Jonathan tells me you've got a presentation all worked out for us. Blythe, you remember Anderson. He's the magician I told you about."

"Oh, yes," she said, gazing at me as if through a lorgnette. "You're the young man who gave me those silly violets."

"I'm sorry you didn't like them," I said. "I'll try diamonds next time."

"I think you're quite an impertinent young man," she said. "I can't imagine what Mark sees in you." She sniffed and departed, drink in hand, toward the library.

Mark Clovis made no move to follow her. "Don't mind Blythe," he said. "She enjoys being rude to people." He flashed me a quick smile, like someone turning a light on and off in an empty room.

"I guess she doesn't respond much either to magic or idle patter," I said. "I didn't mean to offend her."

"Forget it," he said. "The only person my wife approves of is me." Another wintry flash, while his intensely serious, cold gray eyes remained focused on me. "I know we haven't given you much time, Anderson, but I have confidence in you."

"The moves are rough, but once I see a script I can adapt them. By the way, that was an interesting article on America One in the *Times* last week. What did you think of it?"

"Just the sort of liberal rantings I expect from that organization," he answered. "I was pretty angry with our friend McDame, but I realized there isn't much even a skillful spin doctor can do to fend off the jackals of the liberal establishment press. We're going to have to cope with much worse in the months ahead."

"You mean as we get closer to the election."

"Precisely." He looked at me a little more intently, as if he suddenly felt that he hadn't quite sized me up correctly. "What did you think of the piece?"

"I'm not sure what to think," I said. "I found it interesting because I didn't know anything about the background of America One. As for the allegations of possible wrongdoings and ulterior motives, I have no opinion. I just don't know."

"It's an attempt to smear us," Clovis said. "There will be many others. But we're in this for the long haul, Anderson. When I embark on a project, I stay the course. And in this case we have no choice. If the country is going to be saved, then we're going to have to do it and do it right now. We can't take another four years of this socialist tax-and-spend government and that gaggle of criminals who run it."

"Too bad Reagan couldn't run again."

"No, not at all," Clovis said. "He was much too weak. He did a lot of good things for the country and he meant well. He also had some very fine people around him—Bill Casey, Ed Meese, Weinberger, a few others—but when the crunch came, he was too weak. He buckled under pressure just when he should have taken charge. He had his chances and he blew them."

"I've never heard Reagan described as weak before," I said, "even by the left-wing press. Superficial, dumb, but never weak."

"You weren't listening to the right people, Anderson." The flashing smile again. "You know what government is, don't you? It's the art of the impossible practiced by the incompetent for the benefit of the unworthy."

"So you're saying Wayne will be stronger."

"Oh, much. And he'll have a really strong team around him."

"If you want a strong man, what's wrong with Bob Dole?"

"Too old. Too entrenched in old-fashioned politics," Clovis said. "But more important, he can't get elected. Too many people don't like him."

"And everybody likes Wayne."

"You're beginning to get it, aren't you?"

"But what if Dole runs? He could get the nomination, don't you think?"

"I think we can stop him. We have two years to do it. And there's nobody else, really. But we'll run as an independent if we have to."

"Perot tried that."

"He's a ninny," Clovis said. "He had some great ideas, but he self-destructed. He can't keep his mouth shut when he has to, and he's an egomaniac with a strong paranoid streak. Basically, he's a boob. Smart in business, but a boob in politics. He'll be out of it by the time we're organized and rolling along. I fully expect we'll eventually get his support as well."

"Really?"

"And we'll have a role for him to play."

"Like what?"

"Spoiler. We can use him. I think that eventually we can offer him enough to get him to throw in with us during the primaries. If we can do that, and I have reason to think we can, we can get Wayne the nomination. The election itself will be a lot easier."

"In what way is Wayne qualified to be President?" I asked.

Clovis laughed. The sound of it was chilling, a shattering of glass on concrete. His eyes remained coldly fixed on me, no mirth in them at all. "What a question," he said. "Do you think Clinton was qualified? Or Bush or Carter or even Reagan? The truly qualified people don't get elected to anything, Anderson. Who do you imagine really runs this country? The people's elected representatives?"

I heard a stir behind me, mostly a shuffling of feet and a murmur of voices. I turned and saw Wayne Copeland standing in the entryway surrounded by a small party of friends and admirers. He was grinning, shaking hands, waving. Guests from the rest of the house flowed toward him. The band struck up "America the Beautiful." I realized suddenly that I was looking at a small preview of coming attractions. Charisma, that's one quality a man needed to become presidential. I could have shared that insight with Mark Clovis, but he had already moved past me to join the group around the actor. And then, as I stood there watching this scene, Megan Starbuck stepped out of the crowd. She was wearing high heels and an elegant glittery black cocktail dress that ended well above her knees. Her eyes widened when she saw me, but I don't think my wink reassured her. "Come on, everybody, let's join the party," I heard Wayne say as he swept Megan up in his wake and the group moved toward the main body of the gathering.

It was nearly ten o'clock by the time I tried out my act. I had a feeling I might be playing to a tough audience, because it was late and because people tend to lose interest after an excess of food and drink. Luckily, Buck Tender cooperated. He and Jonathan Small rounded up about half the guests and moved them into the living room. I had positioned myself in front of the fireplace, which was so large that it formed a small proscenium to frame me center stage. Wayne Copeland, with Megan by his side, stood at the rear of the room. Mark and Blythe Clovis sat on a sofa to my left, but I decided to ignore them and play to Wayne himself, as if he and I were alone. I still don't know why, but I had a feeling he'd respond favorably, as one performer to another. I'd seen him twirl his six-shooters and accomplish small miracles with them in movie after movie as the fastest draw in the West. Now I was going to show him what manual dexterity was really all about, even if I was a little nervous. Not about the moves themselves, but because I was going to be pandering to this rich, right-wing crowd. Like our friend Vinnie, I was just another hired gun.

"Folks, welcome to Buck Tender's modest little spread out here on the edge of the California desert," I said, projecting to the rear of the room in my finest cowboy-just-in-from-the-range accent. "Sure is good to see you folks here, rallying around old Wayne and gettin' ready to take our town back from the bad *hombres* and their cheatin' ways. Folks, I guess you know that before all the bad and lazy *hombres* came along, this was a pretty little town, peaceful and with real respect for law and order. It was prosperous, too. Let me show you what I mean." I reached into a side pocket of my vest and produced a tiny packet about the size of a large postage stamp. I began to unfold it as I continued my patter. "We started out makin' just a little bit of money from farming and cattle and mining, and pretty soon we had an economy that was just gigantic, so huge that we had to print up these great big bills so people would know that what we had here was worth having."

By this time I had unfolded the packet until I had in my hands a billion-dollar greenback fifteen inches wide by twenty-six inches long. I held it out with both hands so everybody could see it. The denomination of one billion dollars was clearly visible, under the title "The United States of Amurrica," presented in capital letters. The sight of it made a few people in the room laugh, including Wayne Copeland. "You see what I mean, folks," I said. "Money was big in those days. It counted for something. And when you made it, you got a chance to show it off. Then, if you was out on the range somewhere or up in the mountains and it got real cold, hell, you could sleep under it or wear it around your shoulders like a poncho."

This procured me a few more laughs as I began to fold up the bill again. "Then along come all these people wantin' a piece of the action," I continued. "They seen how good we had it here and they had to have some of it. A lot of these people didn't want to work for the money, neither. They figured we had enough of it so's we could support 'em and they wouldn't have to work at all. And there got to be so many of them that by and by there was more of them than there was of us. So any time we got to vote, they got people elected who said, 'Sure, that's right, we ain't got nothin', you got it all, so you got to support us and pay for everything.' The people who now ran the town out here said, 'That's right, you got the money, so you pay these people for doin' nothin'. It's only right, ain't it?' And by that time the money wasn't worth one billion dollars no more, it was worth this much."

By then I had the bill folded back to its original size in packet form. Now I quickly unfolded the packet and displayed a tiny dollar bill about one inch wide and three inches long. "See that?" I said. "That's what's left of our money, folks, after we get through payin' for everything and everyone."

The sight drew quite a lot of laughter and some applause. "But even this probably ain't going to be enough for these people and the government, so here's what's going to happen to our town if nobody does nothin' about it." I crumpled up the bill into a little ball, tossed it into the air, caught it, rubbed it briefly between the palms of my hands, then turned my palms out toward the audience. The little bill had vanished. "See, folks? There'll be nothin' left of it or of our town if things keep goin' on the way they are."

A couple of the women squealed and there was more laughter and applause. I smiled and nodded my appreciation. "What we need, folks," I said, "is a man in this town who can make the money grow again and, as it grows, move it around some, bring life back to our town, put some of these people to work, get their government off our backs, so we can show everybody what we can do."

As I continued my spiel, I was moving two quarters across the backs of my hands, flipping them up in the air, catching them and then holding them out for everyone to look at. "We begin with just a couple of quarters, see, but we put them right to work," I said. "And if you put money to work, folks, it multiplies and it grows." I tossed the two quarters into the air, caught them, clapped them between my hands, and produced four quarters, two in each palm. I put the quarters together, then held out my clenched fingers toward the audience. "Is four quarters enough, folks? No, of course not." I opened my hands to reveal that they were empty. "I put the money I earned to work and now let's see what happened to it." I made two fists again, opened them, and gazed at my hands in mock amazement. "Well, look what my hard-working four quarters turned into." I showed the audience two sparkling silver dollars. "Ain't that something, folks? Doubled my money again. Just goes to show you what the power of money can do if you put it to work instead of lettin' other people spend it for you."

Everyone clapped this time and I bowed. "Thank you very much, folks," I said. Then, as the applause died down, I looked at Copeland. "Wayne, the people in this town need you," I called out. "Take the money and run." And I flipped the silver dollars toward him. He caught them and grinned. "If you get into the White House, frame them!"

More laughter and applause. I thanked everybody and stepped away from the fireplace. Jonathan Small bounced up to me. "That was thrilling," he said. "Superb!"

"A little rough, I think," I said. "I'm glad you liked it."

"Superb! Please call me tomorrow, Anderson. I want you to take me through these tricks step by step so we can adapt a script to them. Can you come in on Tuesday morning?"

"Anytime."

"Superb! Oh, by the way . . ." He reached into his inside pocket, produced a sealed envelope, and handed it to me. "Your fee."

"Thanks," I said, stuffing it into my vest.

"The bar's still open," Small said. "Get yourself a drink."

"I'm going to head home. Glad you liked the moves."

"Oh, yes. Superb!"

Mark and Blythe Clovis caught up to me in the hall. "Thank you, Anderson," he said, fixing me with that wintry gaze of his. "That was better than I'd hoped for."

"I thought it was stupid myself," Blythe Clovis said, "but then I suppose children might find that sort of thing amusing."

"Be quiet, Blythe," Mark Clovis said. "You're being rude to a very fine artist." He shook my hand. "We must talk again sometime. I think you understand more about us than you admit."

"Us? You mean America One?"

"You're not good at playing the fool, Anderson," Clovis said. "Good night. I expect we'll talk again sometime."

"That was very impressive, Lou," Megan Starbuck said.

I was closing up my little bag of wonders at the time and hadn't seen her come into the bedroom, where I was getting ready to leave. I turned around. She was standing inside the doorway, her back to the wall so no one could see her from the corridor. She looked terrific in her black cocktail dress and high heels. I had to resist the impulse to take her in my arms.

"Why didn't you tell me you were coming to this party?" she asked.

"I didn't think I had to ask your permission, Megan," I said. "I wasn't even sure you'd be here."

"You had to figure I would be."

"My being here has nothing to do with you," I said. "This is a paying gig."

"Who contacted you?"

"Jonathan Small, at Old Glory. I assume you know about him."

"Yes, I do. Who put Small up to it?"

"Mark Clovis. He likes my work. They're looking for a magician to shoot a couple of commercials touting the virtues of Wayne Copeland and America One. Tonight was in the nature of an audition."

"You sure told them what they wanted to hear."

"That was the idea, Megan. You get what you pay for. You ought to know about that."

"What do you mean?"

"Skip it."

"Clovis, how does he know you?"

"From Wayne's party during the summer. I did a couple of moves for him. He asked for my card. I gave it to him and he must have told Small to call my agent."

"You shouldn't have accepted."

"Why not? I need the job and they're paying well."

"I told you, I can't see you, Lou," she said. "Not for a while."

"Maybe never, right? Anyway, Megan, this has nothing to do with you. How's the investigation going, now that you're inside the inner circle again? Have you found out who's been stealing the money?"

"I can't talk to you about this."

"No, I guess not. Being in tight with Wayne now, does that protect you?"

She started to answer, but then chose not to. "No comment."

"Anyway, you're not going to get me fired, are you? They don't even know we know each other, do they?"

"Lou, I wish you hadn't done this. You know what's at stake here."

"Well, actually, Megan, I'm not sure. But maybe you can answer one question for me."

She didn't speak, but gazed at me with those beautiful hazel eyes. I had to look away from her. I picked up my bag and my jacket, then turned to face her again. "I guess what I want to know is," I said, "when did you begin fucking Wayne Copeland?"

She gasped, as if I had jabbed her in the stomach. Her mouth opened and shut. "What?"

"I just wondered if it was before or after his wife's death," I said. "Also, whose idea was it, yours or the bureau's?"

She didn't answer. She turned and walked swiftly out of the room. I was left standing there, feeling as if I had somehow disgraced myself. In the wonderful give-and-take world of intelligence, I guess you're not supposed to ask the participants uncomfortable questions.

20
Epiphanies

♠

That Sunday night, after I got home from the party, I reread the long *L.A. Times* piece on America One that I'd clipped and left on my kitchen table. Then, the next morning, after breakfast and the rush hour, I drove to downtown L.A. and spent nearly three hours in the central library. I dredged up every bit of information I could find on America One and the organization's founders and prime movers. By noon I had a pretty good idea about what I was dealing with, but some key questions remained largely unanswered. I went to a public phone and left Megan a recorded message. "Megan, I'm sorry about last night," I said. "I didn't want to be brutal about it, but was I wrong? I'll be home all afternoon, working on my moves. I have an appointment at Old Glory tomorrow."

Megan called me back a little after three. Her voice was cold and businesslike. "Are you going to be there for a while?" she asked.

"Yes. You want to come over?"

"No. How about Dudley's, one of the side booths?"

"Good idea. It'll be empty till the cocktail hour."

"Four o'clock," she said and hung up.

I arrived a few minutes early to find her already there, sitting in the rear booth at the end of the bar. She looked very different from the night before. She was wearing no makeup and was dressed in a conservatively cut dark gray business suit. "Hi," I said, sliding into place opposite her. "What are you having?"

"Coffee."

I looked around. The restaurant was empty, except for a couple of Latino kids playing pool in the back room. I signaled for the waitress, who was talking to the bartender, and ordered a refill for Megan and one for myself. Neither of us said anything until the coffee arrived and the waitress had returned to her conversation at the bar. "All right, Lou," Megan said, "you want to tell me what this is all about?"

"That's what I was going to ask you," I said.

"Let me tell you what I've done," she said. "I discussed your case this morning with the agent in charge—"

"My case?"

"The situation. The bureau wants you uninvolved in any way."

"Did you tell your boss about us?"

"Yes, I had to. Not everything. Just that we knew each other and had gone out on a couple of dates. And about the shooting, of course."

"Oh. So?"

"So, as I said, the bureau has decided you can't be involved."

"What are they going to do, arrest me?"

"Don't be silly, Lou. I told my boss about your deal with Old Glory. We'll pay you whatever Old Glory was going to pay you, but you don't take the job. An agent named Todd Brown was going to contact you today. After you called me, it was decided I could do it instead. I wasn't too happy about seeing you again, after last night, but this seemed the easiest way. How much is Old Glory paying you?"

"Twenty-five hundred dollars a day. It's probably a two-day shoot, so let's say five grand."

"We'll pay you the fee. You turn down the deal."

"Why should I?"

"Because this is a serious investigation involving a national interest and you pose a threat to it," she said. "You're a wild card, Lou. These are dangerous people we're dealing with. Getting involved with you was my mistake. If I weren't so far inside the organization now, they'd pull me off this case. I compromised it by becoming involved with you."

"Aren't FBI agents supposed to have personal lives?"

"Not if it interferes with the job."

"It's like joining a cult."

She made a move to leave. "You'll have the money, in cash, within a week."

"You mean I don't have to declare it to the IRS? How thoughtful of the bureau."

She stood up. "Good-bye, Lou."

"Wait a minute, Megan," I said. "I haven't agreed to do this. Did you hear me agree to do this? Sit down, please."

She sat down again. "We can pay you up to ten thousand. That's it."

I smiled and shook my head. "Money isn't everything," I said. "What I need to know first is why."

"I can't go into that."

"Okay, here's my deal," I said. "I tell you what I think is going on and you either confirm it or deny it. I've done a little research and I've come to a few conclusions. Call them educated guesses, if you like. You don't have to answer any questions. Okay?"

"I don't think so—"

"Then it's no deal, Megan. I take the job, make the little shorts, do my little number, maybe even join America One, get real patriotic, work hard for the great cause. Do you think Wayne would create a government post for me? Say, Secretary of Pretense? Or Commissioner of Misdirection?"

She looked at me in silence for quite a long time, then leaned back in her seat, still staring at me. "I wish I'd never met you," she said.

"Really? Was I so terrible? What did I do that was so awful?" I asked her. "I made the mistake of falling in love with you, right?"

"Lou, this isn't helping. You want to say what you have to say?"

"Okay. Megan, I've done a lot of research. I spent all morning at the central library downtown, reading everything I could get my hands on. I know a lot about America One."

"Like what?"

"That it's not just a charitable organization and hasn't been from the beginning," I said. "It was established from the very first with a political goal in mind: to push the country to the right, either through normal political channels or outside of them. How am I doing?"

"Fine, but I've heard no revelations."

"What's interesting is that the original prime mover was Robert Goldman," I continued. "He wanted to found an organization that would be both political and charitable. The charitable part would serve to propagate the organization's political ends. You do good, you get media coverage, you push your agenda along. He needed a figurehead and he knew Wayne Copeland. Goldman had once owned horses and he'd met Wayne through his involvement with Thoroughbreds. He also knew that Wayne was politically conservative—in fact, way over on the right, where Goldman was. Wayne said yes to the proposition and they decided to use Wayne's potentially great colt, Superpatriot, as their gimmick. Every time the horse won, the purse money would go to provide scholarships for worthy poor students. This helped to combat the image of America One as just another right-wing pressure group. Wayne Copeland is everybody's idea of a great American hero, even though in real life, apart from his movies, he's never done anything of note except speak out from time to time on the conservative side of important issues, like crime or drugs or street gangs. He's a member of the National Rifle Association and he's taken stands in the past on such terrifically controversial issues as not coddling criminals. This is the sort of stuff the public wants to hear these days. Want another coffee?"

"No, thanks," Megan said. "What else?"

"So Goldman put America One together. He approached his rich friends and they approached their rich friends and in a matter of months America One was off the ground and getting just the sort of publicity they wanted. Superpatriot was winning and the worthy kids were getting their scholarships and Wayne Copeland became even more popular than before. Now, among the people Goldman brought in were some real heavyweights, men very high up in the world of international finance and corporate capital. You want me to name them for you?" I pulled a slip of paper out of my pocket and showed it to her. On it I had written down the twenty-seven names I had culled from the *L.A. Times* story and my research. Megan glanced at the list and nodded. "But the key player on that list is Mark Clovis, the chairman of Megatex," I continued, "which, according to *Fortune,* a magazine I never read, is an international colossus, with billions of dollars in assets all over the world—banks, oil companies, vast land holdings in the Third World, communications conglomerates, shipping, arms-manufacturing plants, you name it. Megatex and perhaps another dozen companies like it not only operate entirely free of national controls, but dictate to smaller countries how to run their affairs. The movement of capital around the globe is what now controls the destinies of civilizations, according to *Fortune,* and no one is a bigger player in this power game than Megatex. Furthermore, it's a family-owned company, responsible to no one and largely shielded from public scrutiny. Nobody knows for sure, in other words, just how big and wealthy Megatex is. Mark Clovis, the family head, calls the shots. He *is* Megatex. Have I got it right?"

Megan nodded. "Okay, so what?"

"So this. At some point, quite early in the game, Clovis and his allies—Drumheller, Greenwood, the Hepples in Texas, the Colby brothers, a handful of others—decided to use America One for a bigger power play. They decided to run Wayne Copeland for president. They figure they can capture the Republican nomination through the primaries. If not, they'll go ahead independently. They really think they can win."

"Do you think Copeland can win?"

"Absolutely. Perot got nineteen million votes despite quitting in the middle of his campaign, and he's still got millions of followers," I said. "And what if he throws in with America One and Copeland? Look at what's happening in the country. Clinton's managed to accomplish a few things, but he's compromised and nobody trusts him. The national debt still continues to grow, the crime rate is soaring, the drug traffic flourishes, the inner cities look like scenes out of *Blade Runner*—a great movie, by the way—our foreign policy is a joke, we're threatened on all sides. The public is scared, Megan. A lot of people want a quick fix. Wayne Copeland is a quick fix."

"What are you trying to tell me, Lou? I don't know this?"

"I want you to know I know it."

"Okay, so?"

"So maybe that's enough of a motive for Clovis and his people to want Bob Goldman and his allies out of the way," I said. "It does seem extreme, but then aren't billionaires used to having their own way? They think nothing of ruining the lives of tens of thousands of people every day. They exploit them, they fire them, they pollute their environment, they expose them to toxic elements. I mean, what's a couple of straightforward murders to people like that? A minor inconvenience, with no risk. I've thought a lot about this. Am I making sense?"

She nodded, but said nothing. She continued to look at me out of those beautiful hazel eyes. I resisted an insane impulse to kiss her, tried to fill my mind with a vision of her lying with her legs open under Wayne Copeland. It helped restore my balance.

"All right, so now why is the FBI involved?" I continued, looking away from her to avoid those eyes. "Because millions of dollars may have been diverted or stolen? Maybe that's why Goldman and the others were killed. Either they were doing the stealing or they found out who was and had to be silenced. Then who brought the FBI into the case? Goldman, before he was killed? Clovis? Someone else? That's the part that didn't make sense to me. There had to be another motive, right? What do you think, Megan?" I looked back at her; she hadn't moved.

"I don't know, Lou," she said. "It's your call."

"Right, I forgot," I said. "Okay, if it had to do only with money, then why not just find and arrest our friend Vincent Noranda Portello or whatever his name is. Make a deal with him, get him to spill the beans about who hired him and why. No, the FBI doesn't go after Vinnie yet. Why? Because the case isn't about money. Clovis, Drumheller, Greenwood, these other huge wheeler-dealers, what do they need to worry about a few million for? They're stealing the whole world, why call in a hit man for a missing few million? How am I doing, Megan?"

She stood up. "I'm going now, Lou. Good-bye."

"I'm not through. You agreed to hear me out."

"I've heard enough." She headed swiftly out of the restaurant.

I dropped a five-dollar bill on the table and hurried after her. She had parked halfway up the block by a meter. Her time had expired and there was a ticket tucked under her windshield wiper. "Too bad," I said as I rejoined her, "but maybe the bureau will pay it for you."

She removed the ticket, opened her purse, dropped the ticket inside, then groped about for her car keys.

"So I asked myself, why would this girl I'm crazy about and who obviously likes me compromise herself by going to bed with a principal in the investigation?" I said, talking fast. "She wouldn't do it if it were just a question of people stealing from each other. So what would make her do it? Something more important. Something very big. National security, you indicated. That's it, of course." I leaned down so I could look at her as she settled herself now behind the wheel of her car. "She sacrificed her body on the altar of patriotism," I said. "She kicked a relationship to pieces for love of country. That must be what the boys at the bureau told her. They suspect you, they said, but they won't touch you if you're Wayne's girlfriend. Come on to him, he's vulnerable and he plays around, anyway. His wife was a drunk. Which leads me to one more question, Megan. Why did somebody kill Cheryl Copeland? We know it wasn't really another senseless unconnected happening, one more manifestation of the public rot. So what was it really about?"

She was crying by this time and it shook me, because she wasn't the type to shed tears. She had the key in the ignition, but couldn't close the door because my body was in the way. She looked up at me. "Damn you, Lou," she said. "Please get out of my way."

"One more thing, Megan," I said. "I don't need the bureau's money."

I stepped aside and she slammed the car door shut. I stood there and watched her drive away. It was a warm late-summer evening, but a cold wind was blowing at my back.

♠ ♠ ♠

"What the hell do you mean, you're not going to take the job?" Happy Hal Mancuso barked in my ear. "You don't need the twenty-five hundred bucks a day? What's happening? Is there a big race you can't miss? A hot horse you have to bet on? Don't you know any bookies?"

"Hal, Hal," I said, "calm down, will you? It's nothing like that."

"Well, what the hell is it? Not enough money for you? Who do you think you are, David Copperfield? I got you top dollar and then some. I mean, who the hell has heard of you, Shifty? You know and I know you're a regular Houdini with the junk you use, but who the hell else knows? You know what I'm saying? Who can see a pack of cards or a fifty-cent piece from more than ten feet away? Elephants, tigers, lions, naked women—why don't you work with something people want to look at?"

"Hal, I'm really sorry about this," I said, "but I can't take this job. I can't tell you why, either. I have personal reasons."

"I don't know what's wrong with me," Hal said. "I have a foul-mouthed nightclub comedian who wants to become a rap star. I have a pop singer who wants to go to the Met. I have a scriptwriter who's working on his novel. I have a soap opera actor who wants to do theater. And, worst of all, I've got a magician who's a horseplayer. Where did I go wrong? What god did I insult who does this to me? I could have been a used-car salesman and had a happy life."

"Hal, call up Vince Michaels in Las Vegas. He's a better magician than I am." I gave him Vince's number. "So when you call Mr. Jonathan Smart to tell him I can't take the job, you'll have someone who can step in for me. These people don't know anything about magic or magicians, and you're a great salesman. Vince will do a terrific job. I'll call him myself in the morning and tell him what it's all about."

"Shifty, what's going on? You want to tell me about it?"

"No, Hal, I can't. You're going to have to believe me. I've never walked out on a job before and I hope I never have to again. I'm sorry, really."

"It's about the horses, isn't it? You're mixed up in some bullshit about horses, right?"

"No, you're wrong, Hal. It's personal. I can't talk about it."

He let out a long, soul-wrenching sigh. "My God," he said, "my father wanted me to be a schoolteacher like him. Not only was there no money in it, but I'd have had to deal with bunches of delinquents armed with Uzis. So I became an agent and now I have to cope daily with lunatics. There must be something else I could have done with my life. You want to work or not?"

"Of course. I'll tell Vince I can substitute for him in Vegas next week if he wants this gig."

"You do that, Shifty. Then go back to the horses. What is it you see in them, anyway?"

"They don't cheat, lie, steal, murder, or betray one another," I said. "They're a superior form of life."

"They could never get work in Hollywood, that's for sure," Hal said, and he hung up the phone.

After this call, I sat in my room for nearly an hour, nursing a glass of Chablis and staring at my walls. Houdini and Verdi stared back at me. The horses I had loved flashed across my consciousness, caught there in those great moments when they'd lifted me out of myself with their grace, courage, and power. I tried not to think about Megan Starbuck, but her face, pale and angry, with those wide hazel eyes staring at me in distress, persistently intruded. Had I been wrong? Had I misjudged the situation? Why hadn't she protested her innocence? Finally, when I couldn't cope with my growing depression, I refilled my wineglass and went out to the pool area.

No one was around. It was dark by this time, nearly nine o'clock, and I should have been hungry. I sat down in one of the folding chairs near the diving board and looked at the still water of the swimming pool, then up at the tops of the tall palms and heard the way the wind rustled through the fronds. A half-moon rose above the rooftops. I could hear the noises of traffic in the street, the murmur of distant voices, dishes rattling, a child crying, then, like a stream cascading down a slope, the sound of a string ensemble playing Mozart.

I stood up and walked to Max's half-open door and knocked. The old man answered. He was in his bathrobe, his beret still on his head.

Behind him the music flowed on like a small fountain. "Shifty," he said, "how are you?"

"Who's playing?" I asked. "It's beautiful."

"The Guarneri," Max said. "It's magnificent, yes?"

"Yes."

"You wish to come in?" he asked, peering closely at me in the reflected light. "You look terrible."

"I feel terrible," I said.

I went inside and sat on the edge of the sofa across from Max's stereo. The music filled the room. It made me want to rejoice, not weep or feel sorry for myself. I should have been a musician, I reflected. In what other art form could one lose oneself so entirely? I looked at Max. He was sitting in his favorite armchair beside me. His eyes were closed and he was lost in the music. At the end of the movement, he looked at me. "Max, were you ever in love?" I asked.

"Many times," he said.

"But you never got married."

"Only once, but she died forty years ago in a car accident."

"Do you still miss her?"

"I miss them all, but I have Mozart."

The music filled the room again. I relaxed, shut my eyes, and listened. For the next twenty minutes I managed to stop thinking about Megan Starbuck.

21
Superpatriot

♥

The only thing that horse can beat is the ambulance," Arnie Wolfenden said as the field emerged from under the stands for the fourth at Santa Anita.

"Come on, Arnie," Angles said. "I got this from a real good source."

"Who?"

"I can't tell you because I promised the guy I wouldn't," Angles explained. "You got to take it on faith."

"I gave up faith when I lost my first photo," Arnie said. "Reggie, don't listen to him."

"To try or not to try, that is the question," the actor said.

"Come on, Reggie, let's take a shot," Angles urged him as he stood up. "The horse is eight to one, for Christ's sake. All I can tell you is that my source is very close to the trainer."

"It is a wise trainer that knows his own horse," Reggie said. "If nothing comes amiss, so money comes withal." He rose to his feet and followed Angles away toward the betting windows.

"A tout, having nothing, nothing can he lose," Arnie observed.

Jay turned around in his seat to stare at him. "What the hell is that?" he asked.

"Shakespeare," Arnie answered. "I misspent my youth getting a formal education."

"I'm not sure I can cope with all this erudition," Jay said.

"Don't worry about it," Arnie said, rising to his feet. "It's a one-shot deal. I'm leaving the Bard to Reggie and Angles."

"Where are you going?"

"You said you liked the other horse."

"I do, but not at even money on the rail."

"I like him better than you do," Arnie said. "I'm betting him on top of two horses in exactas, that's all." He shuffled painfully out of the box.

"What's wrong with you, Arnie?" I asked.

"My feet hurt," he said. "I was playing pool at Dudley's till two A.M. It's been a slow meet. But nothing a couple of good winners won't cure."

I was happy to be back and to find that nothing had changed. Nothing much ever does in the world of racing. Somewhere the horses are running, the Dummy God is on his throne, and the great game goes on. I'd been away nearly a month and it was like coming home from a long exile.

"How was the cruise?" Jay asked.

"All three of them were swell," I answered, "but I've seen all I ever want to see of Alaska. I made decent money, especially in tips, and it was a good time to go."

"When did you get back?"

"Last night. I timed it so I'd be sure to make the Norfolk."

"You haven't been able to do much handicapping, obviously."

"No, but I haven't made a bet yet and I'm probably not going to," I said.

"I have a horse in the seventh you could take a small flyer on," Jay said. "He'll be no lower than four to one. Say, how come you're all dressed up?"

"I'm going to the Turf Club in a few minutes."

"To see your girl?"

"She's not my girl, Jay. No, just out of curiosity."

Traveling in a luxurious cruise ship up and down the northwest coast of America to Alaska and back tends to isolate you from the real world. No sooner had I come back from Las Vegas, where I'd filled in at the Four Kings for Vince Michaels while he was in L.A., than Hal had booked me out as part of the onboard entertainment during the fall cruises on the Rainbow Line. I had spent the past few weeks entertaining Rainbow's mostly middle-aged, wealthy white passengers with my repertory of legerdemain and I had enjoyed myself. After my breakup with Megan Starbuck, I had needed desperately to get back to work. It had been a blessing to have heard nothing except from Vince, who had called me in Vancouver to tell me that he'd successfully filled in for me at Old Glory. "The funny part is, Shifty, they only filmed my hands," he said. "I duplicated your moves with the paper money and the coins, but they had an actor do a voice-over. He was like a carnival barker. I gather it's some kind of commercial aimed at putting down the Democrats and promoting the Republicans at the midterm elections."

"That soon?"

"What do you mean?"

"I thought the script would have something to say about Wayne Copeland."

"America One," Vince said. "It was a pitch for them."

"I see."

"Anyway, Shifty, I just wanted to thank you again. I still don't understand why you couldn't do it."

"Personal reasons, Vince."

Angle's hot tip in the fourth ran a dismal fifth. Arnie had the good grace not to say anything, especially since his own selection had won and brought in a modest exacta payoff for him, but Angles was indignant. "Broke slow and then had to check at the eighth pole," he said. "How do you like that, Reggie?"

"Something is rotten in the state of racing," the actor said. "The naked truth is, I have no shirt."

"Want to borrow a few bucks?" I asked him. "You can pay me back tomorrow."

"Neither a borrower nor a lender be, Shifty," Reggie said. "Nay, friends, not one more move into the breach today."

We left the box together. At the head of the escalator, Reggie gave me a cheerful wave as he descended toward the exits. I waved back, then walked into the cool, quiet premises of the Turf Club, where I expected to find Megan.

She wasn't there. Wayne Copeland and his party occupied a row of tables high up just beyond the finish line. I spotted the familiar faces from America One, but not Megan. I retreated inside to the bar, where I ordered a nonalcoholic beer and sat down on a stool to think things over. I've always found the Santa Anita Turf Club a soothing ambience. Patrons can peruse their *Racing Forms* under crystal chandeliers in a spacious room containing comfortable sofas and padded armchairs, as well as great bouquets of fresh flowers. Oil paintings and sculptures of long-vanished human and equine heroes of the turf adorn the premises. I think of it as a church, where you can bask in quiet contemplation of the past while trying to figure out what to do about the rest of your life. So I sat there for about five minutes, sipping my beer and trying to figure out my next move, until I saw Mark Clovis walk past on his way to the men's room.

I set my beer down on the counter and caught up to him as he reached the restroom door. "Mr. Clovis," I said, "I didn't know you were such a fan of the races."

"Well, Anderson," he said, pushing through the door ahead of me, "are you all right now?"

"I'm fine, as you can see." I looked around; the small room was empty.

"Your agent told us you were in the hospital."

"He lied. I just didn't want to shoot your commercial."

"I see. Pity. But he sent us another wonderful magician. It's going to make a very nice spot during the campaign. We may shoot a series of them."

We lined up next to each other at the urinals and let fly. "You know, I've figured it out about Cheryl Copeland," I said.

"Figured it out?"

"Why she was murdered."

"Really? Why?"

"She was a drunk. She also hated publicity and the limelight. Not exactly a great candidate for First Lady."

"Are you sure you're all right, Anderson?"

"Also, by eliminating her, Wayne benefits from aroused public sympathy. It's more effective to talk tough on crime if you've been a victim of it yourself."

"Are you suggesting Wayne had his wife murdered?"

"Not Wayne," I said. "Maybe some of the people around him. I'm not saying you had anything to do with it."

"How perceptive of you, Anderson. I'm impressed."

We shook ourselves off, left the urinals, and moved to the sinks, where we both began washing our hands. "Do you always confront people in the bathroom?" he asked.

"Not usually," I said. "But how else would I get a chance to talk to you? I mean, if I called your offices at Megatex, would I get through to you?"

"Almost certainly not."

"One of the things I like about restrooms and racetracks is that you get to talk to everybody and anybody," I said. "I mean, in your own world you're probably about as remote from down-to-earth events as an ancient Oriental potentate. You're not much concerned about what happens down below in the street, right? But here you are, at the track, and even the very great have to take a piss from time to time."

We both reached for towels and began drying our hands. "You're an odd bird," Clovis said. "Do you really think Cheryl was the victim of an assassination?"

"Oh, not only Cheryl Copeland," I said. "How about the Goldman family? How about the others who've died within the past year and a half?"

"You're amazing, Anderson," Mark Clovis said, bunching up his towel and dropping it into a large basket beside the row of sinks. "I suppose that in your world of magical effects and small illusions, fantasizing the incredible becomes a daily routine."

"Life itself is incredible to me," I said. "I often find even the most ordinary events improbable."

"You're a born fantasist." He started to leave. "Excuse me now."

"Did Goldman steal money or was it something else?" I asked, barring his way. "Is it possible that he and others objected to your political plans? Maybe he thought they were too extreme and threatened to call in the FBI."

"And so we had him eliminated, along with his whole family? Do you find that credible?"

"In your world, yes."

"Would you get out of my way, please?"

He pushed his way past me and I followed him out into the small anteroom where the public phones were. "What *are* your political plans, Clovis?" I asked. "When your bunch takes over the country, are you going to impose martial law?"

He turned around, smiling. "You know, that's a really terrific idea, Anderson," he said. "You think it can't happen here? It can. The president is the commander in chief, isn't he? Do you really know how much power the presidency has at its instant disposal? All this country has ever needed is a chief executive with the balls to exercise that power. You declare a state of national emergency. You call out the troops, you impose curfews, you close the borders, you shut down the rotten areas of this country where the evil comes from, you start putting people in prison who don't behave. You clean up the mess, Anderson. That's called law and order, and we're ready for it at last, don't you think?"

"Tell me something, Clovis," I answered. "Do you think the Bill of Rights would pass today if it were put to a national referendum?"

"No, of course not," he said. "It's antiquated. It no longer works. The whole system no longer works. We're going to make it work. You wait and see." He started to leave, then turned back again. "I'd take it easy about airing these peculiar theories of yours," he said. "I don't know whom you've been talking to, but that kind of chatter could be classified as malicious. It could get you into trouble."

I smiled and held out my open hands. "See? Nothing up my sleeves, nothing to hide." I made a quick pass in the air and produced a single card, the ace of spades. I handed it to him. "I'm just a small-time magician, Clovis," I said. "My job is to entertain people. Who'd pay any attention to me?"

"Exactly," he said, pocketing my card. "I'll keep this, as an interesting memento of our conversation." He started to walk away, but paused in the doorway. "Very nice, the ace of spades. You keep the joker, Anderson."

"*La muerte,*" I said. "You understand Spanish?"

He laughed. "Better than you think. But this is America. We don't speak Spanish here. Anyway, you're an entertaining sort. You're lucky, you know, that no one takes you seriously." He headed back toward Copeland's party.

Jay's horse in the seventh won, but paid only six dollars and twenty cents. Still, it was nice to be back in action with a winner. I cashed my twenty-dollar ticket and went down to the paddock to have a look at Superpatriot and the six other entries in the Norfolk Stakes. It was to be the big colt's last race before the Breeders' Cup in early November and he was expected to win easily. He had reportedly been training well, and his poor performance in the Balboa had been dismissed by the experts as an aberration, a onetime occurrence that had no significance, especially since he'd come back to win the Futurity at Del Mar. He was considered much the best of the West Coast juveniles in training, and he was expected to romp home an easy winner, after which he'd undoubtedly be favored to secure his championship by handling the best the East and the Europeans could throw up against him.

I did not, however, find the sight of him in the paddock reassuring. Lopez led him in first and was having some trouble with him. The big bay colt was tossing his head up and down and looking wildly around as the groom tried to calm him. He patted him on the neck and talked to him as he and a second, younger man, also a Latino, tried to lead him around the walking ring. I also noticed a little lather of sweat between the colt's hind quarters. In the sunlight the horse looked quite spectacular, as always, but he wasn't behaving like a champion. He didn't walk with pride and confidence, well within himself, as the horsemen put it; he acted more like a nervous teenager, an uncomprehending kid about to bust loose in frustration and anger.

"Look at him, he's a damn mess," I heard a woman's voice say to my left. "He's going to explode."

I leaned forward over the railing and looked down the row of watchers next to me. Babs Harper, dressed in scuffed boots, jeans, and a plaid cowboy shirt, was staring with disgust at her ex-charge. I pushed my way toward her. "Hello, Babs, what are you doing here?"

"I came to see Junior," she said, cocking her thumb toward the colt. "I was hoping maybe he would be all right. But he ain't all right. It makes you sick."

"He was nervous before the Futurity, but he won it anyway."

"Yeah, but that was only seven-eighths of a mile," she said. "This time they're asking him to handle two turns. Just look at him! He's a damn basket case!"

"What have you been up to since I last saw you?"

"Don't ask me," she said. "For some reason I'm still with this damn fool husband of mine."

"Where is he?"

"Out riding the circuit again, getting his balls busted on the back of some mustang," she said. "He don't never give up nothin'. I'm about sick to death of him."

"You coming back to the track?"

She shook her head. "No way, not after this. I'm going to find me a ranch somewhere and go back to breaking yearlings. That's what I do best. I don't want no part of the racetrack again, after what I see 'em doing to this colt." She spat into the flower bed at her feet and glared at the goings-on before her.

The Copeland party, about thirty strong, dominated the scene. Wayne was doing his usual number, smiling and waving to the crowd. I thought Megan might have put in an appearance by now, but she was not with him. Neither was Mark Clovis. It was a festive group and obviously brimming with a confidence that was reflected by the odds on their champion, three to five and dropping.

Billy Bob Short had to come to the aid of the two grooms to keep Superpatriot under control. When Kelly McRae mounted him, the colt started to rear up, but Short jerked hard on the lead shank and brought him back down before he could unseat the rider. Snorting and still bobbing his head up and down, Superpatriot led the field out toward the underpass. "Pitiful, just pitiful," Babs commented. "What they've done to this colt is criminal! But then I never did see Billy Bob ever back off an animal."

"Hey, lady," the worn railbird standing next to her observed, "don't fret. He's going to win this thing by ten."

"Save your money, old man," Babs told him. "The one thing this colt ain't got his mind on today is running."

"You going to watch the race?" I asked as we left the paddock.

"No," she said, "I ain't into watching disasters, Shifty. I'm getting out of here."

"It was nice to see you. I'm glad you're okay."

"You still doing that magic shit?"

"Yeah."

"Stick to it. Give up the horses," she said. "They'll break your heart if you let 'em." And she walked away from me toward the parking lot.

Babs was right about Superpatriot. He was so lathered up and nervous by post time that he broke through the gate twice before the start of the race. When it did go off, he rushed to the lead, nearly pulling McRae out of the saddle. He opened up five lengths around the first turn, pulling so hard against the bit that he had his head turned practically sideways against his rider's stranglehold. Finally, McRae was forced to give him his head. Superpatriot opened up ten lengths on the field by the half-mile pole, setting suicidally fast fractions. By the three-quarters pole he was done. The field swept past him on the turn for home and McRae was forced to ease him in the stretch. He jogged painfully back to the stands to a small chorus of boos from the fools who bet heavily on odds-on favorites, while the rest of us watched in stunned silence.

"I wonder if Billy Bob Short will ever be elected to the Hall of Fame," Jay said as the horses came back toward the winner's circle.

"I hate that son of a bitch," Angles said. "I wouldn't piss on him if he was on fire."

"The corruption of talent by greed," Arnie observed, "a recurring theme in American life."

22
Spats

♦

Over the next few weeks I tried not to think too much about Megan, but every now and then her face would pop into view. Sometimes I'd find her in the entertainment section of newspapers and magazines, usually in the company of Wayne Copeland. She was attending an opening night or a gala of some sort, always in a large group of friends and colleagues of the actor. She had already been linked to him romantically in several gossip columns, but the connection had always been promptly denied. It had been made clear to everyone that she was an employee of Flaherty and McDame, the Washington public relations firm representing Wayne and America One. The rumors persisted, however, and much was made in the press of her smashing good looks, but I noticed now that she was always conservatively dressed around him in public and remained on the fringes when the cameras started shooting. "Miss Starbuck works for me," Wayne Copeland told one interviewer from the tabloids. "She's damn good at what she does. Should I fire her just because you guys want to write lies about her and me? Hell, man, I loved my wife. It's going to be a while before I even think about anybody else in my life." For the most part, the press had chosen to accept this disclaimer and to honor the actor's grief over his murdered spouse.

Megan also showed up in the sports pages and the *Racing Form*, where she was on hand to guide Wayne through the intricacies of press conferences. Much was being made of the attempt to get Superpatriot ready for the Breeders' Cup. Billy Bob Short was not an easy interview and prone to lose his temper when pressed too hard about his colt's erratic performance in recent races, especially his disastrous showing in the Norfolk. Wayne Copeland could ride horses but knew nothing about them, and he simply spouted vague generalities regarding his animal when what the racing writers purportedly wanted were facts. Megan supplied those. She'd grown up around racehorses; her father was a well-known horseman, so when she talked about Superpatriot's soundness, conditioning, training regimen, and state of mind, the reporters listened to her. She also had the lingo down pat, the trainer talk with which she could snow them. The colt had been running a slight temperature on the day of the Norfolk, he wasn't himself, but he'd come back just fine, he was doing good, he'd put on a little weight, he was training great, he'd give a good account of himself in the Juvenile on Breeders' Cup day. This was the sort of patter trainers feed their owners and the press. For some reason that has always escaped me, even the most cynical writers report this garbage verbatim in their columns, as if it were gospel truth. Not one of them had yet written or would write that Superpatriot ought not to be running in the Breeders' Cup, that he was obviously off his game and needed some time away from the track. No, he was America's horse, America One's horse, so there was no talk of not running him. Only a top trainer would have had the courage to back off the colt now, threaten to quit if the owner insisted on running him. Billy Bob Short wasn't man enough to do that.

Jay was looking forward to the Breeders' Cup. He knew that Superpatriot would run poorly, but as America's horse and because of his past form, he'd almost certainly be heavily backed again and might even go off the favorite. Jay was planning to make a big bet against him. "It may be my only action of the day," he said. "The Eastern two-year-olds aren't that much this year, but this colt isn't going to be on the board the way he's going. I usually lose on Breeders' Cup day, too many good horses, but this year, Shifty, we can make a killing." Arnie, too, was saving his money for the coup of the year. I mean, if you knew Secretariat wasn't going to be at his best in those five races he lost during his illustrious career, wouldn't you have bet your life savings against him? That's what this game is all about, knowing when to bet and how much.

I wasn't planning to go to the Breeders' Cup this year. I'm not as cold-blooded a gambler as Jay or Arnie, and I don't like to bet against a potentially great horse. I don't feel as deeply about it as Babs Harper, but the sight of a top athlete being mismanaged and perhaps ruined sickens me, too. I don't want to look at it, I don't want to be part of it. Besides, I had another, more compelling reason for wanting to stay away, maybe even get out of town, go abroad for a while. I wasn't sure whether the local cops had enough on Portello to hold him much longer.

I had spotted him absolutely by chance that Friday afternoon. I was late getting to the track, due to an accident on the Pasadena Freeway, and I went from the parking lot directly to the nearest betting windows on the ground floor of the grandstand. The horses in the first race were nearing the starting gate, and my selection in the race, my best bet of the day, was going off at odds of five to one. I found the nearest betting line and stepped into it. I had no sooner taken a twenty-dollar note out of my billfold than I saw him. Or rather I saw his feet first, a snappy-looking pair of black-and-white shoes. I looked up and there he was, a couple of people ahead of me in the line to my left, his face buried in the *Racing Form*.

We reached the betting windows at about the same time. I wagered twenty dollars to win on my horse, tucked my ticket into my breast pocket, and stepped aside, waiting to see where Portello would go. Hoping not to be noticed, I avoided looking directly at him, but saw him head for a TV monitor, his usual method of viewing a race. I took out my wallet, removed everything from it but my driver's license and a fifty-dollar bill, then put the wallet in my side pocket, where I could get at it most easily.

I went up behind him and we watched the race together, standing in a small group of five or six other men. I gathered from Vinnie's grunts that he had wagered on the favorite, as he had also begun to rock back and forth as his horse started a determined stretch run. My animal was well in front by that time, however, and Vinnie's horse came up half a length short. I was a hundred dollars richer, but it was Vinnie I was concentrating on. "Tough beat, Spats," I said as the horses swept past the finish line.

He whirled around, the little pig eyes glittering with surprise. I kicked him in the right shin, then brought my foot down hard on his instep. He grunted and staggered forward. "Help!" I shouted. "Help! I've been robbed! Police! Help!"

The other members of our group looked bewildered. Portello recovered his balance and lunged for me, but I danced away from him, still shouting. Two security guards were running toward us. "Look out!" I shouted. "Look out, he's armed!"

One of the guards drew his gun. "What's going on?" he asked. The other guard was focused on Portello, who was standing in place now, still unsure of my action.

"He stole my wallet!" I shouted. "Look out for him, he's got a gun!"

"He's nuts," Vinnie said. "I didn't do nothin'."

"Search him," I said. "He's got my wallet."

"Okay, you," the first guard said to him. "Put your hands up against this post here and don't move."

"What, are you crazy?" Spats said. "He's nuts."

"Do what I tell you," the guard said.

Another security guard in plainclothes showed up and took charge. He emptied Portello's pockets and immediately found my wallet. "This yours?" he asked me.

"You bet it is," I said. "Look at my driver's license. That's my picture. He came up to me in line and bumped me, then a couple of minutes later I realized he'd stolen my wallet."

"He planted it on me," Portello said. The plainclothes cop now came up with Vinnie's piece, a small automatic tucked into an inside pocket. "You got a license for this?" he asked.

"I can explain," Portello began.

"Yeah, you can explain to the Arcadia police," the cop said.

I didn't see the rest of the card that day. Most of the afternoon was spent in the Arcadia police station, where I signed a formal complaint against Portello and agreed to testify against him. "You better check on this guy," I said to the detective who interviewed me. "I could swear I've seen his picture somewhere, maybe in some post office. I think he's wanted for kidnapping or murder or something."

"Don't worry, we'll check him out," the detective said. "He ain't going anywhere for now."

I went home, called Megan's number, and left a message saying it was urgent. I stayed in that night, but she didn't call me back. The next morning I called the Starbuck ranch and Jim Starbuck answered the phone. I told him I'd been unable to get in touch with Megan and asked him if he could get a message to her. "I figure I can do that," Jim Starbuck said. "She's right here. Maybe the reason you couldn't get through to her is we were all over to the hospital with Matty. She was operated on a couple of days ago."

"I'm sorry to hear that. She all right?"

"She ain't never going to be all right," Jim Starbuck said, "but we may have bought her a little time."

"What kind of surgery?"

"On her heart. She had one of those things they call a cabbage. It's spelled C–A–B–G, but that's how they pronounce it. And they had to replace a valve. Matty's a pretty sick girl, what with the cancer, too. Don't know what we'd have done without Meg. Here, let me see if she'll talk to you."

The line went dead for what seemed like an eternity, then Megan picked up the receiver. "Lou? What do you want?"

"Nothing, Megan. I just thought you ought to know about our friend Vinnie."

"What about him?"

"He's been arrested by the Arcadia police. Seems he was trying to pick somebody's pocket."

"Vinnie?"

"Yeah, that's the guy. I thought you might want to know."

"Is that all?"

"Not quite. One more thing."

"Good-bye, Lou."

"No, wait. Please don't hang up. I'm sorry about your mother."

"Thanks."

"I realize now I got it all wrong, Meg. Well, not all wrong, but I understand it better."

"What do you understand, Lou?"

"About the money. It wasn't FBI money, was it?"

"What money?"

"The money you offered to buy me out of the Old Glory gig. It was your money, Megan, I know that now. I'm sorry."

She didn't say anything, but I had this terrible feeling in my soul that she was crying at the other end of the line. "Megan? You there? Don't hang up on me, please."

"I'm here," she said, in a husky, dead voice.

"Your folks don't have any medical insurance, do they?" I continued. "You paid for your mother's surgery, didn't you? What did it cost? Fifty thousand or so, right, with the hospital and all?"

Again she didn't answer. I plunged on, not knowing where it might take us, but by this time what did I have to lose? The game was all but over, might as well shoot for the moon. "I just hope you're not playing a double game, Megan, not with the FBI," I said. "And I hope it's Wayne's money, not Clovis's. Megan, please watch yourself. I'm so sorry you had to do this."

She did hang up on me then. What else could she do?

About a week later, I found out from my friend Jude Morgan, the homicide detective working out of West L.A., that Spats was still in jail. New York was asking for him and the extradition process was under way. He was wanted on several counts of murder and kidnapping back in the late eighties. It's funny, though. He still hasn't been charged with anything having to do with his activities in California. Maybe nobody can tie him to the Goldman or Copeland cases. Maybe nobody wants to.

I guess I can stop worrying about him. They obviously have enough on him in New York to put him away forever. My guess is he won't last long in prison. If Gotti's people don't get him, Clovis's will. Like me, Portello's just another little mouse scurrying about in an arena of fat cats. They're eating us alive, these people.

Superpatriot never made it to the Breeders' Cup. Two days before the race, during a routine morning gallop, he broke down on the track. Pulled a suspensory, they say. America's horse is being retired to stud in Kentucky.

I wonder if I'll ever hear from Megan again. I doubt it. She's still close to Wayne Copeland, and the rumors concerning their relationship have resurfaced in the gossip columns and the tabloids. She's now referred to in most stories as an ex-police officer, so she must have quit the FBI. Too bad, because there's no doubt in my mind at all that America One is a dangerous, subversive organization. I can tell you one thing. If Wayne Copeland does run for president and is elected, I'm leaving the country. I've been told Costa Rica's a nice place to live. I wonder if it has a racetrack?